The monster held in place for a moment

Then the huge beast staggered, a brief three-step dance across the sand, before bellowing another of its unearthly banshee wails, boiling saliva pluming around its face.

Kane watched in horror as the monster threw the crocodile-masked Incarnate to one side, and the man went head over heels before slumping to the ground, covered in sand. At the same time, the monster seemed to turn, to spin in place, its reverse-hinged legs kicking up great clumps of sand, moving faster and faster.

A blur, and then nothing. The creature was gone.

Kane rushed over before Brigid could stop him, ignoring her pleas to be careful. There was a hole in the ground now, a roughly circular tunnel that appeared to go straight down. Kane could hear scrabbling down there as the nightmarish creature disappeared from view, and he kept his Sin Eater trained on the opening in the sand for a long moment, debating in his mind whether he should follow.

Other titles in this series:

James Axler
Outlanders®

SHADOW BOX

A GOLD EAGLE BOOK FROM
WORLDWIDE®

TORONTO • NEW YORK • LONDON
AMSTERDAM • PARIS • SYDNEY • HAMBURG
STOCKHOLM • ATHENS • TOKYO • MILAN
MADRID • WARSAW • BUDAPEST • AUCKLAND

Recycling programs
for this product may
not exist in your area.

First edition May 2009

ISBN-13: 978-0-373-63862-8
ISBN-10:   0-373-63862-0

SHADOW BOX

Printed in U.S.A.

"Cursed, cursed creator! Why did I live?
Why, in that instant, did I not extinguish the
spark of existence which you had so wantonly
bestowed?"
—Mary Shelley, *Frankenstein*, 1818.

The Road to Outlands—
From Secret Government Files to the Future

Almost two hundred years after the global holocaust, Kane, a former Magistrate of Cobaltville, often thought the world had been lucky to survive at all after a nuclear device detonated in the Russian embassy in Washington, D.C. The aftermath— forever known as skydark—reshaped continents and turned civilization into ashes.

Nearly depopulated, America became the Deathlands— poisoned by radiation, home to chaos and mutated life forms. Feudal rule reappeared in the form of baronies, while remote outposts clung to a brutish existence.

What eventually helped shape this wasteland were the redoubts, the secret preholocaust military installations with stores of weapons, and the home of gateways, the locational matter-transfer facilities. Some of the redoubts hid clues that had once fed wild theories of government cover-ups and alien visitations.

Rearmed from redoubt stockpiles, the barons consolidated their power and reclaimed technology for the villes. Their power, supported by some invisible authority, extended beyond their fortified walls to what was now called the Outlands. It was here that the rootstock of humanity survived, living with hellzones and chemical storms, hounded by Magistrates.

In the villes, rigid laws were enforced—to atone for the sins of the past and prepare the way for a better future. That was the barons' public credo and their right-to-rule.

Kane, along with friend and fellow Magistrate Grant, had upheld that claim until a fateful Outlands expedition. A displaced piece of technology…a question to a keeper of the archives…a vague clue about alien masters—and their world shifted radically. Suddenly, Brigid Baptiste, the archivist, faced summary execution, and Grant a quick termination. For

Kane there was forgiveness if he pledged his unquestioning allegiance to Baron Cobalt and his unknown masters and abandoned his friends.

But that allegiance would make him support a mysterious and alien power and deny loyalty and friends. Then what else was there?

Kane had been brought up solely to serve the ville. Brigid's only link with her family was her mother's red-gold hair, green eyes and supple form. Grant's clues to his lineage were his ebony skin and powerful physique. But Domi, she of the white hair, was an Outlander pressed into sexual servitude in Cobaltville. She at least knew her roots and was a reminder to the exiles that the outcasts belonged in the human family.

Parents, friends, community—the very rootedness of humanity was denied. With no continuity, there was no forward momentum to the future. And that was the crux—when Kane began to wonder if there *was* a future.

For Kane, it wouldn't do. So the only way was out—way, way out.

After their escape, they found shelter at the forgotten Cerberus redoubt headed by Lakesh, a scientist, Cobaltville's head archivist, and secret opponent of the barons.

With their past turned into a lie, their future threatened, only one thing was left to give meaning to the outcasts. The hunger for freedom, the will to resist the hostile influences. And perhaps, by opposing, end them.

Chapter 1

A dog's carcass lay in the middle of the street in the town called Hope. Rats surged around the corpse like a flowing river, yanking off strips of flesh with their needle-sharp teeth.

Brigid Baptiste suppressed a shudder and turned away from the revolting spectacle as she and Kane and Grant followed their diminutive guide through the narrow, twisting streets of the shantytown.

Hope was located somewhere along the southern coast of California, close to what had been the border with Arizona. With the recent fall of several baronies, the small Outland villes had been swamped with refugees seeking food and shelter. Eighteen months ago, Hope had been a quaint fishing ville with a population of less than two hundred. Now its populace had swelled to over five thousand and a vast, makeshift settlement had formed at its outskirts.

Theft and murder were daily occurrences; what people wanted they simply took. That wasn't the whole story, of course. Many of the refugees had come to Hope genuinely looking to create a better life for themselves and their families. But crime had escalated over recent months, and Hope had become a destination for scoundrels of every stripe to hide out and carve a niche for themselves, free from reprisals.

Kane, Grant and Brigid had come to Hope chasing a rumor. Word had it that a black marketer called Tom Carnack possessed some very valuable salvage and was offering it to the highest bidder. Carnack presided over a whole tribe of loyal brigands, and he rarely left the safety of his base in the Hope shantytown.

The Cerberus crew had heard that Carnack was currently in possession of the genetic material from the baron reproduction program. The rulers of the baronies had been hybrids of human and alien DNA, and they had governed with an iron fist. More recently it had come to light that these strange hybrids were in fact the chrysalis state of a higher form of life, a warlike alien race called the Annunaki whose goal was the absolute subjugation of humankind. The ever present threat of the return of the Annunaki hung heavily over every human being on the planet. The objective of the Cerberus team had always been to safeguard humankind. Carnack's promise of reborn barons did not bode well.

"They should have called this pesthole Hopeless," Grant muttered as he stepped over the dog's carcass, punting a rat out of the way with his toe. Dressed in a long leather duster, Grant was a wide-shouldered man with a towering frame, every inch of which was muscle. With skin like polished ebony, Grant wore a drooping, gunslinger's mustache. His coarse black hair was shaved close to the scalp. Beneath the matte-black duster, Grant wore a shadow suit, a black, tightly fitting one-piece garment that served as an artificially controlled environment and offered protection against both radiation and blunt trauma.

As a Magistrate in the barony of Cobaltville, Colorado, Grant had been schooled in many forms of combat and tasked with keeping the strictly tiered human population in its place. Several years ago, the huge man had been convinced that his job was predicated upon a lie, and he had resigned with explosive finality.

Kane looked at his partner and nodded. "It was probably a nice place once," he said quietly. Like Grant, Kane was an ex-Mag from Cobaltville. Wearing a washed-out denim jacket over his shadow suit, Kane was built like a wolf, all muscle piled at the upper half of his body, his arms and legs long and rangy. His partnership with Grant dated back to their days in Cobaltville, and many considered them an inseparable—and unstoppable—team.

The third member of the group, Brigid Baptiste, was another exile from Cobaltville. She had been an archivist, a faceless cog in the bureaucratic machine that kept each barony running smoothly. However, her friendship with Kane, coupled with her insatiable hunger for knowledge, had placed her on the wrong side of the conspiracy to subjugate humankind, and she had been forced to leave Cobaltville along with the ex-Mags when they were enlisted in the Cerberus operation by Mohandas Lakesh Singh.

Brigid was a stunning woman, tall and athletic. She tied her long, red-gold hair back in a ponytail, swept away from a high forehead that suggested strong intellect, while her full lips spoke of a passionate aspect. Her skin was pale and flawless, and her piercing emerald eyes shone as she took in the details of their nightmarish surroundings. Brigid's real weapon was her eidetic, or photographic, memory—an ability to instantly remember the finest details of anything she had observed.

Like Grant and Kane, Brigid wore a black one-piece

shadow suit over her curvaceous body, with tan boots and a brown suede jacket contrasting its stern appearance. A strip of frayed tassels ran across the back of the jacket, midway through her spine, while the boots' Cuban heels added a further two inches to her already statuesque height.

The three of them had been following the boy through the streets for more than ten minutes now. He led them from the outskirts of the shanty community through its warrens to its stinking, rat-infested center. The boy had no shirt and no shoes, and his ribs could be seen clearly drawn along the taut skin of his pigeon chest. He wore a knife at his waistband, the naked blade shoved through a belt loop of his trousers, now and then catching the light as he jogged ahead of them. Brigid had been unable to tell if he could speak English; he had greeted them enthusiastically at the outskirts of the wreckage they called a town, nodded and gestured for them to follow him, but his only words had been, "Carnack, yes-yes, Carnack."

The implication was he had been sent by Tom Carnack to find them, or at least he knew where Carnack was hidden—a fact that they had next to no chance of uncovering on their own. Grant had offered the boy a ration bar from the meager supply he had stashed away in his coat pockets, and the boy had eagerly accepted it, tearing at the foil wrapping and gorging on it with sharp teeth as he ran into the stinking, claustrophobic alleyways of the shantytown.

Finally, the boy led them down a tight alley so narrow that they had to walk single file. Grant was forced to walk sideways to squeeze his wide shoulders through the tightest parts. Three-quarters of the way along the alleyway, the boy pushed back a curtain that covered a doorway and glanced back at his charges before ducking inside, indicating that they should follow. Kane led the way inside, and the three teammates found themselves within a low-ceilinged reception area where two burly, scarred individuals held some heavy-duty automatic weapons on them with studied disinterest.

"You wait here," the boy told them before disappearing through another curtain into the room beyond.

The sweet, cloying stench of marijuana filled Kane's nostrils as he glanced at the weapons the guards held. Big-barreled automatics ending in wide muzzles like a shortened version of the ancient blunderbuss, they were a type he didn't recognize, most likely cobbled together by a local gunsmith.

His eyes flicked to Brigid, standing to his left, and he saw her watching the door through which their guide had disappeared. Her body was relaxed, giving the careful impression that all of this was just another day, nothing out of the ordinary. Behind him, Kane could hear Grant's steady breathing as he stood before the entry door to this ramshackle shelter, ready for a hasty exit if need be.

The curtain before them swished back and the boy returned, accompanied by a short thin man wearing a purple velvet frock coat, a loud Hawaiian shirt and a pencil-thin mustache. Kane mentally tagged the man as "Velvet Coat," and watched as he produced an eight-inch white baton and approached the Cerberus field team.

"You have weapons?" Velvet Coat asked in English dripping with a thick, Mexican accent. He had used some sort of oil to slick back his black hair, and the scent of it assaulted Kane's nostrils as he stepped closer.

"Sure do." Kane nodded. They were all well aware that meeting with this crime boss would necessitate their disarming, but bringing weapons to the scene at least allowed for the possibility of using them. Besides which, everyone knew that entering the ville of Hope unarmed was foolhardy, and Tom Carnack's people wouldn't have expected otherwise. "You want them?"

"Slowly, if you please, and one at a time," Velvet Coat told Kane, sweeping his gaze to address them all as the boy came forward with his empty arms outstretched to take the weapons from them.

Kane pulled a .44 Magnum pistol from the shoulder rig hidden under his jacket, and Grant did the same, producing two pistols—a Heckler & Koch and a dented .38 Police Special with a corroded finish that looked as if it had spent a hundred years in a swamp. As the sentries' guns turned on her, Brigid slowly reached into the leather holster slung low on her hip and pulled out her TP-9 pistol. The TP-9 looked factory new, its matte-black finish unmarred, and both Velvet Coat and one of the sentries nodded their approval.

Once they were finished, Velvet Coat held the white baton before him. "You mind?" he asked Kane. "Just a precaution, nothing personal."

"Go ahead." Kane nodded. "It's a shitty world, and if I were you I'd do the same."

Kane held out his arms as the man ran the baton up and down his sides and between his legs. The baton made a low electronic ticking noise, like a Geiger counter, until Velvet Coat nodded and smiled at Kane. "Okay, you're clean," he confirmed, and Kane brought his arms back down and stepped aside.

Velvet Coat moved across to Brigid, who adopted the same position as Kane with her arms stretched out from her shoulders, tugging her jacket open. She stood almost eight inches taller than the mustached man, and Velvet Coat's eyes narrowed for a moment as he admired the way the shadow suit clung to her breasts, before running the weapons sensor over her limbs and torso.

Then he moved onto Grant, who tried to look disinterested as the man ran the baton down to his feet. As the baton reached about to the level of Grant's knee, the clicking was replaced by a shrill whine. Velvet Coat leaped backward, and the sentries raised their guns and targeted Grant's head, stern expressions on their faces.

"Your boot, *señor?*" Velvet Coat said. "You will remove this for me."

Grant lowered his arms very slowly, his eyes never leaving those of the man, very aware that he stood in the sights of two guns. "Whoa, okay," he said, "everyone just calm down."

"Your boot, *señor,*" the man stated again, his irritation barely suppressed. "Or you can forget the deal and we kill you and your friends right now."

"Now, let's not be hasty," Kane began, but the man in the velvet coat held up a hand to quieten him.

"Your colleague has something in the boot there, a weapon," Velvet Coat explained as he backed toward the curtained doorway, far away from Grant.

Grant lowered his arms slowly, trying to keep his tone calm. "It's just a knife," he said. "Clipped to my boot. For camping."

"We came a long way to see you," Brigid added. "Camped out for three nights in the Outlands."

"Man's gotta cut firewood somehow," Grant explained reasonably.

"*Vamonos.*" Velvet Coat nodded very slowly, the slight trace of a smile on his lips. "You remove and hand over the knife," he said, "and if I find you hiding anything else…" He left the sentence unfinished, but the implication was clear.

Grant knelt and pulled his pant leg up to reveal a scuffed leather boot that ended a little way up his calf. There was a six-inch-long, brown leather sheath there from which the handle of a knife protruded at an angle. Grant unclipped the sheath, not bothering to remove the knife. As he did so he smiled inwardly—it had been a ploy to keep up their appearances. The last thing they had wanted to do was advertise themselves as representatives of Cerberus, here to gather intelligence and shut down Carnack's little DNA trading post, so they had come here posing as traders themselves. And any trading party worth its salt would try to sneak just one weapon into a meeting, no matter what the rules were.

Grant stood and handed the sheathed knife to the shirtless young guide, who placed it atop the little stack of guns he had amassed.

Velvet Coat stepped forward once more, watching Grant warily as he raised the baton. "Arms outstretched, please, *señor,*" he said, and Grant obeyed, waiting as the man ran the baton carefully over his form three full times before he was satisfied.

As a rule, Kane and Grant would each be carrying a Sin Eater pistol each in its distinctive wrist rig. The Sin Eater was the weapon of the Magistrate, a symbol of office as much as a devastating hand cannon. But its very recognizability would have caused problems in this environment, and any rationalization about acquiring the Sin Eaters from storage or from killing Magistrates was too risky to chance. They had opted instead to arm themselves lightly with fairly common pistols that wouldn't draw any undue attention to a supposed group of traders.

Once the trio had been disarmed, Velvet Coat pushed through the curtain into the next room and held it to one side to usher the three Cerberus warriors through.

Kane turned back and shot a look at their young guide as he knelt to stash their weapons in a chest in the corner of the anteroom. "Careful with those," he told the boy. "Family heirlooms."

The boy smiled and nodded, but there was no recognition in his eyes. Kane suspected that he hadn't understood the words.

"Come," Velvet Coat said, "no tricks."

Kane pushed past the dirty curtain and found himself inside a far bigger room. The area was ill-lit, its walls draped with sheets of orange and tan, billowing in the draft and leaving Kane with a confused and uncertain idea of the true size of the room.

The floor space seemed to cover about eighteen square feet. To the back of the room, facing the curtained entry, a young man sat low upon a smattering of cushions, slumped into their enveloping folds and cramming his mouth with berries dipped in syrup. There were two other men in the room, both well-armed and wearing fierce expressions. An attractive woman dressed in shimmering fabrics was dancing in one corner to a light jazz recording piped into the room at low volume, close enough that the man on the cushions could reach out and touch her.

"You would be the interested party," the lounging man announced, still watching the dancing girl.

"That we would," Kane said, impatience in his voice, "depending on what deal you're offering here. All we've heard so far are rumors."

The man's head turned and his blue eyes met with Kane's. He was perhaps twenty-five, lean with sunken eyes but just a little puppy fat around his jowls. He had dark hair, cut short and prematurely balding, and his chin was dark where he hadn't shaved. With his sharp features and swift, twitching movements he reminded Kane of the rats they had seen in the streets outside.

"Rumors are tricky things," the man said cheerfully. "Never really know what the cack you're being told. I'm Tom."

Kane bowed his head slightly and Grant and Brigid did likewise.

Carnack gestured that they take a seat on the cushions before him. "No need to stand on ceremony. We're all brothers under the skin and on and on." He smiled. "You fellas got names, I take it?"

Taking the lead, Kane kneeled on the cushions before Tom. "John Kane," he said, "with my partners, Grant and Brigid." This was a lie. Kane had no first name, and nor, in fact, did Grant. Magistrates were born with one name, bred to take over their father's position in the Magistrate Division in the illusion of continuous service. The need for first names was a luxury Magistrates never enjoyed.

"Nice to meet you, John, Grant and Brigid," Carnack

said genially. "So, why don't you start by telling me these rumors and we'll see if we have any common ground or if you're just pissing your time away."

As Carnack spoke, the woman draped in shimmering silks continued to gyrate provocatively to the soft music, but Carnack appeared to have dismissed her from his mind, suddenly all business. She was tall with straight brown hair and long, shapely legs, and Kane found himself distracted by her movements for a moment.

He blinked and turned his attention back to the trader. "They say you have access to a baron," he stated. "A young baron, ripe for training, for molding. Mentally, I mean."

Again, this wasn't entirely true. The rumor that had reached Cerberus was that Tom Carnack and his brigands had access to hybrid DNA blueprints and the technology to regenerate barons from them—cloning tech or birth pools or whatever. That part of the story changed in the telling from place to place. Since the hybrid barons were sterile, the only way for them to reproduce had been through artificial techniques.

"Well, you're half-right, friend." Carnack nodded, smiling widely. "What I've got is, well—did you hear what happened out in Beausoleil?"

Kane rubbed at his chin thoughtfully. "I don't get out there that much, but I heard there was some kind of aerial bombardment." In actuality, Kane and his colleagues had walked through the rubble just a few months ago. "Maybe leveled the whole ville."

"That's pretty much the long and short of it," Carnack told them. "See, the barons had some sort of disagreement and they started taking shots at one another. Don't ask me what it's all about, I couldn't give a monkey's, I can tell you. The bottom line is, the nine baronies are in turmoil, right?"

Kane nodded, encouraging the man to continue.

"Happens that I knew some folks what were in the flamin' ville when they started bombing Beausoleil." The trader smiled. "Almost got themselves barbecued. One of them has got half a head of hair now—you couldn't miss him."

Kane suppressed a smile at the man's friendly charm. "So, what is it you have?" he asked.

"Well, once the bombing was over there was stuff there that was just ripe for the taking, see?" Carnack explained. "High risk, you know. Magistrates trying to keep out independent traders, honest folk like you and me. Anyway, I happened to acquire some genetic material, very nice stuff. Hybrid DNA. You know what that is?"

Grant snarled. "Yeah, flyboy," he growled, "we know what it is. Nature's building blocks for making new barons."

"Spot on, my friend, spot on." Carnack laughed.

"So, what use is this DNA?" Kane asked.

Carnack adjusted the cushions beneath him and sidled a little closer, holding his hand up to mask his words from the dancing girl. "World's going to hell in a handbasket, friend," he told Kane conspiratorially. "The baronies are all blowing up, and I figure the whole game of marbles is up for grabs for those that want it. Strong people, leaders, like you and me. Am I right?"

Kane dipped his head in a slight nod. "Right. So what do I do with this baron DNA? Just add water?"

"If you want to make baron soup." Carnack guffawed,

slapping his thigh loudly. "You're having a laugh, right? Just add water? What are you, a clown?"

"Then what use is this DNA to me?" Kane asked, his tone somber.

"Like I was saying," Carnack told him, "the world's changing and everything's up for grabs. But you try setting yourself up as a baron, friend—people will lynch you from the nearest tree. They've been indoctrinated, see?" He tapped the side of his head. "In their heads. These ville-raised twits all think that the hybrid barons are their natural leaders—it's like law of the jungle or something."

"So," Kane said, "if I had a baron of my own I could call the shots."

"Exactly," Carnack told him. "If your crew want to live like barons, you set up your puppet in the position of power and you pull his strings. Welcome to John-Kaneville." He looked at Brigid and a smile crossed his lips. "Mind you, your friend there can pull my strings anytime, if you catch my drift."

Brigid smiled tightly at him, narrowing her eyes and saying nothing.

"Suit yourself." Carnack smiled back before turning to address Kane once more. "So, I'm talking a small fortune for the DNA. On top of that, you'll need birthing pods. Now, I've got a lot of DNA but only one set of the pods. For them you pay the motherlode, and it's a rental—there's no buyout option. You get me?"

"And then what?" Grant asked. "DNA in the pods makes us a baron?"

The trader shrugged. "Well, that's the catch. We've got the equipment, but we've yet to produce a real live hybrid."

Brigid leaned forward, suddenly interested. "How are you operating it?"

"What's that?" Carnack asked. "How do you mean? The thing's set up with plenty of juice but, honest, all we've had come out so far is dead babies. Ugly nippers, too."

"You have whitecoats operating this? Scientists?" Brigid urged.

"Some, but they're still working out the kinks," Carnack admitted.

"So, why would we go in with your organization on this?" Kane asked.

"It'll work," Carnack assured them. "Might take another ten goes to get it right, but it'll work. And if you want to set up a barony, you'll need a baron. That's science right there, my friends. Once it works the price triples. Get in early and you nab a bargain, set yourselves up for life."

Kane gestured to Brigid. "My colleague here is a scientist."

"Geneticist," Brigid said by way of clarification as the trader turned to admire her once more.

"What say you to a forty percent drop if she can get your tech working?" Kane suggested.

"Friend," Tom said, smiling, "if she can get my tech working, I'll bloody well marry 'er."

"Forty percent discount will be sufficient." Brigid smiled patronizingly. "When can I look at the birthing pod?"

Carnack's eyes lost focus for a moment, and he looked at Velvet Coat, who stood beside the exit while he thought. "Now you're asking," he said. "Let me go work out some details. You wait here. I won't be a minute."

Carnack stood from the cushions and stepped past the

dancing girl, stroking her hair and kissing her cheek before disappearing through a gap in the veils that hid the contours of the walls.

Kane sat still, watching as the man disappeared. He wanted to turn to address Brigid and Grant where they knelt behind him, but the armed guards were still in the room, along with the dancing girl and Velvet Coat. This was too easy. If they could get access to Carnack's alleged birthing pod, they could assess whether this was a genuine threat and if it was, maybe destroy it then and there.

"Seems like a nice guy," Grant muttered under his breath after a few moments, and he felt the eyes of Carnack's men turn on him, watching warily.

"Just watch the pretty girl, Grant," Kane suggested out of the side of his mouth, and they sat there in silence once more while the long-limbed beauty continued her sensual dance before them.

After a moment, the dark-haired woman leaned down and stretched her arm out to Kane. "You like what you see, yes?" she said, flashing dark eyes at him.

Kane smiled. "You're very pretty," he told her, his eyes flicking back to the curtains where the negotiator had disappeared.

"Would you like to dance?" the girl asked.

"I don't think that would be such a good idea," Kane admitted.

"Tom won't mind," she assured him, leaning in close. Kane felt her warm breath on his cheek as she whispered in his ear, "I'm just his little fancy. You can have me if you want me. Big, strong man like you."

Kane looked at her, admiring the way that the silks

clung to her curved figure like liquid. "I really don't think that I should," he told her quietly.

As he finished speaking, Tom Carnack stepped back into the room brandishing a scarred Kalashnikov AK-47 rifle.

"What's going on?" Grant asked as the other guards in the room leveled their handguns at the Cerberus teammates.

"I'm sorry, Mr. John Kane," Carnack explained, "but Señor Smarts there recognized you the second you walked in the door."

Standing in the doorway holding a tiny revolver, a single-shot .25 with a pearl handle, Velvet Coat mock bowed as Kane looked at him. "I can sniff out a Magistrate at fifty paces, *señor.*"

"What…?" Kane blustered, pulling himself up from the floor. As he did so, the dancing girl swung one of her long legs over his rising shoulder and shoved him down to the cushions so that he was lying on his back. He lay there looking straight up her torso, her legs to either side of his head.

"You should have accepted that dance, Magistrate man," she told him, shifting her palm to reveal a shining stiletto blade. "I would have killed you so beautifully you would have wept for me to continue."

Chapter 2

Lying beneath the dancing girl, Kane flicked his eyes to Tom Carnack. "You think we're Magistrates?" he protested. "This is a joke, right? Little bonding exercise. No, I get it. It's funny." He tried to shift his weight and get the dancing girl off him but she crushed her thighs around either side of his head and gave him a warning look.

"You keep squirming, Magistrate man, and I'll pluck your eyes out," she told him, bringing her blade down toward his face.

Carnack took another step into the room and pointed the AK-47 at Kane's groin. "Now, you have to appreciate that we outlanders have our own special way of dealing with Magistrate scum like you," he snarled.

"Whoa, whoa," Kane said. "Let's all just take a step back and talk about this."

"Yeah," Brigid chipped in as she knelt on the cushions beside Grant, warily watching the two armed guards. "You're making an awfully big mistake." Unnoticed, her hand reached down and her fingers felt around the heel of her right boot.

"Know what?" Carnack said as his gaze took her in. "You, I might just let live. If you're interested in a new position."

Brigid shook her head and laughed. "I'm not your type. You'd only get bored of me."

Suddenly her hand flicked forward as she tossed the Cuban heel from her boot at the man's face. Before Carnack could react, Brigid, Grant and Kane turned away and the heel exploded in a dazzling flash of brightness and noise.

His ears rang and spots swam before Kane's eyes as he opened them and looked around the room once more. Above him, the dancer was shaking her head, eyes balled tight against the sudden pain that Brigid's flash-bang had caused. In the enclosed space and semidarkness of the tentlike room, the flash-bang had an awesome effect, like staring at the sun through a telescope.

Kane tossed the dancing girl off him, slapping her to one side as he stood. "Let's get out of here," he said as he turned to his companions, who were warily getting up from the floor. Even with their eyes closed and their heads turned away, the effects of the flash-bang in the little room had still been strong. Heaven only knew what Carnack's crew had to have been thinking right then.

At the door, the velvet-coated Señor Smarts was reaching for his face, his tiny handgun forgotten as tears streamed from his eyes. "I'm blind, I cannot see," the effete Mexican wailed.

Grant stepped across to him and punched him solidly in the jaw, knocking the man backward into the wall hidden behind the drapes. Smarts slammed against it with the back of his head and crashed down to the floor, unconscious.

A second later, alerted by the noise of the flash-bang, the two burly guards from the anteroom stormed in through the part in the curtains. Grant dropped to the floor and angled a swift leg sweep, knocking both of them onto their backs. He lunged at the closer man, left hand held flat, and rammed him in the throat, bruising his windpipe and sending him into instant unconsciousness.

The second guard struggled to pull his gun out from under him and began to raise it in Grant's direction, but Brigid was already beside him. She kicked her right leg out and up, knocking the pistol from the man's grip. He yelped in pain as the gun disappeared over his shoulder and through the curtain back into the anteroom. Then Grant swung a powerful fist into the man's face, crushing his nose in an explosion of blood. The man shook his head, droplets of blood spraying left and right, struggling to get to his feet so that he could take on Grant. The ex-Mag drove another jab at the man's face and he slumped back, his head lolling on his neck, unconscious like his companion.

Meanwhile, Kane had walked across to Tom Carnack, who was doubled over and clawing at his face with one hand, tears streaming from his eyes. Kane grabbed the Kalashnikov midway along its barrel and yanked it from the man's grip with a single, mighty heave. At the same time, Brigid and Grant disarmed the two other blinded guards.

"Okay, Tom and Tom's people," Kane announced. "I want you all to listen up. See, you really did make a mistake. We're not Magistrates come to haul you in. But we're also not the kind of people you can just screw over like this. So now we're negotiating ourselves some new terms."

Carnack's face was bright red, and his bloodshot eyes were open but unfocused. "Go screw yourself," he snarled.

Kane swung the heavy barrel of the Kalashnikov into the man's face, connecting with a loud crack and knocking the smaller man onto his back. "I don't think we need any more of that attitude," Kane spit. "Here's how it's going down. You, me and my associates are going to walk out of here together, and you're going to take us to wherever it is you have the hybrid DNA and the birthing pod stashed. And in return for handing them over, gratis, I am going to be very generous and let you live, on the basis that you close up shop here in Hope. Okay?"

"What are you?" Carnack growled, wiping blood from his mouth where the blow from the Kalashnikov had loosened a tooth. "Some kind of joker? You're surrounded by a whole bloody ville of my men. I ain't going to give you squat, buddy. Squat, got it?"

Kane smiled humorlessly. "If you tip-off your men, if you so much as breathe funny once we leave this room, I will shoot you in the head. You understand?"

"Do I look like an idiot? You'd never get out of Hope alive, Magistrate," Carnack stated bitterly.

"Ninety seconds ago you had a gun pointed at my crotch and your gal pal here was about to take my eyes out," Kane told him. "I'm thinking that this here is a step up. Now, on your feet, we're leaving."

Tom Carnack spit a gob of blood to the floor as he slowly lifted himself from the disarrayed cushions. Kane noticed there was a single broken tooth shining amid the splash of blood.

Grant slipped through the curtain back into the anteroom while Brigid kicked back her foot until the heel of her left boot snapped free. Kane looked at her and she shrugged.

"I'm not running around on one heel," she told him. "That's a sure ticket to spinal damage."

"I didn't say anything." He held the Kalashnikov steady on Carnack.

Then he raised his voice, calling to Grant, "Everything okay out there?"

Grant's head popped through the drapes a moment later, his brow furrowed with concern. "I got into the trunk but the kid's disappeared."

Carnack nodded knowingly. "Benqhil has gone for help. You're dead men," he snarled.

"Yeah, pal," Kane said, dismissing him, "heard it all before. Distribute the weapons and let's move, Grant," Kane urged, shoving Carnack toward the rift in the drapes.

As they left the room, the dancing girl writhed on the floor, still clawing at her eyes. "Did you hear? They're taking Tom. Are you all buffoons? Stop them."

Her pleas went unacknowledged—the guards in the room were either unconscious or still blind and deaf from the flash-bang.

Outside, the chest on the floor of the anteroom stood open, its lock smashed in two where Grant had either pulled or kicked it apart. Grant handed Brigid her compact TP-9, and she checked its ammo clip was still in place before she led the way into the street outside. The TP-9 was a midsized semiautomatic weapon, roughly the length of Brigid's arm from wrist to elbow. The bulky pistol had a grip just off center beneath the barrel, and a covered targeting scope across the top for pinpoint work. The whole unit was finished in molded, matte black.

Grant clipped the sheathed knife back on his boot and

shoved the corroded Police Special into an inside pocket of his black leather duster, keeping the Heckler & Koch in his right hand. He offered the .44 Magnum weapon to Kane, who shook his head.

"Seems a shame to lose the Kalashnikov," Kane told him, "but it would be bastard conspicuous out on the street."

While Grant held both pistols on their blinded prisoner, Kane removed the clip from the AK-47 and pocketed it before tossing aside the empty rifle.

"They've probably got spare ammo," Grant warned.

"Of course they have," Kane agreed as he took the .44 Magnum weapon from his partner, "but they'll be blind for a couple more minutes yet, and I intend to be long gone by the time they've reloaded it." With that, he shoved a firm hand between Carnack's shoulder blades and pushed him through the curtain into the tight alleyway after Brigid. "Keep going forward, fast as you can," Kane told him, "I'll tell you when to stop."

"I can't see anything, you idiot," Carnack screamed at him as he batted at the wall in front of his face.

"So, run your hand along the wall if it helps," Kane suggested. "Just keep moving."

Brigid Baptiste waited for them in an alcove across the main street at the end of the alleyway, the TP-9 cradled in her hands, partially hidden by the shadows. The whole shantytown reminded the three of them of the Tartarus Pits back in Cobaltville, the ghetto level that sat at the base of every ville structure, both metaphorically and physically, supplying cheap labor and offering dire warning to those who disobeyed the baron.

The whole ville stank of human waste, and people watched warily as they made their way into the light. None of the street people looked well fed. By contrast, the physically powerful Cerberus warriors had to have looked like gods to their eyes.

"We got a way out of here?" Grant asked as he mentally checked off the people milling in the street, reassuring himself that no one was taking any undue interest in their progress.

"Our best bet is to head for the docks and pick up a boat there," Brigid said.

"Do you know where you're going?" Kane asked her.

Brigid smiled, tapping the side of her head with her empty hand. "I saw satellite recon photos before we came," she told them. "I've got a pretty good idea of the layout of this rathole. Soon as we get back on the main thoroughfare I'll find us the right route."

Kane pushed Carnack between the shoulder blades again as they rushed through the narrow streets. "Keep moving," he growled, his finely tuned senses alert, warily watching for signs of possible attack.

"Oy," Carnack yelled behind him, "careful, fella. I can't see, remember? What the bleeding eff was that thing, anyway?"

"Just keep quiet and keep moving," Kane told him sullenly. "Your eyesight will come back soon enough."

"That's reassuring," Carnack muttered, rubbing at his eyes as he rushed forward. "Right now it sounds like everyone's underwater, too, you know? You're a bunch of frackin' idiots."

They had reached an intersection and Brigid had

stopped, looking down each of the routes, trying to fit them together with the map in her mind.

"Come on, Baptiste," Kane urged as he glanced over his shoulder, checking for pursuit, "let's hurry it up."

"This way," she decided, her long legs kicking out as she raced off to the left.

Carnack just stood there, refusing to move. Kane shoved him once more while Grant covered their backs with the Heckler & Koch.

"All right," Tom Carnack yelped, "keep your hair on. I'm disabled, remember?"

"About that," Kane said, checking his wristchron. It had been three minutes since they had exited Carnack's lair, almost five since Brigid had unleashed the flash-bang. Ample time for Carnack to recover, at least enough to see shapes and blurs. "How's your vision?" Kane asked him.

"Completely scragged," Carnack complained.

"You're faking," Kane told him. "You should have recovered by now. If you're deliberately slowing us down I'm going to shoot you in the foot and carry you the rest of the way."

"Genius," Carnack said, snidely. "That'll only slow you down more."

"That's *my* problem," Kane growled, whipping out his .44 Magnum pistol and pointing it at Carnack's stumbling feet.

There was a loud report as he pulled the trigger and buried a slug in the ground between the trader's feet. Carnack leaped aside, pulling his hands over his ears.

"That's your warning shot," Kane told him. "The next one hobbles you."

"All right," Carnack cried, hands up in the air. "I can see

colors and shapes. It's still a bit messed up, though, so I'm going to go slow. Okay?"

"Speed up," Kane responded, "and keep moving."

They turned another corner into a wide thoroughfare, stepping past a man with a burned face and a begging bowl who was lying in the middle of the street. Between the tightly packed shanty buildings Kane saw a glint of sunlight reflecting off water.

Brigid waited while her companions caught up. "We're close," she told Kane as he grabbed Carnack's collar to halt him. "There's a series of jetties down there. It's where the ville folk fish from. Or they used to."

Kane nodded, peering behind and checking to see if anyone was following.

"There's an unmanned motorboat off to the left," Brigid pointed when Kane turned back. "Just a little way along from the pier." Her finger pointed to a small fishing scow with a tiny covered bridge.

"You'll never make it." Carnack laughed fiercely. "My people will ex the lot of you the second you step out there."

Brigid grabbed the man's stubbled chin. "Sorry, Tom. We're home free," she told him. "Didn't you hear—they're not coming for you. There's no honor among thieves."

"Scratch that," Grant chided from the rear of the group. "We've got company."

Brigid and Kane looked in Grant's direction and saw four dark shapes weaving along the narrow street at high speed: three motorcycles and a quad bike followed by a billowing plume of dark exhaust.

Carnack looked at Brigid and laughed. "Before the end

of the day I'll have you right where I want you, red," he said, "bunny hopping across my lap."

"Keep moving," Kane said, ignoring the man's vile comment.

More people were milling where the streets opened up onto the waterfront, and Brigid looked back at Kane as she took them in. "It's too crowded, Kane," she told him. "Someone's going to end up getting hurt."

Kane checked behind him for the approaching gang members, then shoved Carnack toward Brigid. "Cover him," he instructed. "I'm going to clear us a path." With that, he strode forward and raised his pistol in the air, pumping three shots into the sky in quick succession. "Everyone get out of here," Kane shouted over the frightened cries of the crowd.

They didn't need to be told twice. Everyone ran to the edges of the ramshackle street, ducking into doorways and clearing a path for Kane and his team.

Behind him, Kane heard gunshots as Grant began firing at the approaching marauders. He refilled the chambers of the .44 Magnum pistol and turned to face the enemy.

Beside Grant, Brigid raised her TP-9 pistol and blasted off a stream of shots down the street as the motorcyclists and quad riders approached.

Seeing his chance, Tom Carnack took a step away from her, his bloodshot eyes fervently looking around for an escape route. Suddenly, he felt Brigid's elbow slam into his gut and he doubled over, his breath exploding out of his mouth in a coughing whoop.

"Stay still," she told him, thrusting her free arm around his throat and holding him against her hip in a headlock.

Carnack continued to cough and splutter as Brigid pumped the trigger of her pistol, firing shots at the approaching gang members.

Their attackers were the same guards they had seen in Carnack's trading pad. The velvet-coated Señor Smarts sat on a motorcycle behind one of the guardsmen from the main room, a spooky-looking man wearing a bandanna across his head and goggles over his eyes to protect them from flying grit. Beside him, his partner was riding alone on his own motorbike, spinning a chain in one hand as he powered the throttle. A pace behind them, the dark-haired dancing woman rode her own bike. There was a scabbard attached to the side of the bike, the shining hilt of a sword sticking out beside her right knee. Bringing up the rear of the group, the two large guards from the anteroom shared a quad bike that belched a thick cloud of black exhaust into the air around them. While one drove, the other raised a Kalashnikov autorifle and aimed at the Cerberus field team. The muzzle flashed as the guard launched a stream of bullets into the narrow street.

Kane, Grant and Brigid each pulled back, finding what little cover they could at the sides of the street, backs against the walls, with Brigid and her prisoner standing close to Kane. On the other side of the street, Grant took careful aim and his bullet clipped the shoulder of Velvet Coat, almost toppling the bike as he reeled in pain.

Then the vehicles were upon them.

Kane held the .44 Magnum pistol in a two-handed grip, steadying his aim as he blasted three shots into the driver of the quad bike. The man slumped in the saddle and the bike veered off to the side, crashing through the flimsy walls of one of the ramshackle huts that lined the street.

Brigid took aim at the second bike, the one with the guard wielding the chain, as it bore down on her. Carnack's struggling tipped her aim, and her shots skewed wide. Suddenly, the bike was next to her, zipping past at a ferocious speed, the guard's chain spinning through the air with an audible thrumming. She ducked back as the bike passed, and her eyes widened as she saw the chain whip out and snag Grant's ankle, pulling the big man off his feet.

"Eyes front, Baptiste," Kane's bellowing voice warned from behind her as Grant was dragged off onto the pier. She looked back and saw the dancing girl's sword cleave the air at waist height, just barely missing her while the other bike skidded to a halt a few steps ahead.

As the sword cut the air beside him, Kane's empty hand shot out and tangled in the woman's long brown hair. In a fraction of a second, the motorcycle tipped up as the dancing girl was yanked from the saddle, still clinging to her sword.

She appeared to be falling backward, but her momentum dragged her ahead, pulling Kane into a stumbling run for a moment before her snagged hair ripped from her scalp and he let go. She crashed to the ground, slamming hard against it on her back as her bike sped away, the distinctive note of its two-stroke engine rising as it raced out of control.

She was quick; Kane acknowledged that much. She had hit the ground hard, but she rolled and was standing before him in less than two seconds. She stood low, adopting a fighter's stance as she held the heavy sword behind her, readying for attack. There was blood in her hair, and she gritted her teeth in a fierce smile as her eyes met with Kane's.

The bandanna-wearing guard had pulled his bike around, kicking up dirt as the tires tore against the makeshift road surface. Brigid struggled to target him with her TP-9 while Tom Carnack squirmed against her side in the headlock. She seemed only able to watch as the motorcyclist pulled a revolver from his jacket's inside pocket and aimed it directly between her eyes.

Meanwhile, already thirty yards away, racing down the rough wooden slats of the fishing pier, Grant found himself dragged behind the rider of the other motorcycle, his right ankle caught up in the chain that the man held. His back slapped the splintering pier beneath him, tossing him in the air before dropping him back down hard against its surface, knocking the breath out of him and giving him no time to recover.

Realizing that the slats were evenly spread, Grant timed his breaths and tried to focus his vision on the jostling view of the rider. He was momentarily tossed into the air once more, and as his shoulders took the brunt of another hard landing, Grant raised the pistol in his hand and aimed down the length of his body at the motorcycle, praying he would manage to avoid shooting his own foot off.

The Heckler & Koch spit, and three bullets flew through the air. The first one hit the rider just behind the ear, causing him to turn the handlebars violently and forcing the motorbike into a skid. The second shot went wide, flying over the top of Grant's target, but the third bullet hit the bike beneath the saddle, drilling through the chassis and into the fuel tank.

With a blossoming explosion, motorbike and rider caught light as it sped off the side of the pier with Grant still dragging behind it.

The motorbike and its flaming rider hit the blue-green waters of the ocean with a splash, before sinking immediately beneath the waves and pulling Grant along with them as the flames were extinguished.

"Oh, crap," Grant snarled as his head ducked beneath the water and he felt himself plummeting toward the bottom.

Back on the pier, Kane watched as the bike caught fire and Grant disappeared off the side of the wooden structure, dragging behind it. But there was no time to react—the dancing girl was already upon him, swinging the wide blade of her sword in a sweeping arc intended to rip his chest in two. Kane leaped backward, barely an inch out of reach.

"Looks like we get to dance after all, Magistrate man," the dark-haired woman announced, her eyes flashing.

"I've got two left feet," Kane replied, raising his pistol and targeting her head with the heavy Magnum handgun.

And then, with no warning, the ground started shaking, rocking the whole, flimsy ville of Hope. Kane and his beautiful opponent staggered before falling to their knees.

Chapter 3

Pulled down by the weight around his ankle, Grant held his breath as he sank beneath the waves. He opened his eyes, feeling the salty sting of the ocean press against them as he plummeted from the surface. Beneath him, the rider and the motorcycle were sinking rapidly, and the rider still clung to the length of chain that was wrapped around Grant's ankle. The ex-Mag fought for a moment, trying to swim away from his sinking adversary, but the chain was cinched tight and he would have to disentangle himself before he could escape.

Grant looked back down the length of his body, watching the darkness of the ocean envelop the bike and its rider. He discarded the Heckler & Koch, letting it drift away from him on the current as he twisted his body in an effort to reach for his trapped ankle.

The darkness was closing around him now, and his chest was starting to yearn to take its next breath. Soon it would be hard to see the chain.

As he scrambled over himself, plunging his arms toward his weighted foot, Grant felt something slam his body beneath the water, as though he had hit a solid wall. He was thrown about in the ocean depths, spun and shunted, as the wall of pressure hit him. Light followed by darkness, then light again, his breath blurting from his mouth in a rush of bubbles, and suddenly Grant could no longer tell which way was up.

Beneath him, or at least at the end of his foot, the rider clung to the chain as his motorcycle was wrenched from under him, and Grant watched in astonishment as the heavy two-wheeler seemed to dance around then disappear over his head.

Suddenly another wall of pressure collided with Grant's body, and he seemed to pirouette in the dark waters of the Pacific. He felt something pull at his foot as he was tossed around, and suddenly his assailant's face rushed before his eyes before spinning away.

THE MAN IN THE bandanna and goggles was about to pull the trigger of his Beretta when the first tremor hit, shaking the ground violently and throwing Brigid and her prisoner into a staggering, graceless dance.

Brigid heard the gun blast, watched the bullet speed over her head as she toppled over, releasing her headlock grip on Tom Carnack. A moment later, the dirt track of the ground was rushing toward her face and she thrust her hands forward, still clutching the TP-9, and braced for impact.

When Brigid let go, Tom Carnack found his feet wrenched from under him and suddenly he was in the air, sailing across the width of the street. His brief flight was cut short as his frame slammed against the side of one of the makeshift huts, knocking a thin, plywood wall into splinters before he caught the structure's metal support pole in midstomach. His breath spluttered out of him as the brigand leader sank to the floor inside the ruined little hut.

The gunman, meanwhile, found his bike and rider, Señor Smarts, dragged away beneath him, and the handlebars clapped into his pelvis, sending a wave of sudden agony through the top of both legs before flipping him to the ground. His jaw hit the dirt road with a resounding thud, making his ears ring once more.

The motorcycle still beneath him, Señor Smarts became tangled with the vehicle as it flipped over itself, again and again, sliding along the street as though at the top of a sharp incline. Smarts's head cracked repeatedly into the ground as he was dragged backward.

Close by, at the entrance to the pier, Kane and the sword-wielding dancing girl were brought to their knees by the sudden shock. Kane reached forward, his left palm slapping into the wooden slats of the pier as he tried to halt his fall. Beside him, the dancing girl rolled forward, taking the brunt of the fall on her shoulder before turning to face him, still kneeling.

Kane saw the startled look in her eyes, and he was about to question her when a second tremor ran through the pier and he felt the ground shake where it touched his legs and steadying hand. Before his eyes, the dark-haired swordswoman toppled over and rolled down the pier. All around, people and loose items were being tossed about, and Kane heard the crash as several of the poorly constructed buildings collapsed.

Kane clawed the ground as it rumbled beneath him, throwing him onto his side. He lay there, facing the pier as the shock wave thundered through the ground. Abruptly, the pier beneath him disintegrated, and Kane reached frantically behind him to secure a grip on the ground as the whole structure crashed into the ocean, the dancing girl and a handful of fishermen dropping with it. As the pier fell, Kane saw the rising wave behind it, growing from twenty to a monstrous forty feet as he watched, rolling toward him with unstoppable force.

Kane braced himself as the wave crashed over him, the weight of water blocking out the sunlight for a moment before the surge of water crashed down and smothered the seafront buildings.

Kane's grip was broken as the wave swelled all around him, and he found himself being shunted along the street before being pulled backward toward the ocean along with several dozen locals and their belongings as they were caught up in its ferocious torrent.

GRANT FOUND HIMSELF caught up in the immense wave as it crashed down on the buildings that lined the beach. It was like flying, the water streaming all around him, pushing him unstoppably onward as it tossed him high in the air. He gasped, gulping in air and seawater as he hurtled ever onward, and he saw the motorcycle and, separately, its rider, race away as they were caught up in other parts of the colossal wave.

Suddenly, the wave lost integrity and the ground was rushing beneath him, fifteen feet below. Grant looked ahead and saw sunlight glint off of the corrugated tin roof of one of the huts, and, quicker than he could acknowledge it, he was shoved into the roof and sent rolling over and over until the whole single-story structure collapsed in on itself.

BRIGID WATCHED AS, caught up in the huge wave, Grant's familiar form sailed overhead and crashed into a wide hut a little way along the street. She held herself low to the ground as the tremor subsided, remaining there for a few seconds until she was certain that the shock wave had passed.

When she looked up again, she saw that the structure that Grant had hit had collapsed in on itself, and a number of the ramshackle buildings along the street were in a similar state of disrepair. Whatever had hit them had hit hard, like a heavy stone being dropped in a pond, the ripples spreading across its surface until its energy was finally spent.

Carefully, Brigid got back on her feet and, steadying her grip on the pistol with her free hand, checked the street. The motorcyclist who had pointed the gun at her head was nowhere to be seen, nor were his bike and passenger. Tom Carnack lay amid the rubble of a building that now stood on the beachfront, where a minute earlier it had been three buildings back. His eyes were closed, and blood was oozing from a wound around his hairline above the right eye.

The street itself was three inches deep in clear water, swells of foam bobbing along here and there as it ran back toward the ocean.

The pier was gone, and Brigid checked the faces of the shocked and wounded who were recovering all around, trying to locate Kane. Neither he nor his lithe opponent were to be seen, and Brigid tamped down the urge to rush to look for him. Grant was just down the street, and she needed to ensure that he was okay first. Plus, assuming he was all right, the two of them could cover more ground in the search for their teammate.

Still clutching the TP-9, Brigid jogged along the street,

her boots splashing in the carpet of flowing water, until she reached the collapsed building that she had seen Grant thrown through. Her hearing was coming back now, after the colossal crashing of the huge wave had briefly deafened her, and she could hear screaming and crying coming from all around. The burned beggar was gone; he and his bowl had presumably been washed away. Children were running around in the street, a naked toddler wailing as he stumbled through the road, looking for a friendly face.

Brigid leaned down and scooped up the unclothed toddler, lifting him to shoulder height and looking to make sure that he wasn't wounded. "There, there," she told him quietly, "it's okay now. It's okay. Hush now."

Carrying the child over one shoulder, Brigid kicked rubble aside and made her way into the remains of the collapsed hut. "Grant?" she called, raising her voice. "It's Brigid. Are you here?"

She listened for a moment, watching the rubble for signs of her partner. Grant's familiar voice came rumbling from across to the right, and Brigid saw the wreckage move and his hand appear above the mess. She rushed across the rubble, taking care not to trip as she balanced the toddler close to her chest, and leaned down to help shift the debris.

A moment later, Grant was struggling out of the shattered remains of the building, water pouring from his coat and his skin caked with pale dust. He wiped a hand over his face and smiled at Brigid. "What the freak just happened?" he asked her, a snarl replacing his smile.

Brigid shook her head, rocking the toddler in her arms. "I don't know," she told Grant. "Felt like maybe a bomb blast, but I didn't hear the explosion. Earthquake maybe?"

"You think?" Grant asked.

Brigid shrugged. "The San Andreas Fault runs through here," she speculated. "If you look at the old maps, you'll see that it pretty much wiped out most of the West Coast a couple of centuries back, after the nukes fell."

Grant nodded thoughtfully. "I'll see if I can raise Lakesh and get some intel," he told her. Then the huge ex-Mag looked around. "Where's Kane?" he asked.

"He was on the pier when it dropped into the sea," Brigid said, clambering over the rubble and back onto the waterlogged street.

Grant shook his head angrily as he followed her. "This day just keeps getting worse," he growled. With that, he activated the Commtact that was embedded subcutaneously behind his right ear and patched through to Cerberus headquarters.

"This is Grant in the field, Lakesh, Donald? Are you guys receiving me?"

There was a brief pause and then Donald Bry's friendly voice came to Grant, uplinked to a satellite from the operations room in the Bitterroot Mountains of Montana. "Hey, Grant, how are things? Mission accomplished?"

The Commtact units were top-of-the-line communication devices that had been discovered in a military installation called Redoubt Yankee several years before, and they had become standard equipment for the Cerberus field operatives. Commtacts featured sensor circuitry incorporating an analog-to-digital voice encoder that was subcutaneously embedded against the mastoid bone. Once the pintels made contact, transmissions were picked up by the auditory canals, and dermal sensors transmitted the electronic signals directly through the user's skull casing. Theoretically, if a wearer went completely deaf he or she would still be capable of hearing, after a fashion, by using the Commtact.

Permanent usage of the Commtact would involve a minor surgical procedure, something many of the Cerberus staff were understandably reticent to submit to, and so their use had stalled, for the moment, at field-test stage. Besides radio communications, the Commtacts could be used as translation devices, providing a real-time interpretation of spoken foreign language on the proviso that sufficient vocabulary had been programmed into their data banks.

The Commtacts could be uplinked to the Keyhole satellite, allowing communication with the field teams, which was a considerable improvement on the original design parameters of the communications technology.

"Mission parameters may have changed," Grant responded. "We think we were just hit by an earthquake. At least, we're hoping it was an earthquake. You have any info at your end?"

"I'm bringing up the feed data now, Grant," Bry's voice came back crisply over the Commtact.

At the Cerberus redoubt in Montana, Donald Bry had access to a wealth of scrolling data from satellites and ground sensors. In his mind's eye, Grant could almost see the man working to bring up all the available data and extrapolate a logical conclusion.

"No evidence of any aerial bombing raid, Grant, but it might be an underground test, of course," Bry suggested after a moment's thought.

"Of course," Grant replied, his voice heavy with sarcasm.

Ahead of him, Brigid was standing at the edge of the damaged pier, looking over the side at the roiling waters below. People were rushing about, their clothes soaked through, desperately searching for their friends and families.

Bry's voice piped over the Commtact once more. "Grant? I'm going to speak with Lakesh and Dr. Falk, see if they have any insights into the data we're receiving. I'll get back to you as soon as I can."

"Cool," Grant replied laconically as the transmission ended.

Brigid was scanning the water, the toddler clambering over her shoulder, his face still red where he had been crying. "What did Cerberus say?" she asked, not bothering to turn to Grant.

"They're not sure yet," Grant told her as he took in the mass of frightened faces that bobbed in the water. "Bry says there's no evidence of aerial bombing. Beyond that he's as in the dark as we are."

"Earthquake," Brigid said. "I'll bet you."

The water poured between their feet as the Cerberus teammates scanned the water for their missing colleague. Parts of the pier bobbed about amid the people that had been caught up in the enormous wave; almost the whole structure had been reduced to worthless driftwood in the space of five seconds. A strut of the pier still stood at an angle, no longer connected to the shore. As Grant's eyes brushed over it he spotted the familiar lean figure of Kane clambering up its leg and securing himself against it with one arm before reaching with his free hand into the water and pulling a woman up by the arm. He was fifty yards from them, surrounded by water.

Grant tapped Brigid on the shoulder and pointed to the figure. "Kane," he stated.

"Got him." She smiled. There was a special bond between Brigid Baptiste and Kane, something more fundamental than a mere emotional connection. They were *anam-charas*, soul friends destined to be together no matter what configuration they found themselves in, friends throughout eternity.

Still holding the TP-9, Brigid rubbed a reassuring hand over the toddler she was cradling over her left shoulder before she turned to face Grant. "Whatever happened, there's a lot of hurt and frightened people out here, Grant," she told him. "We need to start helping them, set up some kind of program for medical treatment."

"What about the mission?" he asked, and then he checked himself. "No, skip it—you're right. Let's take the slope down to the beach and start hauling people out of the water."

Brigid agreed and together they made their way to the waterfront, which was now littered with the debris that had just recently been a ville called Hope.

WITH ONE ARM stretched around the strut of the pier and his feet resting on the little ledge that surrounded its foot, Kane inhaled deep lungfuls of air before reaching back into the water. The dancing girl was bobbing a little way over from him, eyes closed, floating on her back. He stretched out and guided her to him, lifting her up onto the small sill of the strut. "You okay?" he asked as her eyes fluttered open and she spluttered for breath.

Her sword was long gone, but as soon as she saw him,

her mouth broke into a snarl and she spun around, reaching for his face with hands formed into claws. As she did so, she began slipping from the ledge and Kane reached out to steady her. "Take it easy." he told her. "Fight's over."

"What are you talking about, Magistrate man?" she spit as he held her firmly by the shoulder.

"Something hit us, I think," he explained. "Whatever it was it's done plenty of damage. Look." He pointed to the coastal ville stretched out before them.

The dancing girl followed where he had indicated, and Kane heard her sharp intake of breath. The makeshift shanty structures of the settlement had been ripped apart by the tidal wave, and at least seventy percent of the ville had been reduced to rubble. From their vantage point they could see people running about like ants, desperately searching for missing loved ones.

"What happened?" the dark-haired woman asked, bewildered.

"I have no idea," Kane admitted. "Whatever it was, it doesn't matter right now. Some of these people will need help getting out of the water. Can you swim?"

"What?" she responded. "Saving people and their shit? Is this, like, the Magistrate code?"

"No," Kane declared, fixing her with his no-nonsense stare. "It's called being a fucking human being. Now, can you swim?"

She nodded, chastised.

Kane looked out at the people struggling all around them in the water. "You're young and fit," Kane told the dancing girl. "You get in there and you save some lives, you understand?"

She nodded once more and followed Kane as he dived into the churning waters.

TOM CARNACK WATCHED as the redhead and the dark-skinned Magistrate—or *whatever* he was—disappeared down the slope leading to the beach. He felt cold and nervous, on edge, and there was a pain below his ribs where he had collided with the metal strut.

Slowly, carefully he grasped the pole that had winded him and he pulled himself up to a standing position, albeit bent over like an elderly man. Teeth gritted, he winced as pain ran through his gut. He had to have taken quite a hit, though the memory was abating, already vague and insubstantial.

Carnack looked around, taking in his surroundings. He remembered that there had been a loud noise, and the world had turned upside down as he was tossed through the air before... He shook his head, trying to piece the episode together. He was standing in the collapsed ruin of a hut. He could make out the square of the floor plan, what looked like a two-room dwelling constructed of the flimsiest of materials. Sheets of plywood were split and splintered. They had doubtless formed the walls of the habitation before whatever it was had knocked them over. Was it him? Had he done this?

I have to get out of here, Carnack realized, his thoughts slow and fuzzy. His head ached, a low-level buzzing, like when he hadn't had enough sleep, or sometimes when he'd had too much. He stood there, doubled over himself, his hand clinging to the metal pole that had once supported the roof of the hut, and he drew in a long, slow breath, feeling the clawing pain as his diaphragm moved. Whatever had just happened had given him an opportunity for escape, and Tom Carnack was one man who knew when to exploit an opportunity.

In a stumbling, lurching walk, Carnack made his way back into the ruins of Hope, disappearing among the frightened crowds.

THE SUN HAD SET and risen and set once more, and a half moon was rising in the clear sky at the end of their second day in Hope. Kane, Grant and Brigid had worked solidly through that first afternoon, organizing a temporary camp for the survivors of the quake and providing what little medical attention they could for the wounded. A lot of people had been shaken up quite badly by the massive earth tremor, but there were only nine reported deaths, mostly where the makeshift buildings had collapsed on people, although two more had drowned in the savage tidal wave that had followed the quake.

Kane had watched with growing admiration as the swordswoman, whose name was Rosalia, had turned her attention to first rescuing those people stuck in the water who had either never learned or were too panicked to swim, and then helping to entertain the lost children by teaching them the flowing movements that came naturally to her as a dancer.

"You have quite a way with children," he remarked as they sat eating breakfast together after that first, long night.

"Children are the same as men," she told him with a malicious gleam in her eyes, "easily captivated by simple movements."

Kane laughed at that. "Well, I suppose it depends on who's doing the movements," he admitted.

The dozen or so lost and unclaimed children had slept in a storeroom behind the main hall. Kane watched the roll of her hips as Rosalia walked to the room to wake them up. As he watched, the dark-eyed woman looked back at him over her shoulder, and her hair fell over her face, adding to her exotic allure as she offered him a warm smile before leaving the hall.

Señor Smarts had offered to help, too, once he had recovered from the pounding his body had taken when he had been thrown down the street astride the motorcycle. Initially, he had wandered the now brackish streets in a daze, but when he had heard that people were getting organized at the robust church buildings, he had arrived at the door and asked how he might assist. Along with Brigid, Smarts had helped organize a reception system at the church hall where lost family members might be found.

The steady stream of lost and weary people seemed never-ending, but finally, as the sun disappeared over the horizon for the second time since the quake, their numbers started to dwindle as people began making their way back to their ruined dwellings and thinking about picking up their lives again.

While the church hall was quiet, Brigid peeled back the bandage that was wrapped around Smarts's head and took a proper look at the wound there. "You took quite a beating," she said, dabbing at the dried blood with a damp cloth while Grant looked on.

Across the hall, Kane was busy with the onerous task of helping frightened relatives identify the handful of dead bodies. Rosalia was sitting with five children, telling them an old story she recalled from her own childhood. There were other locals there, too, officials and selfless do-gooders who had stepped in to man the recovery operation with no thought of their own concerns. It was remarkable how well the locals and the refugees had pulled together, a testament to the resilience of the human spirit in adverse circumstances.

Señor Smarts shot a fierce look at Grant as he addressed Brigid. "I think your friend shot me," he told her.

Grant looked apologetic. "Well," he said, shrugging.

Smarts held his gaze a moment longer before his expression mellowed a little. "What's done is done, *señor,*" he admitted, "and I'm sure I was intending to do the same given the circumstances of our meeting."

Kane joined them as Brigid sterilized and dressed Smarts's head wound from the church's meager supplies. "Yeah, about that," Kane said, "what made you think that we were Magistrates?"

"It's obvious." The olive-skinned Mexican smiled. "You and Señor Grant here have a certain manner about you, a way of walking, your heads held high. An air of authority, arrogance that comes only with the badge of office."

Kane smiled bitterly, shaking his head as Rosalia walked over to join the group, having finally found a family to take care of the last of her young charges. "I'm not a Mag," Kane told Señor Smarts. "We're not Mags."

The man smiled again in a display of yellowing teeth. "The way that the three of you took command here, organizing and taking care of the local people, tells me different, *señor*. If you are not Magistrates, then you almost certainly trained to be, at some point in your past."

Grant flicked a warning look at Kane, as if to tell him it wasn't a topic of conversation worth pursuing.

After a moment, Kane spoke again. "Any idea what happened to the rest of your crew? Where Carnack disappeared to?"

"I'm sorry, Señor Kane." Smarts sighed. "I was unconscious for quite a while. When I realized what had happened I felt it my duty to help out. That's all I can tell you."

"Very admirable," Grant muttered before he stood up and took Kane to one side. They stood together, looking at the devastation outside the open church hall doors for a few moments, and then he spoke to Kane in a low voice. "This doesn't change anything. That hybrid DNA is still in the hands of their extended clan. We can't ignore that just because these two helped out."

Kane nodded, a haunted look in his gray-blue eyes. "No good deed goes unpunished," he said quietly.

"You reckon the girl knows anything?" Grant asked.

"I'd guess Smarts is Carnack's majordomo," Kane reasoned. "If anyone knows the location of the gang and the DNA, it's him. But Rosalia is more than she seems. I'd dismissed her as a—" he shrugged "—companion when I first saw her, but the way she came at me with that sword yesterday afternoon—she's trained and she's deadly."

"We'll take both of them back to Cerberus," Grant suggested. "We can interrogate them there, see what we turn up." He glanced back at the Mexican in the loud shirt and stained velvet coat, and at the dark-haired enchantress who stood beside him. "Who knows? Maybe they'll be more forthcoming after all that's happened."

Kane chewed at his lip thoughtfully for a moment. "I wouldn't bet on it," he told Grant.

As the two ex-Mags were striding back to where Brigid taped gauze to Señor Smarts's head, their Commtacts came to life and the three Cerberus teammates heard the voice of Dr. Mohandas Lakesh Singh inside their heads.

Lakesh was the nominal leader of the Cerberus exiles, although his suitability to that role was somewhat contentious. Their early meetings with Lakesh had shown Kane, Grant and Brigid that the accomplished cyberneticist had orchestrated a Machiavellian plan to destroy their lives in Cobaltville, albeit for the greater good, and his methods had often proved to be supremely devious. However reluctantly, Lakesh had conceded his singleminded control of Cerberus and its exiles undermined the united front necessary to battle the Annunaki and the threat they posed to humankind.

Lakesh's mellifluous voice piped directly to their ear canals with crystal clarity. "It seems that we may have an additional problem, and I wondered how the three of you would feel about taking a little detour to look into it?"

Kane held up his index finger to let his companions know that he would deal with the transmission. "Kane here," he said. "What seems to be the problem?"

"Decard has just got in touch with us from over in Aten," Lakesh explained. "He's stumbled across something on one of his regular patrols, and he thinks we might want to take a look."

Decard, like Kane and Grant, was also an ex-Magistrate. He had been adopted into the strange culture of the hidden city-kingdom of Aten, out in the wilderness of the California desert. His path had crossed that of the Cerberus crew on several occasions. Initially hostile, the people of Aten had come to respect the Cerberus exiles, and Decard had proved himself to be a faithful friend and valuable ally.

"Did Decard say what it was?" Kane asked, aware that the ex-Mag wasn't one to jump at shadows.

"He seemed mystified," Lakesh explained, "but the report he gave describes a group of people who apparently have no independent will. He called them 'mindless, soulless wretches.'"

Kane considered this for a moment before responding. "Don't want to be callous here, but is that such a big deal?" he asked.

"It is when the same people were vibrant and very much alive just three days earlier," Lakesh told him, "or so Decard indicates."

"Okay," Kane agreed. "We'll arrange transportation and get over there before dawn. Warn Decard that we're bringing a couple of stragglers with us, and we might need to use his hoosegow."

"I'm sending Domi over there now via mat-trans," Lakesh replied. "She'll pass on the message and meet you close to Aten. Take care."

"Will do." Kane signed off. He turned to the others, who had been able to hear the whole conversation on their own Commtact. "Well, troops, looks like we're moving out."

Señor Smarts, who had only heard Kane's half of the

conversation, smiled tightly. "Leaving so soon?" he said in a patronizing tone.

"Yeah," Grant growled, reaching for the man's elbow and helping him up, "and you're coming with us, Charlie."

Kane looked across at Rosalia the dancing girl and smiled. "You, too, Princess."

Chapter 4

The five of them skulked through the alleyways of Hope, hidden in the shadows of the ruined ville. Kane walked close to Señor Smarts, leading the party, the Magnum handgun held tightly in his hand. Behind him, Grant accompanied Rosalia, pulling her by the elbow, his own pistol hidden under the folds of his leather duster. Brigid brought up the rear a few paces behind the rest of the group, her handgun drawn and held low, muzzle pointing to the ground.

As they made their way to the outskirts of the shantytown, Rosalia's eyes flashed with anger. She pulled from Grant's grip and strode ahead, catching up with Smarts and Kane. She glared at Kane. "Where are you taking us, Magistrate man?" she demanded.

"We're needed elsewhere," Kane replied laconically, while Grant reached for the woman's elbow once more.

Rosalia pulled away and glared fiercely at them both, standing in place until Brigid caught up. "After all we have done for you," Rosalia snapped, "you still treat us like... criminals?"

Grant suppressed a laugh when he heard that. Kane looked at him sternly before addressing the dancing girl.

"We need that hybrid DNA," Kane explained, "and right now, the two of you are our only link to finding it."

Brigid made eye contact with Rosalia and Señor Smarts as she joined them. "We all have a lot of admiration for what you both did back there," she told them, indicating the buildings ruined by the quake. "You stepped in to help when it was needed. We don't need to be enemies. Perhaps we can reach a mutually beneficial agreement with regards to the DNA."

Smarts reached up to scratch at the gauze that had been attached to his head before stopping himself with a pained intake of breath through his teeth. "This puts us in a difficult position, *señorita*," he lamented, his eyes warily watching the shadows around them. "It would be inadvisable for Rosalia and I to engage in dealings that might be considered traitorous to our group," he added quietly.

Kane nodded in understanding. "Would that still hold true outside of ville limits?"

Smarts considered this for a few seconds, smoothing down his pencil-thin mustache while, Kane noticed, Rosalia's dark eyes scanned the alleyway in a predatory fashion. "Perhaps," Smarts said eventually, "we would reconsider our position if placed in such a situation."

Kane smiled. "Then let's keep moving."

"And where exactly is it that we are going, Señor Kane?" Smarts asked.

"Just a little walk in the desert," Kane explained. "Friends out there need our help, but you can just watch if you want."

Rosalia looked at the half-moon rising in the sky. "It is almost midnight, Magistrate man," she told Kane, "not a good time to be walking across the desert."

"Gets mighty cold out there," Smarts added.

Along with his companions, Kane had arrived in Hope from the desert. The three of them had used the interphaser to jump close to the ville location, but they had still been forced to walk the last eight miles for the sake of appearances as much as anything else. That had been in the daytime, in the rising heat. At night the temperature in the California desert dropped significantly, and the chill wind could catch a traveler unawares.

"There's never a good time to cross the desert," Grant said practically, tilting the pistol in his hands so that it caught the light for just a moment. "Hence the argument's over."

"I think not," Smarts told them. "We could borrow a vehicle from one of the people here without too much trouble."

"By 'borrow' you mean steal?" Kane asked. "We don't do that."

"Señor Magistrate," Smarts argued, "many people here have lost their homes, their loved ones, some even their lives. The loss of a cart, an automobile would be of little—"

"Doesn't matter." Kane silenced him with a firm look. "You have legs, so we walk."

Rosalia smiled. "We have reconditioned Sandcats," she said, "ideal for desert travel."

"And where would these Sandcats be?" Kane asked.

"Back at the base," Rosalia said lightly, gesturing toward the depths of the shantytown labyrinth. "If we went there, we could—"

Kane held up a finger to stop her. "No. Nice try, but we won't be walking into any traps tonight. Now, let's get moving."

Kane and Grant urged their charges on as Brigid sank

back to cover the rear of the party. What Kane hadn't told Smarts and Rosalia was that he had his own special transport located outside the ville. They weren't safe here, and he had feared being overheard, but soon enough the group would be traveling a whole lot faster than the two street thieves could imagine.

IT WAS THREE in the morning by the time the group stopped. The ville was long since behind them, now just a speckling of lighted dots on the far horizon. Ahead and all around, Death Valley and the empty California desert stretched relentlessly onward. Stars twinkled in the night sky, and the cool air seemed to drill through their bones as the group strode across the open sand. Rosalia shook, cold and miserable, hugging herself as she pulled Smarts's bright frock coat over her shoulders. Smarts himself was cold, too, but he prided himself on being nothing if not a gentleman.

"Where are we heading, *señor?*" Smarts asked, looking at the distant rock formations, the endless swathe of sand around them.

"We're almost there," Kane assured him.

"It has been a long day," Smarts told Kane. "We could stop. If not for ourselves, perhaps we should consider the ladies?"

"We're not going much farther," Kane told him.

Then he raised his voice. "Baptiste?"

Brigid had drifted a little farther behind the others, and she was looking around carefully as they crossed the bleak desert. "It's just over there," she called back, pointing with the muzzle of her handgun toward a rising sand dune.

Kane held a hand to stop Smarts and the rest of the party, while Brigid ran toward the dune that she had indicated.

"Be a minute, people," Kane explained, ignoring the quizzical looks of his captives.

Exhausted, Rosalia sat on the dry sand and shook her head. "Magistrate clowns," she muttered under her breath.

Hearing this, Grant smiled and caught her eye, shaking his own head in chastisement. "Oh, you are in for such a sweet surprise," he told her.

Smarts's head twitched like a bird's as he watched Brigid disappear behind the dune. "What is going on?" he demanded.

Deciding that there was nowhere his prisoners could run to, Kane placed his handgun back in his low-slung hip holster before addressing the small Mexican. "It's time we traveled in style," he said.

Smarts narrowed his eyes, peering at the dune, his head jutting forward, until Brigid reappeared carrying a small case. The case was caked with sand, which Brigid brushed away with her hand as she approached. Smarts realized immediately that this item had been hidden out here, buried somewhere in the empty, featureless desert.

Brigid stopped before them and knelt, placing the case on the ground. Then she began to work at its twin catches. The carrying case folded open and a squat, broad-based pyramid-shaped object was revealed. Made of a dull metal that shimmered with the blurred reflections of the bright stars, the pyramid's base was barely one foot square, and its peak was about twelve inches above the ground. This was the interphaser.

"What is this thing?" Smarts inquired.

Kane smiled tightly. "A little shortcut," he said enigmatically.

Smarts gestured around them at the featureless desert. "You left this thing here, yes?" he asked. "How could you possibly find it? It is a—what you call it?—needle in the haystack."

"Brigid's our needle finder," Kane said as Grant helped Rosalia to her feet behind him.

Smarts looked baffled as he assessed the beautiful woman with the shimmering red-gold hair.

Brigid smiled and tapped the side of her head. "I remember things," she told him.

The Cerberus team had opted to bury the interphaser in its protective carrying case close to where they had first appeared in the desert. This was, on reflection, much safer than carrying the astonishing piece of technology into a covert meeting with Carnack's merciless thieves and brigands. They had needed no marker for the location. One of the advantages of Brigid's phenomenal memory was her ability to recall the smallest details of anything she had seen. While the desert appeared featureless and largely unchanging to most people, Brigid would recall the tiniest details, a ridge here, a dead tree stump there. Finding the burial spot for this particular treasure chest was as easy to Brigid as finding the toes on the end of her feet.

The interphaser interacted with naturally occurring hyperdimensional vortices to create an instantaneous teleportation system. In simple terms, the little pyramid opened dimensional rifts through which one could travel from point A to point B, despite the two points being dozens, hundreds or even thousands of miles apart.

The Parallax Points Program provided a map of these naturally occurring vortices, which could be found around the world and even on other planets.

The success of the interphaser was the combined work of Brigid Baptiste and a Cerberus scientist called Brewster Philboyd, and had taken many months of trial and error to achieve. While a useful device, their interphaser still depended on the location of a parallax point, as opposed to the mat-trans units, which had been installed in military redoubts. As Grant had put it when they had arrived in Death Valley with an eight-mile walk still ahead of them, "What good's having a personal mat-trans if we still have to walk halfway?"

While Brigid readied the pyramid-shaped device, Kane probed the sand around them with the toe of his boot until he found what he was looking for. He kicked at the sand and used his instep to brush it away until he had uncovered a flat, stone disk. The stone disk was approximately two feet square and showed cuneiform carvings around its outer ring. Brigid stepped across and carefully placed the interphaser unit in the center of the stone ring.

"What is that?" Smarts asked once more, absolutely out of his depth with the progression of events before his eyes.

"We think it was some kind of grave marker." Kane shrugged. "Probably Navaho or Apache."

"Or whatever those peoples called themselves way back when," Brigid added, mostly to herself.

Rosalia took a step closer and peered at the stone circle with the pyramid now protruding from it. Then she looked at Smarts, a quizzical frown on her beautiful brow. "What is all this?" she asked him.

"I admit," Smarts responded, "to being mystified. Seems the Magistrates don't want to share their secrets today."

Kane confirmed with Brigid that the interphaser was ready for use, then he turned to address Smarts and Rosalia. "Okay, here's the skinny," he began. "What we have here is a transport network like you folks can only dream of. The whole thing is instantaneous—"

"Like a mat-trans only portable," Smarts broke into Kane's explanation with a knowing smile.

"You've used a mat-trans?" Kane asked him, intrigued. The mat-trans units were mostly the realm of Cerberus and similar covert outfits who had penetrated the secret military redoubts to access the hidden technology there; their existence was hardly common knowledge.

"I have seen them in action once or twice," Smarts confirmed.

"Good," Kane affirmed. "That makes it easier for all of us. Rosie?" he asked, turning to the dancing girl.

She nodded, her face solemn. "I am aware of the mat-trans machines," she said quietly, "though only through anecdotal evidence."

"These are smaller," Kane explained, "and there's no chamber to enter. But they function in much the same way."

He encouraged the pair to step forward, closer to the foot-high pyramid resting on the stone circle on the ground. The stone circle was a parallax point, and would work as a secure entry point for their jump.

Grant stepped across from the others, so that the team now formed a rough circle around the interphaser as the stars twinkled in the sky above.

Still kneeling, Brigid tapped out a brief sequence on the interphaser's miniature keypad. As she stood, a waxy, illuminated cone fanned up from the metal apex of the foot-high pyramid. It had the appearance of mist, with flashes of light swirling within its depths.

Smarts's jaw opened in astonishment as the cone of light grew larger, taking over not just more geographical space, but, in some way, swamping his mind like the onrush of a migraine, blurring everything around him to insignificance as it overwhelmed his comprehension. A glowing lotus flower blossomed from the base of the pyramid. The radiance stretched into the night sky, filled with sparks of lightning witch fire.

"Just walk into the light," Kane's calm voice came to his ears, and Smarts turned from the cone of brilliance to look at the hard face of the ex-Mag. The light was dancing in Kane's gray-blue eyes, playing across the stubbled chin and sharp planes of his face.

"I don't think this is such a good idea, Señor Kane," Smarts admitted, rising fear in his voice.

Then Grant's bearlike arm whipped behind Smarts, slapping so hard across his back that the little Mexican stumbled forward. "Man up," he heard the dark-skinned man say, "you're going first."

There was a rush of sensation, energy crackling all around him, colors so bright and vibrant that Smarts didn't have names for all of them. And then his senses rebelled at the unfamiliarity of the situation, and the next thing Smarts saw was his shadow grow as he stepped out of the cone of light behind him. Then he was joined by his four companions.

They had arrived.

"Did we do it?" Rosalia asked, her voice breathless with wonder.

"Sixty, seventy miles in a footstep," Kane assured her. "We did it."

"Sixty-eight miles," Brigid confirmed as the interphaser powered down, its lotus blossom of colors sucked back inside the unit like liquid swirling down a drain. She crouched beside the device, which now rested on an otherwise unremarkable section of sand, and placed the carrying case beside it, undoing the catches. There was another circle of stone there, almost entirely buried in the sand, its cuneiform markings long since worn away.

Having packed up the interphaser in its carrying case, Brigid scanned the sky around them, looking at the constellations and assessing their position in her head.

Kane triggered the Commtact and spoke in a subdued tone, "Domi, we are on-site. Please respond."

A few seconds passed before Domi's enticing, husky voice was audible over the subcutaneous Commtacts.

"Hi, Kane. I'm with Decard's team. We're sending up a tracer on three."

"Aten should be somewhere over that way," Brigid decided, pointing off to the east.

Almost as soon as she said it, they saw a scarlet-colored firework whoosh into the sky, leaving a bright point high over their heads as the flare beacon floated on the wind currents.

"Guess that's them." Kane smiled.

IT TOOK ANOTHER fifteen minutes to cover the ground on foot, but Kane, Brigid, Grant and their two prisoners finally found their way to the temporary campsite that Decard's crew had set up among the windswept dunes.

When she saw them approaching, Domi broke into a run and met the Cerberus team halfway.

"Madre de dios!" Smarts exclaimed as Domi raced toward them, startled by the woman's unique appearance.

Though a fully grown woman, Domi still had the diminutive frame of a girl just entering her teens. Her limbs were thin and birdlike, yet she was a superb athlete and robust hand-to-hand combatant. Most significantly, however, Domi looked like no one else that Smarts had ever seen. She had the chalk-white skin and bone-white hair of an albino, and her eyes blazed a burning ruby-red like the flames of hell. She wore her hair in a short, pixieish style, enhancing her skeleton-like appearance, and she had chosen the briefest of clothes—a halter top and cutoff shorts—leaving her midriff, limbs and feet bare. Her clothing was beige, matching the sandy desert beneath the dark sky, its light color making her white skin seem somehow more pale than ever.

Like the other members of Kane's field team, Cobaltville played a prominent part in Domi's past. Domi had been forced into sexual servitude in the lowest echelons of the ville. She had grown up as a wild child of the Outlands, and her wits and decision making still had something of the instinctive to them.

"Kane," she cried, running up to the ex-Mag and wrapping her arms around him. Kane hugged her back, looking like a giant holding a tiny, china doll. "I heard you ran into that quake over on the coast. You're okay?"

As Domi let go of him, Kane nodded. "I think the quake

really ran into us," he told her with a smile. Kane and Domi had a strange history between them, but above all else they were bound by a mutual respect as warriors. "Brought some friends for you to meet," Kane continued, gesturing to Señor Smarts and Rosalia, who stood beside Grant, her jaw jutting at a haughty angle as she observed the albino woman.

"This is Rosalia and the gentleman is called Smarts."

Smarts took Domi's hand and brushed it lightly with his lips. "Enchanted, *señorita,*" he said, his eyes meeting hers.

After the introductions had been made, the group headed back to the camp where Decard and his team were stationed. It was a simple affair, just a bivouac created from a couple of sheets of tarpaulin propped over a small area atop posts pushed into the sand. Once he was close enough, Kane recognized the posts that Decard's crew had used. They were the slender silver rods that the security force of Aten used as their primary weapons. The long poles were tipped by V-shaped prongs, and they were capable of unleashing a charge of energy that could fell a man, knocking him into unconsciousness or worse, depending upon the setting employed by the user.

The makeshift nature of the camp reminded Kane of the shantytown that they had just left on the outskirts of Hope. Two armed guards nodded in acknowledgment as Domi passed, leading the group beneath the slanted roof sheets. The guards were Incarnates, and both came from similar stock. They were sturdy-looking individuals, their skin a shining coffee-bean brown from the sun. Their clothing was identical—naked but for loosely woven white linen kilts threaded with golden wire, coupled with glittering collars of hammered gold that embraced their necks. The only thing to differentiate them were the unique adornments on their faces. Both men wore masks that entirely covered their heads, remarkable helmets carved of painted and varnished wood. The mask of the sec man to the left bore a fierce caricature of a crocodile, its long snout pointing down to the ground, its rows of teeth highlighted in white paint. The man to the right wore the mask of a bug, an idealized version of a beetle, with large eyes and pincers that resembled the drooping lines of Grant's gunslinger mustache.

As Domi led the way into the small, makeshift shelter, Decard got up from his resting position on the floor and called to them. The tent was lit by three small, oil-burning lamps that had been placed around the floor space. There were more guards inside, eight in all, and several had removed their helms and were dozing.

Decard was a fresh-faced young man, about twenty years old, and with close-cropped, sandy-blond hair. He wore the armor of a Magistrate, a familiar black polycarbonate exoskeleton, and it added a sense of authority to his five-foot-ten-inch frame.

Both Smarts and Rosalia backed away when they saw the Mag armor, but Grant was standing behind them, and Rosalia let out a quiet yelp as she bumped into his chest. "Nothing to get worked up about," Grant told her quietly.

On closer inspection, they saw that the Magistrate armor was lacking the red insignia that usually graced the left pectoral; it looked to have been torn from the outfit.

Decard himself bore a friendly expression as he walked across the tent to meet with his old comrades. The man walked with a slight limp, favoring his left leg as he came over to greet them.

"Hello, Kane," Decard said, acknowledging the other Cerberus personnel briefly. "Glad you could all make it out here."

"What's going on, Decard?" Kane asked, not a man for small talk.

"I was on patrol three days ago," Decard explained as he led the way to the back of the small shelter, "when I came across a group of Roamers. Just a family, refugees, I think, crossing the desert. They'd set up camp quite close to the city entrance, and I brought some men out here to shoo them away." Decard looked at Kane as though hoping for approval.

Kane understood what the man meant. Decard, like himself and Grant, may have retired prematurely, but he still had the old Magistrate instincts. In Decard's case, he had been accidentally caught up in a conspiracy involving the welfare of new hybrids, and had somehow found himself on the run. He had landed on his feet in the hidden city-kingdom of Aten, California, where he had gone native and married into royalty. Decard had found a better life than most Magistrates, and his world was generally far more sedate than that of Kane or Grant. Aten treasured its secrecy, a community hidden away from the harsh realities of the world, and Decard had become the de facto leader of the Incarnates, the guardians of the city. He still made patrols around the city-kingdom, though he used his skills as a diplomat far more often than his handgun these days.

Kane nodded, encouraging the man to continue.

"I was doing a surveillance swoop around dusk when I

came across one of the same folks," Decard told him. "Only this time she looked like this…"

Decard gestured to a figure crouching on the ground behind two standing, helmeted guards. As the guards parted, Kane saw a young woman with long blond hair, probably still in her teenage years, bearing the swollen belly of pregnancy. Her hair was damp with sweat, curtained over her eyes, and she rocked back and forth on her heels, her jaw slack. Drool oozed down her chin from her open mouth.

As Kane stepped closer, he felt something nudge him and saw that Decard was handing him a flashlight. "Go on," Decard urged him, "she won't bite."

Kane leaned down and switched on the flashlight, pointing it away from the woman before turning it gradually to illuminate her clearly. She just crouched there, rocking back and forth, not reacting in the slightest to his approach. "You okay, ma'am?" he said.

The woman seemed to be ignoring him. She just rocked, back and forth repeatedly. Now that he was closer, Kane could detect a low humming, too, the noise coming from the woman, not her mouth but pushed from deep in her throat and out of her nose.

Kane reached forward with his free hand and made to tentatively touch the woman's face. She didn't flinch, didn't move at all, and before Kane's fingers met with her he turned back to Decard. "Do I need gloves?"

"Hell if I know." Decard shrugged. He shook off one of his gloves and passed it to Kane. "Use this if you want."

Kane took the Mag gauntlet and pulled it over his right hand before reaching for the young woman again. Crouching before her, Kane used the black fingers of the glove to stroke her hair gently from where it obscured her face. Beneath her mop of hair, as he had somehow suspected, her eyes were wide open.

Her eyes were blank, pure white orbs, white on white, all color drained away.

Chapter 5

After a moment, Kane turned away from the woman, removing his gloved hand and letting her blond bangs fall back over her face. He turned to Decard with a look of concern. "Do you know what's wrong with her?" he asked.

Decard held up his hands. "No idea. I've never seen anything like this before," he said. "She's running a high temperature, just like the others we found."

"There are others?" Brigid spoke up.

"There were eight in the original party that we chased off," Decard told her, "and we found three of them running around out here at dusk. I say 'running,' but I don't mean that literally, of course," he added.

"'Mindless, soulless wretches,'" Kane quoted from the report that Lakesh had passed on to him over the Commtact when they had received word back in Hope. "Isn't that what you said?"

Decard took his glove back from Kane as he spoke. "It wasn't intended as a medical diagnosis," he said with good humor, "but it was about the best way I could think of to describe them."

Brigid Baptiste produced a pair of thin polymer gloves from her jacket pocket and placed them over her hands. They were disposable gloves, transparent and reaching just past her wrists. Then she crouched before the pregnant woman and started speaking to her softly as she gently pushed back the woman's hair. "You said there were others?" Brigid asked Decard, her voice calm.

"Two others. What you see here is pretty accurate to how they were," Decard said. "We found the three of them wandering about the desert here, aimless as a leaf on the wind, just walking around in circles. I think they're a family, or at least they were."

"Where are the others now?" Kane asked.

Decard placed an arm around Kane's shoulders and pulled him toward the closest opening of the bivouac. "Let's talk about that outside," he said quietly.

Leaving Grant, Domi and the Incarnates to watch their prisoners, Kane and Decard stood outside the tent waiting for Brigid to join them.

"Her temperature's running at 108," Brigid said as she walked out of the tent, brandishing a pocket thermometer that the Incarnate medic had loaned her. She sounded astonished. "She must be burning up inside."

"Not burning," Kane said solemnly, "melting. Can a body even take that kind of temperature?"

Brigid nodded slowly. "The human body can take greater extremes than we give it credit for," she said, "but I don't like her long-term chances, especially with the baby."

Decard interjected at that point, all humor drained from his face. "The other two went like that," he said quietly, "first they were walking about like they'd been concussed, then they sat down, mumbling and drooling."

"And then?" Kane prompted.

"They're dead, Kane," Decard told him.

"Shit," Kane spit as he noticed the mounds of earth where Decard and his team had buried two bodies. "What have you stumbled on here?"

Decard shook his head. "We're four miles from Aten," he said. "Far as I'm concerned, this is the very limit of my jurisdiction. I called Cerberus in because I don't have the time or resources to deal with it. Figured maybe you do."

"That's mighty brave of you," Kane growled.

Decard looked away, refusing to meet the man's gray-blue eyes. "We look after our own, Kane," he said, "that's the rule of the Outlands, and you know it. These freaks get closer to the city and I'll do what I have to, but I'm in way over my depth here."

"What if it's a plague," Kane said, "an airborne virus, something you can't just pretend doesn't exist? What then?"

Decard paced across the sand for a moment, head low, absorbed by his thoughts.

"I've got four people and two prisoners," Kane urged. "We need manpower, and your people are on the scene, Decard. Will you help us?"

Decard's gaze swept past Kane and Brigid, and he looked off into the distance. "None of this can be brought back to the city," he said quietly. "No prisoners, none of the infected. I am not having this spread through Aten."

"None of us wants that," Brigid assured him.

"I'm out here with a twelve-man team," Decard said. "You get me and them and that's it. Okay?"

Kane nodded. "You just keep your gun loaded."

"Don't worry," Brigid told them both. "We'll find out what it is. No one else needs to get hurt."

BACK INSIDE the bivouac, Rosalia was peering at the far end of the tent, watching the pregnant woman rocking back and forth on her heels. "What is wrong with that lady?" she asked in an urgent whisper.

"That's what we're here to find out," Domi said. "Friends of ours found her wandering the desert, figured we'd be able to help."

"And what is it that you do?" Smarts chipped in politely.

"None of your nose," Domi said, flashing him her feral smile.

Leaving Grant with the prisoners, Domi made her way to a small, tan-colored rucksack to the side of the tent and rummaged through its contents. A moment later she returned with a Sin Eater handgun in a black leather holster. "Thought you might need this," she told Grant. "Brought one for Kane, too."

Grant shrugged out of the right sleeve of his coat and clipped the wrist holster to his right forearm. The Sin Eater was the official sidearm of the Magistrate Division, and the weapon with which Grant and Kane felt most comfortable. Less than fourteen inches in length at full extension, the automatic handblaster folded in on itself to be stored in the bulky holster just above the wrist. The holsters reacted to a specific tensing of the wrist tendons, snapping the pistol automatically into the user's hand.

The trigger of the Sin Eater had no guard; the necessity for any kind of safety features had never been foreseen when the weapon had been assigned to the infallible Magistrates. While both Grant and Kane were schooled in numerous forms of unarmed and armed combat, the Sin Eater was an old friend, a natural weight that their movements accommodated, like wearing a wristwatch.

Smarts watched with amusement as Grant finished clipping the Sin Eater in place. "I said you were Magistrates, did I not, *señor?*"

Grant looked at him, no hint of amusement or pity in his features. "Why don't you help yourselves out here and give us the information we want about the hybrid DNA. You can see that you're nothing more than deadweight to us right now. You give us the info and we'll let you walk out of here, no questions asked."

Smarts nodded slowly, considering the offer. "I would need to discuss this with my colleague, you understand?" he said, indicating Rosalia.

"Discuss away," Grant said, ejecting and returning the Sin Eater to its holster in the Magistrate's standard test routine.

"In private, if you would be so kind." Smarts grinned.

Grant flicked the Sin Eater into his hand again and gestured to the open doorway of the tent covering. "Let's go outside," he said.

Smarts and Rosalia led the way into the cool night air, with Grant and Domi following. They made their way past the guards and walked for a half minute until Grant instructed the group to stop. He indicated vaguely in the direction ahead, where a few dried-up bushes dotted the sand. "Take ten paces off in that direction," Grant said, "and have your discussion. I'll be right here."

"Me, too," Domi added, producing a Detonics .45 pistol with a chrome finish from the rear of her waistband.

"As you wish, Señor Grant." Smarts bowed subtly to Grant before walking with Rosalia toward the dried-up brush.

The pair of brigands walked a dozen paces before

stopping, trying to create as much distance from their captors without stoking their ire.

"We need to get out of here, Axel," Rosalia whispered, keeping her voice low and her eyes on Grant and Domi.

"Not yet," Smarts told her, his own eyes also fixed on their guardians. "You saw that device they used, the portable mat-trans unit."

"Of course." Rosalia nodded.

"Such a device would be of inestimable value to our people," Smarts told her.

"It would doubtless sell for a pretty penny." Rosalia smiled. "A very pretty, shiny penny indeed."

"Forget your magpie instincts," Smarts chastised her, subtly repositioning himself so that she masked his body from their captors' watching eyes. "With that unit we could go anywhere, take anything. We could be the new masters of the world."

Rosalia laughed. "You're a fool," she said. "You over-estimate its value to Tom."

"A gateway to anywhere on the planet, arriving and de-parting without warning or preamble," Smarts rationalized as he pulled a pocket chron on a thin metal chain from his pants pocket. "I think not. You saw the case in which the woman put it. She has it with her. We must steal that case before we depart. Can you do this, Sweet Rose?"

Rosalia pondered this for a moment, thinking about the small size and apparent light weight of the device. "That won't be a problem," she assured her colleague, "if the right opportunity presents itself."

"They are busy worrying about the sick woman with no sight," Smarts said in a rush. "We're no longer their primary concern. They'll let their guard down soon enough, I am sure of it." The plastic face of the pocket chron had misted up where water had been caught inside it during the tidal wave in Hope. The front was still blurred, and Smarts tapped it lightly with the tip of his manicured nail.

"And in the meantime?" Rosalia asked. "They will keep pestering us for the information about the hidden base."

"Let them pester," Smarts told her, checking the chron carefully. Though disguised as an old-fashioned fob watch, the item that Smarts had produced from his pocket wasn't simply that. It was, in fact, a compass with electronic range finder. Smarts looked at the spinning needle that appeared to be a loose minute hand for a moment, before glancing back at their captors to reassure himself that neither Grant nor Domi was taking any notice; they weren't. With Rosalia still standing before him, Smarts replaced the compass in his pocket.

"A little sleight of hand, the illusion of progress…they'll soon get bored and sloppy."

"The dark-skinned one is like a wall, impenetrable," Rosalia decided. "But Kane is a soft touch. He lets emotions rule him."

"I think you like him," Smarts observed with a smile.

"He has a certain way about him," Rosalia said, nodding, "but a knife still fits between his ribs."

Smarts nodded firmly, once, before leading the way back to Grant and Domi.

As Smarts and Rosalia were talking between themselves, Domi turned and nudged Grant. "Do you trust them?" she asked quietly.

"They're a pair of brigands who deal in stolen genetic material," Grant answered sarcastically. "What's not to trust?"

"Touché," Domi muttered as she watched the pair approach.

THE ELECTRONIC thermometer beeped, and Brigid took it from the woman's ear and checked its reading before looking up at Kane. "One-ten," she said solemnly.

Brigid looked at the slick sheen of sweat that covered the pregnant woman's face and made her clothes dark. The woman crouched there as when they had first seen her, but she no longer hummed and her rocking was slowing, more of an occasional shift of balance now.

"What can we do," Kane asked, "to cool her down?"

"I don't think there's anything," Brigid replied sadly.

"What about going outside the tent?" Kane suggested. "No cloud cover, and that desert wind—it's pretty damn chilly out there."

"No." Brigid shook her head. "That won't work. This is something inside her. Something eating away at her."

"The baby?" Kane asked.

"I don't think so," Brigid said thoughtfully.

"Then what about—?" Kane began, but Brigid silenced him with a stern look from her emerald eyes.

"The baby's dead, Kane," Brigid told him. "Whatever trauma her body's going through here, the infant's going through it ten times worse. Horrible as it is, we have to face facts."

Kane glanced at Brigid before casting his eyes over the crouching woman again. "We could call in Reba DeFore," he suggested.

DeFore was the Cerberus healer, tasked to care for every member of the redoubt's staff. In her time with Cerberus she had dealt capably with hybrid and alien physiognomy, as well as human.

Brigid shook her head. "I suspect there's nothing Reba could do even if she were here. I'm sorry, Kane."

Brigid had worked with Kane for a long time. Whether it was simply knowing the man the way she did, or something deeper, she knew that Kane drove himself hardest in the pursuit of saving true innocents like this woman and her unborn child.

"We could still save the baby," Kane stated.

"No, we can't," Brigid said, all emotion drained from her voice.

"We can try. Cut her belly…"

"No, Kane."

Kane looked at the girl as she shook in place, a shiver running through her fragile body, and his lips parted in a snarl. He turned away then, and Brigid caught and held his gaze with her own. "No," she told him.

Twenty minutes later the young woman and her unborn child were dead. She had moaned and shook violently for a brief period, less than half a minute in all, and a trickle of blood had oozed momentarily from her left ear, working its way down her cheek, where it mixed with the viscous goo that had once been her eyes as they melted from their sockets.

"Do you think she was in much pain?" Grant asked as Decard's men placed a sheet over the victim's body.

Brigid looked at him and smiled sadly. "I don't think she felt anything," she answered, addressing everyone in the tent. "I don't think she even knew who she was in the end."

The Incarnate who doubled as a field medic caught Kane's attention and asked if he wanted to examine the body. Beside him, Brigid Baptiste shook her head.

"Just bury her," Kane said before striding out of the tent.

Fifteen minutes later, once the body had been given a shallow grave and the prisoners placed under armed guard, Grant found Kane standing a little way from the bivouac, gazing off into the heavens. "Clear sky," he said as he approached his longtime friend and partner.

"It's the desert." Kane shrugged. "Clearest skies you ever did see."

Grant stood with Kane for a while, observing the twinkling stars in companionable silence. Finally he spoke again. "You okay?"

Kane looked at his partner then, and Grant saw that familiar steely gaze. "I'm fine," he muttered.

"The girl?" Grant probed.

"It's not the girl," Kane told him. "At least, it's not just the girl. I mean, that's a terrible thing to happen, especially to an unborn child, like that. But it's not that."

Grant looked up at the sky again, following Kane's gaze. "Wasn't so long ago that we were up there, fighting aliens and causing a ruckus."

Kane laughed. "Yeah," he said, "and it's the ruckus that bothers me. Where are the Annunaki? We're down here, chasing around after hybrid DNA and the latest strain of fever and we've not heard zip from the overlords."

The Annunaki were an alien race who had evolved through the genetic manipulation of the nine barons who had controlled mainland America in the early years of the twenty-third century. The Annunaki were a bored, alien race who had first appeared on Earth many millennia before. Their saga was literally the stuff of legend—they had subjugated humankind and had been revered as gods by the earliest of humanity's cultures. But in reality the Annunaki were little more than a technically superior race of bored, cruel monsters who enjoyed playing with the primitive creatures that they found on the Earth.

A division within the ranks of the Annunaki themselves had brought about the near destruction of humankind when the aliens unleashed the catastrophe that the Bible recounted in the tale of the Great Flood. The flood was intended by Enlil, prince of the Annunaki, to wash away the remnants of the primitive playthings that dotted the Earth like a rash. Later Enlil had discovered that tenacious humanity had survived, with a little help from the dissenters within the ranks of the Annunaki themselves, led by his own brother, Enki. Enlil's purge had been unsuccessful and, amused by the survival of his playthings, Enlil and his fellow Annunaki had devised whole new ways to manipulate their enduring, rebellious toys.

Nobody could really say how long the Annunaki had shaped world events, but it was understood that they had orchestrated the second great cataclysm in the form of the nuclear war that had devastated the planet in January 2001. The nukecaust had culled the human population and allowed for the emergence of the new ruling elite called the barons, whose DNA Tom Carnack's people claimed to be holding. The baronial elite were merely a chrysalis form for the Annunaki, however, and a download from the organic computer in the starship *Tiamat,* stationed in orbit around the Earth, had regenerated the godlike Annunaki pantheon from their shells.

The Cerberus warriors had spent much of the past few years battling with Enlil and the other reptilian Annunaki, and every victory was bittersweet. As Kane reasoned, any file download could be opened and accessed again—defeat one Annunaki and another could appear in its place. As such, any lull in the ongoing war felt like nothing more than a temporary reprieve.

"There's an old saying," Grant told Kane as they gazed into the heavens, "make hay while the sun shines."

"I prefer the other one," Kane told his partner, "about the calm before the storm." With that, Kane turned and paced back to the camp, with Grant at his side. "Pack your waterproofs, partner," Kane warned, "we're in for a shitstorm."

Chapter 6

"What's the story with your two friends?" Decard asked Kane as they sat together under the rippling canvas roof of the tent. Besides four Incarnates left standing guard, everyone in the group was asleep, catching a few hours of rest before sunrise.

"They're a pair of street thieves," Kane told him in a hushed voice.

Decard smiled. "Seems a bit low rent for you, Kane," he said. "They must have stolen something real big."

"Word from the rumor mill has it that they're holding hybrid DNA out of Beausoleil," Kane told him, "along with the means to reproduce little barons from it. We leave crap like that unchecked, and suddenly we've got a whole new spate of the tyrannical bastards cropping up to push people around like pawns on a chessboard."

"Have you seen this genetic material?" Decard asked thoughtfully.

"It's all just rumor," Kane admitted, "but their leader spun a pretty good yarn."

"These people always talk big," Decard pointed out, "trying to jack up the price for something that turns out to be a whole load of nothing."

"Throw enough bait and you get your fish, right?" Kane agreed. "Still, Lakesh didn't want it going unchecked."

"Which one's the leader?" Decard asked.

"We lost him," Kane explained. "Got caught up in an earthquake out on the coast. Guy called Tom Carnack—escaped during the confusion."

"Yeah," Decard affirmed, "we felt it in Aten, too."

"Baptiste figures it shook the whole fault line," Kane elaborated. "Spoke to Cerberus yesterday. Mariah thinks it went as far as Arizona."

Decard raised his eyebrows. "That's one monster quake," he muttered in astonishment.

Kane shrugged. "It's not unknown around here."

Decard glanced across at the sleeping prisoners where they lay, their hands cuffed, in the middle of the bivouac. "So what about these two?" he asked. "You have something in mind?"

"Just got caught up in the moment," Kane admitted. "Priorities went haywire during the earthquake. Seemed the prudent thing to do was bring them with us and interrogate them when we get back to Cerberus. Otherwise we'd have likely lost the trading gang for good."

"They dangerous?" Decard asked.

"Don't know about the guy," Kane admitted. "Doesn't seem much of a fighter, but he thinks quick. Had me and Grant pegged for Mags as soon as he saw us. The chica's a different story. Seems pretty enough till you put a knife in her hand. Cut you as soon as look at you."

"Just knives?" Decard queried.

"Knives, swords." Kane reeled off the list in a bored tone. "I figure she knows her way around anything with a sharp edge. Haven't seen her use a gun, but I wouldn't be surprised if she can hit a target at fifty paces."

"You always did keep exciting company, Kane." Decard smiled.

Kane nodded. "Keep an eye on them and tell your men to do the same. If we're not careful, they'll turn into trouble."

"We're in the middle of the desert," Decard reminded him. "Where are they going to go?"

"They're survivors, Decard," Kane advised him. "Maybe you've been living in Aten too long to remember what that's like."

Chastised, Decard nodded slowly once more. "I'll keep my eyes open."

WITH THE ARRIVAL of dawn came two more Incarnates, riding one of the strange, motorized chariot-like vehicles that Aten produced for its people. Dressed as the other men, in white kilts and gold neck braces, these two wore the carved masks of a hawk and ibis. They had been scouting the area while the rest of the group rested, and now they returned to bring their morning report to Decard.

"We have found the rest of the Roamers," Ibis said after removing his mask to reveal a hard-looking face with a haughty, imperious aspect to his lantern jaw and a nasty scar just above his left eye.

Bleary eyed, Decard yawned behind his hand as he listened, and Brigid and Kane came to join the discussion after a moment.

"There, off to the east," Ibis continued. "There is evidence of a campfire, and their wags remain intact. We followed the tracks, and found all five of them about a mile farther on from their fire. They were lying in the sand, and there were signs of a scuffle—sand had been kicked up."

"Any clue what did this?" Kane asked.

Ibis looked at him fiercely until Decard signaled that he could speak freely to the man. "There are more tracks out there, something big," he explained.

"Any idea what?" Kane probed. "A Sandcat maybe?"

"They were scuffed but they looked like footprints," the man reported, "a little haphazard. We followed them for a while but nothing came of it."

"What, you quit or you lost them?" Kane asked.

"We made a strategic decision," Ibis told him, looking at Decard for confirmation and support, "that the distance was becoming too far from Aten to pose a threat."

"Which is to say," Kane summarized, irritation in his tone, "that you thought you were wasting your time."

"My orders are to protect the city-kingdom," Ibis told him hotly, "though I don't see that it's any business of yours."

Across the tent, Smarts's head lifted as he heard the angry words of the Incarnate and for just a moment a smile creased his thin lips.

Decard held his outstretched arms between Ibis and Kane making them step back from each other. "I called Kane's team in," Decard told the ibis-masked Incarnate, "and he will benefit from knowing all of the facts."

Kane shrugged and put on a gleeful, innocent expression. "Just following orders, same as you," he said, looking at the ibis-masked Incarnate.

Brigid addressed Decard and the others. "We need to look at this site, examine the bodies, see where those tracks lead."

"Agreed," Decard said firmly. "We have some dried fruit with us. What say we breakfast, then move out in an hour?"

"Sounds civilized," Kane acquiesced as he made his way across the floor of the tent. Crouching beside Domi's rucksack, Kane attached the spare Sin Eater and wrist holster that his albino colleague had brought him. "One hour."

THE CAMPSITE WAS much as the Incarnate guard had described it: the ashy remains of a fire pit in the sand, two wagons that had been left untended, disturbed sand here and there that obliquely suggested some frantic movement.

The Cerberus field team and their prisoners traveled to the site using the chariot-like vehicles that the Incarnates drove. There were ten of the vehicles in all, large enough to carry two men comfortably, four if they didn't mind being cramped. The chariots were carts with two large wheels on a single axle and no visible means of locomotion. Using an array of mirrored panels, the two-wheeled vehicles converted solar power into electricity and could run indefinitely as long as they had a charge. Elegant and functional, while the chariots traveled at a fairly low speed, they made the journey across the great swathes of desert that much more palatable.

Kane had considered it most prudent to split the prisoners on the journey to the campsite, and he sat in one of the little buggies talking with Smarts while Grant sat with Rosalia on the back of another chariot while the Incarnates ferried them across the sand.

Smarts showed irritation as the wind of their passage blew his lacquered hair about his face. "This is kidnapping, Señor Kane," he said in a low voice. "It seems a little beneath a Magistrate like yourself."

Kane looked at the man sternly, but he was tired of constantly correcting the man. Smarts was only doing this to get under his skin, Kane knew. "Things have moved a bit faster than I'd have preferred," Kane told the man, "but you can get yourself free passage as soon as you're ready to hand over the hybrid DNA."

"Which I don't have on me," Smarts argued, "so your offer is worthless."

"Where's it being kept?" Kane asked. "You have got to know that much, right?"

Smarts smiled enigmatically.

Kane glanced at the clear blue sky overhead as the flotilla of chariots progressed across the dunes, then he turned back to Smarts. "Look," he said, "neither of us is in a great negotiating position here, but I am not going to let you or the girl go until I have a decent lead on the location."

"So, we're stuck together," Smarts concluded.

Kane's eyes flicked to their driver for a moment before he spoke again. "I'm willing to make you an offer, Señor Smarts," he said quietly, "safe passage, a vehicle— whatever it is you need. We can negotiate the details and I'll be as amenable as possible. I need this information and you have it. You think about what it is you want and we'll go from there, okay?"

Smarts smiled and nodded. "You are a generous man, perhaps?" he said.

"This baron DNA could be a lot of trouble," Kane told him. "Not just for me. We get a whole new spate of baronies growing up, and operations like yours will be seized upon in an instant—you'll all be thrown in the Tartarus Pits. Carnack should have taken up my colleague's offer when he had the chance—you'd have all been rich men right now."

"Is that so, Señor Magistrate?" Smarts asked, a tinge of sarcasm in his tone.

Kane's gray-blue eyes locked with the Mexican's. "Figure out a way to make this work," he said, "before I get impatient."

As Kane finished, the group of chariots pulled to a stop a short distance from two parked wagons and the remains of the campfire, and the Cerberus personnel disembarked to take a closer look, leaving the Incarnates guarding their prisoners.

Brigid and Kane walked over to examine the wagons while Grant kicked through the ash of the fire, looking to see if anything peculiar had been burned. Domi stood with Decard by the parked chariots, a little way from the main camp, her eyes on the two prisoners while Decard's Incarnates patrolled the surrounding area.

The wagons were old-fashioned carts pulled by a raggedy mule and a tired horse with bowed legs and a swollen belly that sagged almost to the ground. The animals seemed bored, although Kane could see where the horse had become tangled in its reins, probably when whatever disrupted the Roamers appeared. The wagons were covered by simple canvas sheets, uncolored but dirty-looking from age and travels. One of the coverings had a rent across it, running the whole length of the mule's wagon.

Kane pointed it out to Brigid. "That looks new," he observed.

She nodded. Roamers were used to making do, and they would repair such a tear immediately, even if the fabric they used was a poor match.

"Reckon it has something to do with this?" Kane asked her.

Brigid took a closer look, pulling at the torn material, examining the length of the rip. "Hard to say for certain," she told him. "Are you thinking the Roamers did this themselves in a fit of madness, or that something attacked them? Because that depends on whether this is some airborne plague or something else."

"Well, little Miss Mom-to-be back there wasn't in much of a ripping-cloth mood by the time we saw her," Kane reminded Brigid.

"Decard said that his men came across her and the others just wandering aimlessly, remember?" Brigid told him. "Could have had a flurry of activity before they reached the state of catatonia that resulted in death."

"Lot of coulds," Kane grunted.

"Be a few more before we're done," Brigid lamented.

They checked inside the wag and found the usual supplies for long-distance travel—pots, pans, a kettle, a sealed tin of fire lighters and another full of dried strips of meat, blankets, unwashed clothes, a little collection of children's books full of once bright illustrations that had been pawed to dullness by many hands. As they looked around, Grant came over to join them, standing beside the mule outside the open front entrance to the long wagon.

"You guys need any help?" he asked.

"No." Kane sighed. "There's nothing here."

"Same story with the ash, I'm afraid," Grant told them.

Brigid glanced up at the sun—a colorless orb in the sky out here in the desert—as she stepped from the back of the wagon and into its fierce light once more. "Guess we go look at the bodies," she said.

Kane agreed. "Next stop—corpse central."

While the Incarnates started up the electric motors of their chariots, Kane and Grant released the mule and the swollen-bellied horse from their reins and shooed them off away from the site. Left tied up, they would just starve—at least this way they had a fighting chance at survival.

THE ROAMERS HAD MADE it almost three-quarters of a mile farther, though whether they had been running from something or after something it was impossible to say. A flock of scrawny-looking vultures had appeared to pick over the corpses of the five people, and Kane and Grant fired a salvo from their Sin Eaters into the air to scare them away before Brigid and the Incarnate field medic examined the bodies.

The vultures and sand-dwelling insects had already made a feast of the tender parts of the dead, and peck marks and burrowed holes speckled their open flesh.

While Brigid was busy examining the corpses, Grant and Kane paced around the area along with Decard and the two scouts who had alerted them to their location. The scouts pointed out what they had noticed, and the three ex-Mags evaluated everything they saw.

"The sand's pitted and kicked up all over," Kane observed. "Like someone was wrestling."

Decard agreed. "The wind's tossed new sand over the area here and there, but it's still pretty clear that something happened here. If I saw this on one of my patrols, without the corpses, I'd assume it had been a campsite the night before and I'd be looking out for Roamers."

"What do you think happened?" Grant asked as he sifted a handful of sand through his fingers.

"Big prints around this way," the ibis-masked Incarnate said, showing tracks that led off to the north.

Kane led the way, taking in the tracks and tracing them with his finger to way over the horizon. The two tracks were side-by-side, like footprints, deep indentations that had packed the sand tight. In some parts, the evidence had been covered by new sand picked up by the wind, but there was enough evidence to assess the basic direction that their maker had taken.

"Something big made these," Kane said as he bent to study the closest of the prints. "That's a shoe size of—" he rested his forearm on the ground beside the track and saw that the print stretched almost the whole length, from elbow to his second knuckle "—massive."

Grant whistled in astonishment. "Size extra-extra-large," he muttered.

There had been occasions where the Cerberus warriors had faced huge creatures, time-lost dinosaurs, vast mechanical monsters and even ancient creatures whose size and endurance far outstripped that of man. Whatever had left these prints was not in that league. And yet it sent a disquieting shiver down Kane's spine as he considered the implications of the large footprints embedded in the sand.

As the three ex-Mags pondered the vast markings, Brigid and the medic walked over to join them. As they did so, the circling vultures squawked and cried, flapping their wings and rushing earthward to return to their feast.

"Find anything?" Decard asked.

"Nothing we hadn't already seen in the girl," Brigid admitted, irritation in her voice. The Incarnate beside her nodded his assent to her summary, saying nothing further.

"We have ourselves a set of tracks," Grant told Brigid, pointing off into the distance where they led. "I'm guessing we follow them and see what shakes out of the trees."

Kane glanced up from his crouching position beside the closest print. "We bury the dead first," he decided in a tone that brooked no argument.

While the others discussed their plan of action, Smarts got Rosalia's attention and indicated off to the side of the group while Domi's back was turned. Rosalia followed his gesture, masking the move as though trying to shield her eyes from the bright sun, and she saw the little carrying case for the interphaser, left unguarded about thirty feet from the dead bodies and their attendant birds, resting on the floor of one of the open-topped chariots. Silently she turned to Smarts and shook her head just a fraction of an inch. It's not the time. Not yet.

Smarts assented with a long, heavy blink of his eyes, saying nothing. He trusted Rosalia. She would know when the time was right.

As THE GROUP of solar-powered chariots traversed the sandy swells of the California desert, Kane engaged his Commtact and sent a call to the Cerberus redoubt. He had left Domi guarding Smarts for this run, securing what little privacy he could for this conversation.

"Kane to Cerberus. Come in, Cerberus," Kane said quietly.

Because of the way in which the vocal pickup was embedded into its user, the Commtact could operate clearly from the lowest of whispers. Often, caught in tight situations, Kane and his team had switched to subvocalizing commands into the Commtacts, keeping in touch with one another despite the need for silence.

A few moments passed before Donald Bry's voice responded. "This is Cerberus," Bry said confidently. "How is everything going?"

Kane gave a concise sitrep. "We're out in the desert now," he concluded, "and it's hot and getting hotter. Currently traveling in a northwesterly direction following the tracks. Any chance you can scan the area up ahead of us, Donald?"

"Affirmative, Kane," Bry responded. "It'll take a few minutes to get our eyes in position. I'll get back to you as soon as I can."

Bry was referring to the Vela-class satellite that Cerberus controlled. With it, Donald Bry could monitor the Earth from orbit with just a few instructions to his desktop computer.

Kane glanced up at the rising sun, pulling the collar of the shadow suit away from his neck for a moment as though to relieve himself of the increasing heat. In actuality, the shadow suit's artificial environment was keeping Kane and his team wonderfully cool, but there was something subliminal about being in the desert as the sun approached its midday zenith that made one feel too hot, Kane realized. The power of persuasion.

"We'll be making a stopover shortly," Kane said into the Commtact, "give everyone a chance to cool down some."

"Understood," Bry replied. "I'll get whatever information I can glean before you take off again."

"Acknowledged," Kane said.

Kane shouted for Decard's attention and signaled that

they should pull over for a while. Steering his jostling chariot over the humps of the dunes, Decard scowled for a moment until he saw Kane give the okay signal, thumb to forefinger, before repeating his instruction to pull the chariots to a halt.

As the engine of his chariot powered down, Decard stepped from the open rear and walked swiftly over Kane's chariot. "What's going on?" he asked urgently. "You see something?"

"No," Kane replied, stepping from his chariot, "I just figure it's approaching midday and maybe some of these folks will want to find some shade and take a rest for an hour or so."

"My Incarnates don't mind this heat, Kane," Decard explained patiently. "They're used to it and they'll keep on mission until I tell them differently."

"Well, I'm sure your royal command is good," Kane said with a friendly laugh as he ribbed his old friend, "but I'm guessing my charges are starting to flag." He gestured toward the two prisoners who sat on the rear steps of their respective chariots as Domi and Grant watched over them.

Decard scanned the horizon for a moment before pointing to a tan-colored outcropping a little way from them, to the right of the heavy footprints. "Shady spot," he suggested. "No need to set up the tents that way."

Kane nodded. "I like your thinking."

The group of little vehicles started up once more and traveled over the rough sand until they reached the shade of the low mesa. They would continue the hunt once the sun had passed its peak.

Chapter 7

Concealed within the rocky clefts of Montana's Bitterroot Mountain Range, tucked beneath camouflage netting, hidden uplinks chattered in their continuous electronic conversation with two orbiting satellites that provided the Cerberus redoubt with a wealth of information about the outside world. Within the redoubt itself—a foreboding three-story structure of concrete and metal, hidden by the mountains—communications expert Donald Bry was studying their data feed on the screen of his computer terminal. A round-shouldered man of small stature, Bry wore a constant expression of consternation beneath his curly mop of unruly, copper-colored hair. A long-serving and trusted member of the Cerberus team, Bry acted as lieutenant and apprentice—in all things technological, at least—to Lakesh.

Bry's computer was one of more than two dozen arranged in twin aisles inside the vast operations room of the military redoubt. The control center was the brains of the Cerberus operation, and the room was constantly manned by scientists and communications experts. A number of these staff members had come to Cerberus from cryogenic stasis in the Manitius Moon Base, and the redoubt could now boast some of the sharpest scientific and military minds of the late twentieth century, time displaced and awoken to fill its swelling ranks.

Back when it was first operational, Cerberus had been called Redoubt Bravo, adhering to the standard military convention of using the phonetic letter of the alphabet in naming. The huge complex had undergone a number of changes since then, but it still retained something of its original purposes—to safeguard the freedom of humankind.

As Bry scanned the feed from the Vela-class satellite's camera and thermal sensors, he was unaware that he was being watched by Lakesh. Though he looked to be a man of perhaps fifty years of age, Lakesh was in fact much older. Having spent over a century in cryogenic suspension, Lakesh was truthfully a man of 250 years, and until quite recently he had looked to be exactly that. A contrivance of circumstances had seen a would-be ally of the Cerberus exiles court their favor by reversing the aging process and granting the physicist and cybernetics expert a new lease on life.

With studied politeness, Lakesh quietly cleared his throat to get Bry's attention.

Bry looked up from the screen as the satellite scanned the California desert for the coordinates that Kane's subcutaneous transponder was broadcasting. The transponders provided the Cerberus nerve center with a constant stream of information about a field operative's health and well-being, monitoring heart rate, blood pressure and brain-wave activity.

"How's Kane?" Lakesh asked.

Bry pointed to the screen as the satellite zeroed in on Kane's transponder. "Kane's squad is in Death Valley, chasing footprints in the sand. He's asked me to look ahead to try to clue them in on what's making those prints."

Lakesh nodded thoughtfully. "I see. That's quite close to where the quake hit, isn't it?" he asked.

Bry turned in his swivel chair and pointed to the large Mercator-relief map that spanned one whole wall of the ops room. The Mercator map included dozens of tiny lights, each indicating a point where a known operational mat-trans unit was located. A plethora of colored lines linked each of these lights, somewhat in the manner of an old-fashioned flight plan, showing the many connections between gateways. The map was a legacy of the time when the Cerberus redoubt had been dedicated to the exploration of the viability and military application of a mat-trans system. Dominating the vast operations room, the map was a handy reference that the personnel often examined. Bry's extended finger traced along the West Coast of North America, a coastline that had been remade by quakes in the past two hundred years.

"The quake struck a fault line that ran through Arizona and across into California, culminating somewhere out in the Pacific," Bry told his chief. "Mariah says it topped seven on the Richter scale, and estimates it went far beyond that before it had played out."

Lakesh spoke after a moment, still looking pensively at the map. "So, Kane is definitely within the little pocket that it disturbed," he said.

"He is," Bry confirmed, "but there's no reason to assume there will be another quake anytime soon."

Lakesh turned to his copper-haired assistant, indulging him with a friendly smile. "Of course there's not, Donald," he said. "It was merely an observation."

Bry moved back to his terminal and set about tracking ahead of Kane's team in the direction of the deep footprints that the man had described in his communiqué. As the satellite traced slowly along the area, Bry turned back to Lakesh, who was still studying the Mercator map, his thoughts his own.

"If I may be so bold," Bry proposed, "when you make what you call 'a mere observation,' it usually means you have something in mind."

Lakesh turned to Bry, an enigmatic smile playing across his lips. "In my long years I have noticed one thing above all else," he explained. "Coincidence is a very tricky thing."

Bry nodded knowingly before returning to the task of scanning the live satellite feed.

DECARD'S INCARNATES, the Cerberus warriors and their prisoners waited in the lee of the outcropping as the blazing sun dawdled high overhead. Señor Smarts sat beside Rosalia, his jacket hanging from a jagged part of the rock face, while she fanned at her face with long, languid strokes of one of the silks that had made up the veils of her costume. The wispy costume itself was now stained from her dunking in the sea and muddied by the kicked-up sand of their passage, but it still clung to her curvaceous body enticingly. To fan herself, she had pulled away a strip that wrapped across her belly, leaving her midriff exposed.

While things were quiet, Kane took the opportunity to speak with Brigid and the rest of his allies.

"I'll be honest," Brigid explained, "and say I've never seen anything quite like it. The Roamers, like the girl, appeared to have just burned up from within, as though struck by a massive surge of energy."

Grant nodded thoughtfully, looking from Brigid to Keb, the Incarnate medic. "Could it be some kind of spontaneous combustion?" he proposed.

Keb and Brigid shook their heads doubtfully. "This has the nature of a disease," Keb explained, "or an infection of some sort. But, like your companion, it is something the likes of which I have never witnessed before."

"A fever," Kane said darkly, "that burns people from the inside. Is such a thing even possible?"

Brigid smiled tightly. "The human body is capable of a great many things," she stated. "Just because we haven't seen it before doesn't mean it's impossible."

"How about calling in DeFore?" Domi proposed. "Lakesh might even want to take a look."

"We have no idea how this thing started," Kane said, "nor where. For now, let's keep the number of personnel who come into contact with it to a minimum."

Domi's lips pulled back in a feral smile. "You're just scared of what I'd do if Lakesh got hurt," she said, staring at Kane with her fierce scarlet eyes.

"Maybe a little," Kane conceded amiably.

"Off the top of my head," Brigid said, addressing everyone in the group, "I'd go so far as to say that this is something not seen in medical dictionaries. Which means it's something new and we cannot discount the possibility that it has been intentionally unleashed."

One of the Incarnates scoffed as he heard her words. "You recall the details of every disease? Such a feat is beyond credibility."

Brigid's emerald eyes held the man's gaze in silence for a few seconds before she spoke. "I remember a lot," she told him, "and seeing these symptoms didn't trigger any kind of recall."

Decard shot the Incarnate a warning look, urging the man to back down.

WHILE THE OTHERS were immersed in their discussion, Smarts reached into his pocket and withdrew the pocket chron, flipping open its ornate brass cover. The clock face had cleared now, the condensation—evidence of its dunking in the tsunami—all gone. His dark eyes flicked up to assess his captors before he clicked the watch's winder once, holding it in for the count of three. The compass and range finder took effect, and the hands on the dial spun as they gave a reading. Smarts smiled. Flipping the cover back in place, he turned to Rosalia as she rested against the cool, shady rock, waving her silk at her face to create a breeze.

"We are just nine miles from camp," Smarts told her under his breath.

Rosalia's eyes flashed to him and a broad smile crossed her features. "That close?" she wondered. "Which direction?"

Smarts leaned back, yawning and stretching his arms above his head. Rosalia watched carefully as his right arm pointed to the west. "There are markers as one gets closer," he told her. "Things that would be missed by others."

She nodded once, solidly, sweeping the silk back and forth again to fan her face. The time was drawing near.

AS THE CERBERUS field team waited in the shade of the vast rocks, swigging water and taking salt supplements, Bry's voice came over their Commtacts.

"Satellite surveillance isn't showing much," he admitted. "I've tracked along the basic direction you're heading in, northwest, but there's not much going on. Looks like a small settlement about five miles ahead of you, just a handful of shacks, could be temporary."

"Any people?" Kane asked over his Commtact.

"Some movement," Bry told him, "but nothing struck me as out of the ordinary. No fires or signs of destruction. Just a normal little settlement, five small buildings, people eking out a living. Looks like a horse in a corral there, too."

"Anything farther?" Kane asked.

"I'm panning ahead now, continuing northwest, but it's hard to tell," Bry explained. "I can't see the prints from this distance, just can't get that kind of level of detail into the image. Far as I can see, I'm looking at sand on sand, so if your bogey has changed course, then I've lost him."

"Pull back," Grant chipped in. "See if anything else is out of the ordinary. Something as big and heavy as this shouldn't be that hard to miss."

"I could lose it in a shadow, or it could be undercover," Bry said, "but I'll try my best."

"Thanks, Donald," Kane said before he broke the connection.

Then he addressed everyone in the group, aware that Decard and the Incarnates hadn't been privy to both sides of the discussion with Cerberus. "Our surveillance tells us there's a settlement about five miles up ahead. No signs of trouble, but it's right in the path of our mysterious quarry. I think it's worth checking out."

Decard nodded. "We're farther out than my men usually come," he explained, "so any settlements out this way will be as new to us as they are to you."

"Then let's all keep our eyes open and watch one another's backs," Kane instructed.

Decard looked across at the ragtag pair of street thieves as they waited patiently in the shade of the rocks. "What about your two friends?" he asked Kane. "I predict they'll start flagging if we're going as far as this settlement."

"We'll keep moving forward for now," Kane announced, "and they'll have to keep up."

"Why don't you just force them to give you the information?" Decard wondered.

"If we put too much pressure on them, they'll only give us a false lead and rabbit as soon as they see an opportunity," Kane told everyone.

Domi's hand stroked the hilt of the large knife she had strapped against her calf. "I could cut the information out of them," she told Kane. "Bet the man would start speaking pretty soon once he started bleeding his own blood."

"No." Kane shook his head. "You have to understand these people. They lie and swindle for a living. No amount of pressure will change that in them—it's instinctive. But if they realize they're not going anywhere until they give us what they want—and they maybe see an opportunity to get something out of it in the process—they'll cave. Just give it time."

"That's showing a lot of patience," Domi said dismissively.

"And a lot of faith in your skills of second-guessing people," Decard added.

"Well," Kane replied, looking at Domi, "if it comes to it, we'll use *your* way."

MARIAH FALK SAT at the computer in the Cerberus redoubt, puzzling over the figures that were displayed before her. A very experienced geologist, Falk was a slender woman in her midforties with short brown hair streaked with gray. Though not especially attractive, she had an ingratiating smile that always put others at their ease. She sat at her desk, idly chewing at her pen as she tried to map out the readings.

She was looking at a variety of data regarding the earthquake from two days before. Earthquakes, in fact, a half dozen in quick succession had rippled across the tectonic plates to the west of the old United States. The Cerberus operation was geared up for study in a number of fields, but acquiring accurate readings for an unexpected phenomenon like this was difficult.

Mariah leaned forward in her seat, pulling a printout from the stack that sat in her In tray and noting the peaks that the crazy logarithmic wave had hit when the quake rocked the California coast. Her fingers played across her keyboard for a moment, and she brought up a relief map of the western side of the continent of North America. If her data was correct, this quake had reached over four hundred miles from the effects that had been felt by Kane and his teammates on the California coast. She fed the data into the computer simulation program and watched as concentric circles grew from a point about one hundred miles north of Phoenix, Arizona.

She tapped at the keys for a few moments, switching the epicenter farther to the north and incorporating the limited data that she had amassed. Then she sat back and watched as the quake pattern was mapped.

"Monstrous," she muttered when the program had finished mapping the quakes' effects.

She was still sitting there, staring in astonishment at the computer screen, when Clem Bryant strode up to her desk carrying a tray with several covered dishes.

Mariah gasped with surprise when Bryant's shadow crossed over her computer screen. "Clem, I didn't hear you," she began.

"Quite all right," Clem said in his genial manner. He was a quiet man in his late thirties, with dark hair swept back from a high forehead, a neatly trimmed goatee and intelligent blue eyes. Bryant was an expert in oceanography and had been part of the scientific brain trust that had been placed in suspended animation shortly before the nukecaust. However, upon his awakening at the Manitius Moon Base, Bryant had found little application for his chosen discipline, and had instead begun devoting a large amount of his time to working in Cerberus redoubt's canteen. Much to everyone's surprise—not the least his own—Bryant had turned out to be a natural chef, and he had thrown himself into this new discipline with gusto. He took great pride in his culinary creations, adding a personal touch despite being called upon to feed more than sixty personnel per meal most days.

Mariah cleared a space at her desk and Bryant set the

tray down. "Thank you," she told him. "I had planned to come up to the canteen…"

"An army marches on its stomach," Clem reminded her as he gazed at the map on Mariah's terminal. "Plotting your empire?" he asked in his friendly way.

Despite his easy manner and his diverse fields of expertise, Clem Bryant was very much a scientist at heart. In his quieter moments, he could be found hovering around the empty corners of the large canteen or the redoubt archives working at a logic problem that he had found in an old book or newspaper, a mathematical question, a chess puzzle or a crossword of the devious, cryptic variety popular in Great Britain before the end of civilization early in the twenty-first century. In short, Clem Bryant was an obsessive thinker, and his insights had served the Cerberus personnel well over the past few months.

Mariah pointed at the screen with her pen as Bryant pulled over a spare chair to sit beside her. "If my estimates are correct," she explained, "this quake was at least an eight on the Richter scale."

"That certainly sounds like a lot of quake," Clem agreed jovially.

"It's almost unheard-of. Eight was the level recorded for the infamous San Francisco quake of 1906," Mariah told him.

Clem nodded. "Quite the cocktail hour." He chuckled. "Shaken, not stirred."

"Factor in estimated levels on the Mercalli scale," Mariah said, but Clem held up a hand to stop her. "The Mercalli scale registers the intensity of earthquake phenomenon," Mariah explained. "It's subjective, based on observable levels, but with six or seven quakes one after the other like this, we can safely assume it's pretty high."

"Assume away." Clem smiled.

Mariah had lifted the lid from the bowl that Clem had brought, and the rich smell of vegetable soup filled the office. Mariah took a taste, blowing on her spoon to cool it, then looked at Clem with appreciation. "This is great," she told him.

"That's very kind of you to say." Clem nodded. "But what about this whole Mercalli-scale business?"

"If we could locate the epicenter of the first quake," Mariah said, "we would find some very definite evidence of a whole change in the lay of the land. This is the sort of tremor that levels buildings and moves mountains, Clem."

"And where is the epicenter?" he asked her, thoughtfully running finger and thumb over his dark goatee.

"Here," Mariah pointed out, "Humphreys Peak, Arizona."

Bryant's blue eyes looked at the map thoughtfully. "Meaning?" he asked her.

"I don't know yet," she said, sighing, "but I can't help worrying about what comes out of the woodwork when mountains get shaken so dramatically."

Clem nodded in wary agreement. The Cerberus personnel had been involved in more than one situation where a military or otherworldly base was located in a mountain hideaway. Indeed, the Cerberus redoubt itself was one such facility, and myths had sprung up around the immediate area that surrounded it.

"Perhaps you might show this evidence to Lakesh," Clem suggested, "and impress upon him the importance of sending a field team to investigate. Just as a precaution, you understand?"

"Mmm," Mariah began through a mouthful of soup, "I think that would be…"

"Prudent," Clem finished for her as she swallowed.

Chapter 8

Using the solar-powered chariots, the Cerberus warriors and Decard's men made good time, reaching the settlement inside of forty minutes despite the rough terrain. The settlement was made up of five shacks, along with a deep well at the side of which was a bucket on a rope-and-pulley system. The roughly constructed buildings had been painted white to reflect the heat of the desert sun, though their sides had been discolored by the grains of sand that the winds had thrown against them over time.

As the chariots approached the settlement, Kane indicated to Decard that they stop here, waiting a little way out. Once the electric chariots had pulled to a halt, Kane hopped from the back of the one he was riding and jogged over to Decard. "I think we should go in on foot," he explained.

"Any special reason?" the younger man asked, though he clearly trusted Kane's judgment.

"I'm seeing five dwellings but no people," Kane said, looking at the desert hamlet. "Might want to take that as a bad sign."

Decard nodded. "Fair point," he said. "How do you want to approach this, then?"

"Me and Grant will go in," Kane decided. "We're both

wearing armor. Think you can spare a couple of your men to cover our backs?"

"I'll go myself if you want," Decard told him in a tone of utter seriousness.

"You stay here," Kane said. "If there's any trouble, I'd just as soon have a trained Mag leading my backup."

"As you wish," Decard said amiably before walking across to address the group.

A few moments later, Kane, Grant and two of the fiercely masked Incarnates walked the last 150 yards to the settlement. As they got closer they heard a bleating, and Grant pointed out two goats tethered beside one of the buildings, sheltering in its shadow from the bright sunlight. Kane scanned the horizon, watching the buildings for movements. A corral at the far side of the hamlet held a single, tired horse, chestnut-brown with sweat foaming on its flanks.

The Sin Eater pistol was already in Kane's hand, held pointing straight down in a safety position, as he stepped between the closest two buildings. "Anyone home?" he called.

Having discarded his heavy coat, the shadow suit molded to Grant's muscular body as he walked carefully ahead of Kane, eyes alert, his own Sin Eater in hand. Following the two ex-Mags, the Incarnates took up wary positions, their silver, stafflike weapons held ready.

Giving a signal to Grant, Kane took a step toward the nearest building and rapped his fist against the door before stepping to one side, out of the potential line of fire.

For a moment, all was silent. Then, as they listened, a noise came from inside—a voice.

"Hello?" Kane raised his voice but remained to the side of the door. "I'm not here to hurt you. Can you open the door?"

The voice continued from inside, but Kane couldn't make out the words, just glottal sounds and sibilance.

Kane and Grant shared a look, and everything that needed to be said between them passed in that silent instant. Then Grant took up a defensive position, targeting the doorway with his Sin Eater as Kane stepped back.

Kane raised his voice once again. "I'm coming in. I have concerns about your safety, and I'm going to enter on the count of three. I must warn you that both my partner and myself are armed."

After five seconds, during which all they could hear was the muttering from inside the shack, Kane began his countdown, loud enough that his words carried across the dusty plain. On "one," Kane shoved at the closed door with a swift slap of his palm, knocking it so hard that it visibly shook on its hinges as it shuddered open. Nothing appeared to greet them.

Through the doorway, away from the intense desert sunshine, all that could be seen was darkness. Kane stood there a moment, Sin Eater trained on the open doorway, waiting for his eyes to adjust. After a moment, not needing to inform Grant, he stepped forward and disappeared into the shadows.

Kane was two steps into the room, his eyes narrowed, staring into the greeny blackness of the shadowed room as his eyes began to make out its details. There was a window to one side, but a heavy drape had been drawn across it, with only the thinnest lances of sunlight seeping through around its right edge. Kane could make out furniture, a simple wooden table, several chairs, a box of some sort—crate or chest he wasn't sure—against one wall. There was another door farther into the room, probably leading to the bedroom of the tiny, single-story dwelling.

Kane felt Grant's presence behind him as the imposing man stepped into the room. He looked back and saw Grant sweep the room in a single glance before gesturing to the far door with his Sin Eater. Kane nodded, stepping toward the door on silent, catlike feet.

The voices were coming from the far room. Kane could make out two of them distinctly, a man's deep basso and a woman's or child's higher pitch. But it was like listening to a badly tuned radio; the voices were muffled and their sense lost through the dampening barrier of the closed door.

Warily, Kane followed the same procedure that he and Grant had used for the exterior door, advising the people inside of his intentions and his armed status before counting himself in. As he shoved back the door, his nostrils were assaulted by a tremendous stench, and he reared back without intending to.

There were three people in the room, what looked like a husband and wife with their newborn child. All three were dressed in the old, worn clothing of farmers leading a tough but honest life. The child was tiny, no more than a month old, lying in its crib. Or, at least, that's how Kane remembered it afterward, before he looked more closely and saw that the baby was dead, putrefying on its blanket. The husband and wife were shouting, but not at each other. Their voices were raised, yelling and crying, but they seemed oblivious to the other's presence in the room—oblivious, too, to Kane's and Grant's entrance.

Kane took a step closer, trying to make sense of their words, but nothing seemed to stick. There were noises here, patterns that he associated with speech, but the language was a mystery to him. He lowered his Sin Eater but kept it gripped in his hand.

"My name is Kane," he said slowly, addressing the couple, "and I'm here to help."

They didn't even look at him. Their movements were just twitches, flinches, looking around like crows pecking for spilled seeds on the ground. They looked this way and that, speaking in their loud, strained voices, the sounds reverberating off the close walls of the bedroom.

Behind him, Grant spoke quietly to Kane. "Use the Commtact," he suggested, engaging his own.

Their Commtacts were capable of real-time translation of the many known languages that they had been programmed with, and, as such, their intelligent systems could generally discern a degree of meaning from any spoken language.

The stream of words went on and on, but Kane could make no sense of it. He switched off the Commtact's translation program, looking at Grant in confusion. Grant had a finger up to his ear, listening intensely to the words, a vexed frown across his brow. "What the fuck language is that?" he asked.

"Something the Commtact doesn't know," Kane suggested.

"Freaking me out," Grant muttered as he switched off his own Commtact.

Perversely, the couple apparently remained completely unaware of Kane's and Grant's intrusion. They were like clockwork things, going through their actions with no sense of reality, no break in their movements.

Kane stepped across the room and his hand reached up to draw back the heavy drape that blocked out the harsh sunlight. He pushed back the single drape, letting the light fill the room. The couple's reaction was, at most, muted. Kane thought that they turned toward the window for a moment, but he couldn't be sure. It may have been coincidence, and their robotic movements just continued with unceasing motion.

Grant had stepped closer, and he held his face close to the woman's as she sat at the edge of the bed, blinking in long, sleepy sweeps of her eyelids.

"Their eyes, Kane," Grant said, moving to look at the man who sat across from her on the bed, "there's nothing there."

Kane cursed himself that, in that moment, he felt a sense of triumph. "We're on the right trail," was all he could think to say.

THE OTHER BUILDINGS yielded five more adults and three children, all of them in a similar state to the young couple. One of the adults was an older man, perhaps in his late sixties, hardy from an outdoor life. He was shaking as though with fever when Grant found him, and he had expired before Kane came to see.

"Hot as an oven," Grant said, holding his hand to the old man's forehead.

Kane took a long look at the old man where he was

slumped beside a simple wooden table that still had the evidence of a meal strewed across it, a shattered plate in the corner of the room. "What about his eyes?" he asked after a moment.

"White," Grant confirmed. "Pure white."

There were still nine living in the settlement, Kane realized, and time clearly took a heavy toll on the victims of whatever they had stumbled upon. He postulated that these people would not last more than a few hours. As he and Grant exited the house, leaving the old man as they had found him, Kane activated his Commtact and called Brigid over to join them.

"I think this needs some medical expertise," he told her. "Bring Keb, and tell Decard to bring in a little muscle, too. Whatever's eating these people up is making them tough to restrain."

"Are they violent?" Brigid's query came over the Commtact.

"Not so far," Kane admitted, "but we may have got here after that part of the cycle had passed. There's some signs of activity—old guy tossed his dinner into the wall."

"Maybe he saw a roach jump on it," Brigid proposed reasonably.

"That would assume that he had eyes at the time," Kane told her darkly, before cutting the communication.

As they waited for the others to join them, Grant surveyed the little settlement before letting out a long, low whistle. "You have to wonder what these people lived on," he said to Kane.

Hearing his statement, one of the Incarnates—a man in an adder's helm—turned to him and indicated the land all around. "People mistake the desert for a bad place to live," he said jovially. "There is wildlife here, fauna and flora. The lack of rainfall does not make it a dead environment."

"Guess not," Grant said. "Still seems pretty damn rugged to me."

Kane smiled as he caught his partner's eye. "We both grew up as big ville boys," he said. "Different strokes for different folks."

"The people out here keep goats, sheep, chickens sometimes," the adder-masked Incarnate told them. "They treasure their independence, away from the barons. Much as my people."

Brigid came to join them at the outskirts of the hamlet, with Decard and six burly Incarnates, slick with sweat in the afternoon sun. Brigid had pulled her damp red-gold hair from her face with a white headband, and its color caught the sun like a halo around her beautiful, porcelain-skinned face.

"Where's the patient?" she asked.

Kane pointed to each of the lightly colored buildings in turn. "Take your pick," he told her. "We've got a crazy babbling couple behind door number one here. Then, behind door number two, we have a crazy babbling young man and his babbling teenage daughter, closely followed by a babbling couple and their two babbling kids over there behind door number three."

"And four and five?" Brigid asked as she made her way toward the first shack, the one Kane and Grant had initially entered.

"Well, that's where it gets exciting," Kane told her. "House number four is empty, though it looks like someone went through it with a sledgehammer. Then, over at number five we have the old dead guy who had a fight with his dinner."

There was a swift discussion between Brigid and Keb, and they decided to split the duties of examining the crazed people in the little settlement, taking opposite sides of the street and leaving the dead man to last. Incarnates went with each of them, while Kane and Grant decided to take a closer look at the empty, fourth house.

Kane's description, that someone had been through it with a sledgehammer, didn't seem so far from the truth. The people led a meager life, with few possessions or adornments to their little houses. But what little was in this shack had been overturned, tossed aside, thrown against walls, broken and destroyed, almost as if a whirlwind had traveled through the dwelling.

"Someone looking for something, maybe?" Grant suggested as they sifted through the wreckage of plates, torn books and smashed furniture that covered the floor of the main room.

"It just looks like destruction to me," Kane answered after a few seconds. "Destruction for the sake of destruction."

"Maybe they couldn't find what they were looking for," Grant proposed, "or maybe they wanted to cover their tracks."

Kane swept a broken jug aside with the back of his hand. "I don't buy it," he said. "Look at the way these people live. They don't have anything worth stealing."

"There's always something worth stealing to somebody," Grant told him. "And if nothing else, there's always that perennial favorite—the virgin sacrifice."

Kane shook his head. "This is more like someone was having a fit. Epilepsy times one thousand."

"Then where's our epileptic?" Grant asked.

The other rooms of the shack were empty, Kane knew, so he called on Bry's satellite surveillance once more, from the Cerberus redoubt. "Donald? It's Kane. Do you think you could zero in on my reading and search the immediate area? We're looking for one or more stragglers who've left this settlement not more than, say, three hours ago. Most likely on foot."

"On it, Kane," came Bry's efficient response over the Commtact. Kane stood there a moment, gazing out the back window at a wooden kennel. The kennel, he saw, was empty.

While they waited for Bry's report, Kane and Grant made their way out of the shack and across the dusty street to learn whether Brigid had made any progress. The couple in the first house had become more agitated since Kane had last seen them, more manic in their relentless, shouted stream of babble and their crazy, frantic movements. The man was standing now, swaying to and fro in one corner of the room. Brigid was trying to keep the woman still as she examined her with whatever medical equipment Keb had to spare. Kane watched from the door, standing with the three masked Incarnate guards for more than a minute as Brigid tried to get the woman to close her mouth long enough to take a temperature reading from a little glass thermometer. But the woman was oblivious, her jaw opening and closing as she wailed and hollered at the top of her lungs. Eventually, Brigid shook the thermometer and placed it atop a rudimentary homemade bedside cabinet.

"Anything?" Kane asked as Brigid's emerald eyes flicked up from her examination of the woman to take him in.

"They're showing the same symptoms as the young woman Decard's crew found yesterday," Brigid said. "We're seeing it earlier, but I'd accept that it's the same…disease."

"Disease?" Kane asked, shouting to be heard over the peculiar, agitated couple.

"Infection, then." Brigid shrugged. "Kane, I don't know."

Grant poked his head around the doorway as the Incarnates surveyed him warily. "They sound louder than earlier," he pointed out, and Kane agreed.

"This one here closed his mouth long enough for me to get a decent body temp reading," Brigid said, indicating the husband with her thumb. "Their temperature is rising rapidly. He's already at 103."

"They're burning up," Kane said, bitterness in his voice from his own helplessness. "The baby already boiled, and they're following suit."

"Shit deal," Grant muttered, "everyone loses." With that, he led the way from the cramped bedroom, having heard enough of the incessant shouting from the strangely altered couple.

A moment later, Brigid and Kane followed with the Incarnates in tow, pulling the bedroom door closed behind them so as to drown out the racket.

"What is it that they're shouting about?" Grant asked uncomfortably, looking back to the bedroom door.

"I don't know," Brigid answered. "I couldn't make sense of it."

"Did you try the Commtact's translation program?" Kane asked and Brigid nodded.

Grant chuckled. "I haven't been so freaked out in a long time," he admitted.

"It's just babble," Brigid said. "Nonsense words. The translation program tries to pick up specific sounds, but it's a deception. There's nothing there, just noise."

"The girl, the pregnant one in the tent, she was muttering," Kane said, "quietly, under her breath. Didn't seem to be anything, just a humming. You remember?"

Brigid nodded. "Could be the same thing, petering out at the end, as they get closer to expiring. What about the old man? You said he was alive when you found him."

"Nothing, no noise," Grant told her.

"He was alive for maybe two minutes max before we lost him," Kane said. "He was dead by the time I joined Grant in the room."

Brigid took a deep breath as she looked at the bedroom door, hearing the muffled shouting through its solid wood. "It's glossolalia," she announced.

"It's what?" Grant asked.

"Glossolalia," Brigid repeated. "At least, I think that's what it is." She turned back to Grant and Kane, dismissing the noise coming from the next room. "They used to think it was some religious thing, communing with the Lord. They called it speaking in tongues. But it's just a chemical imbalance, the brain not getting enough of this and too much of that."

"So, what are you saying, Baptiste?" Kane pondered aloud. "That these dust farmers have got a big dose of 'that,' and it's messed with their balance of 'this'? Because, if that's the case, we need to know where the 'that' is coming from."

"It doesn't take much," Brigid assured the ex-Mags. "Voices, visions in the head, nonsense speak. These are all things you find in chronic anorexics. Stop supplying your body with protein for long enough, and it begins to eat at itself. Back in the fourteenth century, French nuns used to starve themselves to achieve this very effect."

"Did they get hot?" Kane asked.

"Fever's a possibility," Brigid stated, "but not to the kind of extent that we're seeing. I mean, this isn't even fever. This is like an explosion of energy from inside the body, completely using it up, wearing it out. It's like nothing I've ever heard of."

"So, are we looking at two things," Kane asked, "that happen to be hitting people at the same time, or one thing with multiple symptoms?"

"Medically?" Brigid began. "I think it's all one thing. It's the same essential effect, manifesting in different ways. Kane, Grant—these people are just being used up at a fantastic rate. That's the only way I can think to describe it."

Grant nodded and Kane glanced ruefully at the closed bedroom door for a moment before turning his gaze back to Brigid.

"That's something I can understand," Kane decided. "Awful, but it makes sense. So, one, where did it originate? Two, is it catching? Three, how do we stop it?"

Brigid checked her pockets for a moment before realizing that the thermometer was still inside the room. "Let me go grab the thermometer and we'll figure out some kind of plan of action with Keb," she told them as she walked back to the bedroom and pushed open the door.

Grant tsked. "Eaten up from the inside," he muttered. "What a way for a baby to go."

"Those people are next and, if we don't move fast, we could follow them," Kane told him.

Grant breathed heavily through clenched teeth. "Thanks for putting that positive spin on things, Kane," he said.

As they paused in thought for a moment, there was a loud thump and suddenly the barren little shack shook. Everyone in the room stumbled, and one of the Incarnates tumbled face-first into a wall.

"What the crap—?" Kane began, but Domi's voice cut into his thoughts from the Commtact link.

"Kane, you have company."

Kane and Grant were already moving, running to the exterior door and rushing out of the little shack, Brigid and the Incarnates right behind them. "Another quake maybe?" Grant asked as they ran.

"What is it, Domi? What do you see?" Kane asked, patching to her over the Commtact. They had left Domi along with four of the fierce Incarnates guarding Smarts, Rosalia and the chariots. Over one hundred yards from the little settlement, Domi was able to provide a better tactical viewpoint of the area.

"I have no..." Domi began, before halting and trying again. "It's big, it's humanoid and there's just one of them. Beyond that, your guess is as good as mine."

"Where?" Kane demanded, flipping the Sin Eater into his hand as he stepped into the tiny sun-drenched street.

"Northmost corner, behind the farthest house," Domi responded. "In the corral."

Kane was already running forward, his body held low,

arms pumping as he raced along the short stretch between the shacks. He could hear Grant's heavy footsteps just behind him as his partner followed, and he held up his empty left hand to tell the man to hold back.

A second later, Kane rounded the corner of the farthest shack, and then he saw it. The creature stood eight feet tall, its legs bent, slightly hunched, its back to Kane. Its proportions matched its height, a huge, hulking figure, with thick protrusions coming from elbows and running down its spine. Its arms and legs were as thick as tree trunks. It was wrapped in some kind of gauze material, an off-white color, stained with dirt and blood, torn in parts to reveal patches of coal-black skin, and Kane saw what he at first took to be a cloud of small flies and insects hovering around it.

Kane stood there, pistol raised, watching for a startled moment as the creature slapped the horse aside, knocking the defenseless animal across the length of the small corral until it slammed into the fencing and fell to its side on the dusty ground, kicking up sand in its frantic efforts to recover. The huge, mysterious creature remained there for a moment, its back to Kane, its shoulders moving heavily as it took deep lungfuls of air.

"Domi?" Kane whispered, activating his Commtact pickup. "Where did it come from? Did you see?"

"It was just there," Domi said, her voice sounding worried. "Like it mat-transed in or something."

Grant stepped forward, his voice an urgent whisper beside Kane's ear. "Kane," he prompted.

Kane looked and saw that Grant was pointing to the little well that sat to the edge of the settlement. Its mouth had become bigger, one side distended where the walls had caved in from heavy turmoil belowground. Kane nodded once before turning his full attention back to the beast.

"We think it came from underground," Kane stated over the Commtact. "Burrower of some kind."

Slowly, the creature turned, as though sensing Kane's presence at last. Head low, it looked at the two ex-Mags where they stood beside the edge of the shack. Its face was black, like shadow, and twin green eyes burned within. Smoke billowed from those eyes, streams of rising chartreuse cloud, before dissipating just above its head. Other parts of it seemed somehow ethereal, too, now that Kane had got past his initial shock and had the chance to assess it more carefully. It wasn't a cloud of insects that hovered about it; the dark cloud was made from aspects of the creature itself. Its face smoldered and where the gauze coverings were broken, its exposed skin flaked away like burning ashes. And yet, it never seemed to lose any body mass. The thing remained huge and imposing, staring at Kane with those vibrant, unearthly eyes.

"What the hell is that thing?" Grant muttered, training his Sin Eater on the huge creature as it surveyed them.

Brigid and the Incarnates were just behind them now, staring in astonishment at the huge figure.

"Kane," Brigid whispered, "I think we need to get out of here."

"Weapons up," Kane instructed everyone loudly, not bothering to turn to look at her.

Suddenly, the creature was moving. It took three long strides in a rush, racing across the sand toward Kane and Grant at a furious pace, almost quicker than the eye could follow, and it unleashed a noise from its open mouth that sounded like a combination of a wolf's howl and a parrot's caw. White mist billowed from its open mouth, a cloud of boiling-hot saliva.

Kane and Grant skipped backward as the creature ran at them. "Domi," Kane called into the Commtact, "we're going to need backup. Get over here now."

The hulking brute's arm lunged toward Kane, cleaving through the air at head height, a misting rush of black flecks following in its wake like the afterimage on a motion picture. Kane ducked, and the creature's fist sailed over his head, just two inches above him, before crashing into the side of the shack with a loud splintering of wood.

"Hostile," Kane concluded as he continued dashing backward, his party spreading out around him, holding the monster in their weapons' sights.

Decard was coming out of another shack now, accompanied by Keb and three Incarnates, with two more rushing down the street to take up defensive positions with their tubular silver staffs. Where Decard had opened the door to the shack, that awful, strained wailing could be heard coming from inside, the infected becoming more and more agitated.

"Domi, get over here," Kane repeated into the Commtact, conscious that she hadn't replied to his previous request.

Domi's response sounded woozy, as though she had just been woken from a nap.

"Kane," she slurred, "we have a second problem. The Mexican and the girl just slugged me and the guards here. Our rabbits are on the run!"

Chapter 9

Kane rushed backward on light feet, gun at the ready, eyes never leaving the huge creature that loomed before him. Behind him, Grant, Brigid and the Incarnates rushed in all directions, taking up defensive positions, finding what meager cover they could in doorways and between the ramshackle buildings.

"Domi?" Kane called over the Commtact. "Repeat message. Did you say we've lost the prisoners?"

"Worse than that." Domi's voice still sounded strained and sleepy. "They've taken the interphaser."

"Damn," Kane cursed. "Can you see them? Do you know what direction they went in?"

As he spoke, the hulking creature took a slow, wary step down the street toward Kane and the others, its head low as its burning green eyes surveyed them. Closer now, Kane could see that its legs featured a reverse knee, like a grasshopper's or a horse's hind legs, and it seemed to totter forward as though set to overbalance at any moment. Its coal-colored face looked up the street, calculating the scene that it was presented with. Then it unleashed another of those terrible wolf-parrot cries, the noise reverberating off the walls of the shacks to either side, before it began running toward them once more, arms out and back as it prepared to swing for Kane.

Kane was listening to Domi's report over the Commtact. "They took two chariots and headed off to the west, I think. Trying to locate—"

Suddenly, Grant's voice snapped Kane back into the present. "Kane, head in the game, stat!"

Kane spun backward, dropping low as the monster's right arm rocketed toward his throat, a cloud of black flecks left in its wake. Kane found himself stumbling, falling to the hard-packed sand of the street as the creature continued swinging its mighty arms at him. He looked up as the creature towered over him, tossing its head back and unleashing another of those unearthly banshee wails, a cloud of misting saliva bursting from its open jaws. This close, Kane could see a pattern on the creature's face and exposed skin—ridges of scales like those of a fish or reptile. Then it turned back to look at Kane on the ground as he scrambled to get away.

A loud report came from off to Kane's right, and he watched from the corner of his eye as Grant pumped a stream of 9 mm lead at the monster from the barrel of his Sin Eater. The creature turned, momentarily staggered as the bullets slapped its chest and shoulder.

Behind Kane, Decard and the Incarnates joined Grant in unleashing a barrage at the creature. From all sides of the tiny street, beams of energy zapped toward the huge beast as the Incarnates fired high-density energy beams from their silver-colored staffs. Once the Incarnates' weapons were engaged, a familiar tickling sensation came to Kane's eardrums, a slight buzzing like an insect's wings.

The energy beams were almost invisible in the sunlight, just lighter streams across a watcher's vision, like sunspots playing across the eyes. Decard, too, was using his weapon—a reconditioned Sin Eater handblaster similar to those carried by Kane and Grant, his old weapon of office. He crouched on one knee to steady himself, his free hand under the muzzle of the compact weapon as he drove shot after shot into the monster's abdomen.

Under the barrage of fire, the hulking creature reared to its full, impressive height—eight feet of solid, jet-black muscle. It struggled against the onslaught, shook momentarily as though flicking raindrops from its skin, then turned its gaze on the multiple attackers, its fierce eyes smoldering.

Still lying beneath it, Kane drew his Sin Eater pistol up and targeted the creature's chin, between jaw and neck, where its soft palate should be located. As he took aim, he heard scrambling, and then Brigid Baptiste was in the sand next to him, pulling him away.

"What are you doing, Baptiste?" he raged at her. "I can make the shot."

"You're too close, Kane," she chastised him. "Let's put some distance between us and that monster before it's too late."

Fuming, Kane struggled to his feet and followed Brigid down the little street as the Incarnates, Decard and Grant covered his back, holding the monster at bay with their continuous barrage of fire.

"I was about to turn that to my advantage. I could have done it," Kane argued with Brigid as they rounded a corner at the far end of the street.

"You would have been dead," Brigid told him angrily.

Kane bit back a curse as the redheaded woman checked around the corner of the building, her TP-9 pistol in hand. Kane followed her, watching as the translucent beams from the Incarnates' staffs blasted into the monster, tentatively holding it in place.

"Did you hear Domi's report?" Kane asked.

"Yes," Brigid snapped. "One problem at a time, Kane."

"No, we need to get after them," Kane argued. "Smarts and Rosalia are our only lead to Carnack's gang, and they have our interphaser now, too."

"They'll never get it working," Brigid told him as she watched the creature from the cover of the shack's wall.

"Oh, sure," Kane growled. "You can build another one, right? You and Brewster."

Brigid looked at him, eyes narrowed. "Kane, can we just deal with the monster first?"

Kane stepped back, holding a hand to one ear to better hear his Commtact over the ruckus all around him. "Tell me if it gets close," he instructed Brigid before hailing Domi once more.

"Domi, I need you to go after the duo right now," he told her.

A LITTLE MORE THAN one hundred yards away, Domi was wincing as she rubbed at a bump that was forming on the back of her skull. Three of the Incarnates who accompanied her now lay unconscious, while the fourth had removed his bird-faced helmet and was using water from his leather drinking pouch to rinse a bloody cut just above his eye. Her head felt like cotton wool, and she tried to blink away the sensation of nausea as Kane's voice came in, all too loud, over the Commtact.

"Domi," Kane was instructing her, "I need you to go after the duo right now."

"No need to shout," Domi muttered.

"What's that?" Kane's voice came back, still too loud to be comfortable. "Domi, we've got a lot going on here right now...."

"I'll get on it," she agreed, cutting him short. "It's just my head, y'know?"

"Don't let them get away," Kane instructed. "How are the Incarnates?"

Domi looked around, gasping at the renewed sensation of pain as she turned her head. "We've got three unconscious and at least one wounded here, not including myself," she replied. "Kane, I swear to you, that girl moved like lightning."

"I'll send backup to follow you as soon as I can," Kane promised.

At that moment, Grant's voice piped over the Commtact, his breath coming hard as he continued to pump the trigger of his Sin Eater. "Hey, people," he said, "I can double back and join Domi in two minutes."

"Sounds good," Kane agreed.

"Stay where you are and I'll pick you up, hotshot," Domi said playfully as she ran to one of the untended chariots. She leaped aboard, flipping switches until she found the engine ignition.

A moment later, the chariot was kicking up sand as Domi swung it around and steered it toward the east flank of the little hamlet where the rest of her teammates were battling the monster.

THE INCARNATES continued to blast the tall creature with energy beams from their staffs, and it reared back, then seemed to shrug, flicking the beams aside like insects. Its head bowed once again, and Grant, who had taken a position close to the beast, tucked inside the doorway of one of the roughly constructed shacks, warning everybody to get back. A moment later, the monstrous thing bellowed once again as it began to charge down the short street.

Sand was kicked up in the wake of those huge feet as its powerful legs drilled it across the ground at an unbelievable pace. Grant pulled his weapon back and withdrew into the shelter of the doorway as the creature rushed past him, a trail of black flakes of skin floating on the air behind it like ashes. It ignored him, and it ran straight past Decard as he followed the same procedure, ducking between buildings as the monster raced at its attackers.

The Incarnates danced away, rushing to their own shelters as the creature charged them. The two at the far end of the street remained, attempting to hold the monster at bay with the energy lances of their staffs. To the side of the street, Kane and Brigid ducked back as the black-faced monster lunged into view. Its huge left arm, still wrapped in gauze bindings, swung out, driving through the side of the far building. The roof began to cave in, the whole structure compromised, but the creature had already passed. Its other arm reached forward as the two Incarnates ran for cover, and it snagged one of them by his crocodile-styled helmet, sweeping him backward and off his feet. The Incarnate screamed as he fell and was dragged across the ground toward the huge creature.

Standing just six feet away, Kane leveled his Sin Eater between the monster's shoulder blades and held down the trigger, blasting a stream of bullets into its back. Sparks of fire spewed up as the bullets struck the monster's hard carapace, but it didn't even seem to react. Instead, it continued to pull the crocodile-masked Incarnate toward its face, lifting him high off the ground. Its grip tightened, and Kane watched in horror as the Incarnate's elaborate wooden mask splintered, collapsing in on itself. Beneath the shattered helmet, the Incarnate was screaming.

The other Incarnates had emerged from their hiding places and began to blast at the monster with their powered staffs once more, smothering it with energy beams.

At the far end of the street, Decard was shouting orders to his men to pull back, not to get too close to the monster. Too late for that, Kane thought sourly.

Kane turned to Brigid, his expression fierce. "We have to do something," he told her. The pair of them were now the closest to the attack.

Brigid nodded once, taking a two-handed grip on her TP-9 before stepping away from the wall of the shack to get a better aim at the hulking brute.

Just then, Kane heard a low whining coming from down the street, and a blur of wood and reflected sunlight raced past, before plowing into the monster. It was Domi, riding one of the Incarnates' solar-powered chariots at top speed. She had to have doubled around the tiny ville to get her speed up, Kane realized as the athletic albino woman leaped from the vehicle and away from the monster.

There was a loud crunch as the chariot slammed into the thick legs of the black-faced monstrosity, the top of the chariot reaching roughly to its waist. The monster held it in place for a moment, and the chariot's engine whined louder as it tried to drive forward before bouncing back on crippled wheels where the axle had split. Then the huge beast staggered, a brief three-step dance across the sand, before bellowing another of its banshee wails, boiling saliva pluming around its face.

Kane watched in horror as the monster threw the crocodile-masked Incarnate to one side, and the man tumbled head over heels before slumping to the ground, covered in sand. At the same time, the monster itself seemed to spin in place, its reverse-hinged legs kicking up great clumps of sand, moving faster and faster.

A blur, and then nothing. The creature was gone.

Kane rushed over before Brigid could stop him, ignoring her pleas to be careful. There was a hole in the ground now, a roughly circular tunnel that appeared to go straight down. Kane could hear scrabbling down there as the nightmarish creature disappeared from view, and he kept his Sin Eater trained on the opening in the sand for a long moment, debating in his mind whether he should follow.

"Whatever it is, it's gone, Kane."

Brigid's voice was close to his ear. Kane turned and saw Brigid standing beside him, with Grant jogging up the street toward them, his blaster held high in the standard ready position. Incarnates were checking themselves while Decard helped Domi up from her tumble on the sand where she had leaped from the moving chariot.

"If we don't follow it, we'll lose it," Kane stated, preparing to make his way into the tunnel.

"Forget it," Brigid told him. "Our weapons weren't doing anything. You'll just get yourself killed."

Kane stood at the edge of the tunnel for a few seconds

before tensing his wrist tendons and sending his Sin Eater back into its wrist holster. "You're right, Baptiste." He nodded. "We need a battle plan."

Just then, the shouted voice of one of the Incarnates came from across the sand. "Medic!"

All eyes turned and saw that the crocodile-masked Incarnate was lying like a rag doll, his limbs at awkward angles, blood streaming over the cracked plates of his ornate helmet.

FIVE MILES AWAY, two stolen chariots leaped over the dunes as Rosalia and Smarts raced away from their captors.

Smarts was still trying to comprehend what had occurred. One moment, they were standing with the petite albino woman and four of the animal-masked guards watching as something humanoid yet inhuman attacked the tiny ville barely one hundred yards from them. The next moment, Rosalia's lips peeled back and she let out an ear-splitting whistle. Even as Smarts turned, the deadly Rosalia was already a flurry of motion. She had bent and spun, reaching behind her and pulling the arm of the closest of the Incarnates, a man in a stylized bug mask. The bug-man was tossed over her shoulder, landing on his back with a whoop of expended breath, and Rosalia kicked the back of her bare heel into the man's nose through the mask, destroying it in an explosion of blood.

Smarts had leaped for the carrying case of the interphaser, grabbing it from the rear step of an open-backed chariot and swinging the solid box around until it connected with the side of another Incarnate's head before slamming into the back of the albino woman's own head.

As the white-skinned woman sank to her knees, Smarts had shoved the case straight down, bluntly knocking into her skull again to be sure that she was out.

By that time, Rosalia had already disarmed the next Incarnate and was just landing a face kick to the wooden helm of the one beside him before she flipped the first Incarnate's stolen staff and jabbed it into its owner's solar plexus.

Smarts remembered standing in awe as he looked at the devastation that Rosalia had caused in a matter of seconds. Three well-built, armed men had fallen to her blows. He himself had taken out another one along with their female jailer.

As he stood catching his breath, the dark-haired woman had let out that penetrating whistle once again and grabbed the case containing the interphaser from his hands.

"Quickly, before they awaken," she instructed, bringing him out of his daze.

Together, the pair of them had mounted separate chariots and gunned their engines before heading to the west at top speed. Rosalia had rested the Incarnate's staff beside her in her chariot as they took off.

Now, Smarts checked behind him, confirming that the swells and drops of the uneven desert had given them cover from the settlement and its monster. He held his hand aloft, indicating to Rosalia that they needed to halt.

"We're not far enough from them," she shouted to him over the rush of wind from their passage.

"We don't know where we're running," Smarts called back, powering down the throttle and killing his speed.

Rosalia sped on for a moment before setting her

chariot into a tight turn and drawing it to a halt beside him. When she joined him, Smarts already had his pocket chron out and was adjusting it to provide a range finder for them.

Rosalia's dark hair blew over her face, and she tossed her head back before speaking to him. "Where are we, Axel?" she asked.

"Not far from a safehouse," he assured her. "Just let me work out…" he said, his sentence drifting to nothingness as he began the calculations in his head.

She butted into his thoughts after a moment, an urgent tone to her voice. "What was that thing? Did you see?" she asked.

"I saw it." He nodded, his tone evincing deep concern.

"What was it, Axel?" she asked again.

"I have no idea," Smarts admitted. "It would appear that Señor Kane and his *compadres* involve themselves in many things that I do not as yet understand."

"It looked like it was attacking them," Rosalia stated. She and Smarts had begun their attack almost as soon as the monstrous thing had begun to move, just after it had swatted the horse aside, when all their captors' attention was focused on it. They had not stayed around long enough to see what happened next; it was simple speculation from Rosalia.

Even so, Smarts nodded slowly in agreement. He had seen the thing shriek as it turned to face the three Magistrate men and their troops. He was fairly certain that he could guess what had followed.

"We need to circle around," Smarts told Rosalia as he closed his pocket chron. "There is a dugout entrance in this direction, three and three-quarter miles—" he pointed

"—but we can't leave tracks like these. It will lead Señor Kane and his people straight to us."

"We dump these primitive vehicles, then," Rosalia said dismissively. "They've given us some distance already. I'll run the rest." She hoisted the carrying case and stepped from the chariot, passing him the procured silver staff.

"You may be able to, dear Sweet Rose," Smarts said, "but I am afraid that that is more than a little beyond my capabilities."

"Follow," she told him as she began running in the direction he had indicated. "I will bring reinforcements as soon as I can."

Smarts bowed his head in acknowledgment as the woman began running across the sand at a fast jog. "We may not need them, if that monster was successful."

Rosalia's long strides seemed to eat up the desert, and Smarts watched as her right arm pumped forward and back with each graceful stride. In her left she held the solid carrying case away from her body, careful not to knock it into her leg as she ran toward the horizon. Reluctantly Smarts glanced at the sun beating down overhead before beginning the long walk in the same direction as his colleague, using the staff as a walking stick to assist his progress over the shifting sand.

KEB AND DECARD were the first to tend to their fallen colleague, while Brigid and Kane followed. When Keb removed the crocodile mask, the wounded Incarnate's face was a tapestry of blood. A shard of wood was jabbed through his cheek, and he would be unable to close his jaw until it was removed.

"What the hell did we just see?" Kane asked, eyeing Decard warily.

"I don't know, Kane," Decard told him hotly. "All I know is that I have a man down here. What, you think I brought you into this knowing that...*thing* was going to turn up?"

Kane checked himself, scanning the horizon. "You've got four more wounded," he told Decard after a moment. "There was a prison break while we were all involved with the floor show here."

Decard swore as he glanced at his team over by the chariots. Brigid laid a consoling hand on his shoulder. "I'll take a look at them," she told him before striding toward the other wounded. Decard followed her a moment later, after checking with the medic tending to the fallen Incarnate in the crocodile mask.

Kane watched for a few more seconds as Keb worked at the hurt Incarnate. His wounds looked bad, and the man was shrieking with pain.

Kane shook his head, trying to clear his thoughts before he turned to Domi and Grant who waited by the side of the nearest building.

"What now?" Domi asked, all sign of wooziness gone from her voice.

"Didn't I tell you to get after Smarts and Rosalia?" Kane growled.

Grant held up a hand. "Whoa," he told Kane, "you may want to back down a little there, partner. Domi just damn near saved all our lives with that little stunt she pulled."

Kane's body was tense with frustration. "Yeah," he

admitted. "I'm sorry, Domi. I'm just real annoyed at losing that whatever-it-was."

"We're all annoyed," Grant told him. "You got pretty close there, Kane. Get a good look at it?"

Kane pointed off vaguely into the distance. "We'll talk about it later," he instructed. "First, you and Domi get our 'jackalopes' back."

Domi and Grant ran off in the direction of the chariots. As they caught up with Decard, Grant explained that they were going to borrow two vehicles.

"We'll be down to five," Decard lamented, "and I still have a fifteen-man crew to take care of out here."

Domi smiled, glistening white teeth amid chalk-white skin. "We'll bring them back," she assured him.

A moment later, Grant and Domi were racing off into the distance, following the wheel ruts left by their prisoners' escape. As they tore over the sand dunes, bumping up into the air and landing heavily in a manner that the chariots had never been designed for, Grant called Cerberus headquarters over his Commtact.

"This is Grant. Fix on my position and give me a satellite sweep."

A moment later Brewster Philboyd's voice piped into Grant's ear over his Commtact. "Grant, this is Brewster. What can I do for you?"

Brewster Philboyd was another of the trusted inner circle of the Cerberus operation. Philboyd was an astrophysicist by discipline, aged somewhere in his midforties. A scientist first and a fighter very much last, Philboyd worked shifts at many of the desk jobs, helping out where he could at the Cerberus redoubt.

"Long story short," Grant explained, "our two prisoners have absconded on solar-powered chariots on a westerly heading. They won't have got far. Can you find them?"

There was a pause, and Grant imagined that Philboyd was working the computer keys to access the data.

"Bear with me," Philboyd muttered.

Grant snarled as his chariot crested another hillock of sand. These street thieves may think they've got all the answers, but they reckoned without the resources at our disposal.

"I've got one," Philboyd said triumphantly. "Turn a little more to the north and you'll see two abandoned chariots, maybe two miles ahead of you. There's a figure making its way from these toward the west."

"Keep scanning," Grant told Brewster. "There should be a second one out there."

As their chariots reared up another of the steep dunes, Domi cried out in surprise, "I see them, Grant! The buggies."

Grant saw the two little dark blots on the landscape. He fed the throttle of his own chariot more power, urging the little vehicle ahead.

Philboyd's voice came over the Commtact once again. "I've spotted a second figure," he explained, "moving at some speed in the same basic direction. He's put quite a distance between himself and the first."

"*She,*" Grant corrected automatically. Somehow he knew it was Rosalia. There was something about that damn woman that was more than anyone had expected on first look.

Domi looked across from her chariot, raising her voice to be heard over the whining engines, the rush of wind and the churning sand in their wheels. "I'll take the nearest," she shouted. "You keep on, okay?"

They whipped past the abandoned chariots and could see the struggling figure of Señor Smarts as he used the staff to walk briskly away to the west, glancing over his shoulder every dozen or so paces. When he saw Domi's and Grant's chariots, he began running, changing his direction and heading for a dead tree that sprouted from the hard-packed ground to his left.

Grant ignored him, standing high in the chariot as he continued off to the west, determined to catch up with Rosalia. His head flicked to his left as Domi's chariot peeled out of formation and she prepared to run him down.

"Be careful, Domi," Grant warned. Then he was racing away, narrowed eyes scanning the horizon.

The wheels of Domi's chariot kicked up sand as she bore down on the running Mexican. "Keep away from me, Señorita Magistrate," Smarts shouted as he ducked behind the dried trunk of the tree.

The back of Domi's chariot fishtailed as she applied the brake, swinging her from side to side as she clung to the steering column. The vehicle was still moving forward, zipping past the dead tree, when Domi leaped from it in a tuck-and-roll across the sand. She saw now that the man before her had a familiar silver staff in his hand, one of the Incarnate's strange weapons, and he was frantically fiddling with the controls as he tried to work the thing.

Domi's hand reached for the Detonics Combat Master tucked into her waistband, and she brought it up in a fluid movement as she got to her knees. "Drop it," she shouted.

Smarts ignored her, finding the correct button at last and

blasting off a stream of energy from the twin prongs atop the Incarnate's staff. The blast went up into the air, shimmering like heat haze, its noise reverberating against Domi's eardrums. Then Smarts brought the staff down, aiming its near invisible beam at the albino woman.

Domi was rolling without conscious thought, moving herself out of the beam as it cleaved the air toward her. Her finger pulled at the trigger of her handgun, and a single bullet blasted from its chamber, cutting through the air and burrowing into the fleshy upper part of Smarts's left leg. With a howl, Smarts toppled, falling hard on his left shoulder, the staff still blasting energy in a crazy arc as it swayed in his hands.

"Next one takes head off scrawny shoulders, wide boy," Domi shouted as Smarts struggled to regain his composure. "Not fooling." In her anxiousness, Domi's speech patterns had reverted to the clipped, broken form of English that was a legacy of her wild past.

Smarts cursed as he tried to swing the staff around, the burning pain of the bullet wound throbbing in his leg. Suddenly, he heard the loud report of Domi's pistol once again, and a bullet whizzed just past his ear, burying itself in the sand above his head.

"Drop it!" was all he heard her say.

His hazel eyes looked down the length of his body, seeing the strange albino crouched there, poised with her pistol aimed between his legs. He flipped the switch on the side of the silver staff and tossed it to one side, raising his hands in the air.

The barrel of Domi's gun followed the deactivated staff as it dropped, then whipped back to point at Smarts as he lay there in the sand, blood seeping from the wound in his leg.

"I had to try," the Mexican said with a disarming grin. "It's the rules of the game, is it not, *señorita?*"

Domi's ruby eyes narrowed as she held the gun on him. "Just don't move," she advised him.

BACK AT THE DESERT hamlet, Brigid Baptiste and Keb the field medic had rounded up all the wounded Incarnates in the shade of one of the shacks and were checking on each in turn. The four Incarnates who had been with Domi when Smarts and Rosalia had made their break for freedom were okay barring a few scrapes and bruises, and one of them had had his bloodied nose strapped down with gauze.

"Next time, you'll wear your helmet strapped tight when in the field," Decard told him sternly, and the man nodded in silent agreement.

A fifth Incarnate, the man who had tussled with the monster itself, lay unmoving, his breathing coming in a painful wheeze.

The other Incarnates had helped shift all of the strangely altered locals into one shack, so that they could be more easily guarded and monitored.

In another of the shady rooms within the shack, Brigid and Keb compared notes on the strangely disoriented people. Their conclusion was depressingly familiar. "We're no closer to knowing what this thing is," Brigid stated.

Kane looked sour as he stood against the wall, the baying calls of the infected a haunting sound in his ears as they wailed in the neighboring room. "We need to do a proper laboratory examination," he grumbled.

"Using what?" Brigid asked. "We don't even have a means of transport right now."

"A temporary setback," Kane said firmly.

Brigid's emerald eyes held his as she looked at him in utter seriousness. "These people don't have a lot of time, Kane."

Kane bit back a curse, looking at the closed door to the next room. His gaze shifted and he addressed the medic. "Keb, how far are we from Aten?"

Keb shook his head. "I see what you are thinking, Kane, but Decard wouldn't allow it."

"You have facilities there," Kane told him. "We need to nail down what this thing is."

Brigid looked at Kane sadly. "No, Kane, Keb's right. We made a deal with Decard that he wouldn't have to take this back home with him."

Kane nodded sourly, making clear that this didn't sit well with him. "I didn't come here expecting the monster from the depths," he grumbled.

"No one did," Brigid said, pacifying him, resting her hand on his arm, her face close to his.

As they stood there, considering their next move, there was a sudden cry from outside and Keb rushed to see what the disturbance was. A look passed between Brigid and Kane before they followed.

Outside, at the shady spot by the wall of the shack, the four wounded Incarnates had all moved away from their companion—the one who had been tossed aside by the dark-skinned monster less than thirty minutes before. The man was tossing around like a beached fish, his bent body flipping despite his broken limbs. And he was screaming, issuing guttural sounds that began from somewhere deep in his throat.

Decard was rushing across from where he had been examining the tunnel at the edge of the settlement, his limping more pronounced now after all the action of the day. "What happened to him?" he asked.

One of the wounded Incarnates spoke up, pointing to his fallen colleague. "He just started screaming, moving about. It's like he woke up all of a sudden," he explained. There was a distinct note of fear in his voice.

Kane stepped closer, looking at the fallen man as he writhed on the ground. His teeth snapped together, and his eyes balled tight as he moaned at his pains. "It's okay," Kane told him. "Help's here, we have painkillers."

The Incarnate ignored him, and then Kane heard words amid the man's shrieks of agony, words that chilled him to the very marrow.

"Get off the planet, ape-thing," the Incarnate said in a voice not his own, a voice coming from deep within his throat. "Make room."

Kane crouched, using his left forearm to hold the writhing man still. With his right hand, the ex-Mag reached for the man's face.

"Kane?" Decard cried. "What the hell do you think you're doing?"

Kane ignored him, snatching at the man's forehead to hold his head down. He shifted his weight, holding the writhing, howling Incarnate as still as he was able. It was like holding an enraged steer, and Kane was thrown about a little, his booted foot and knee shifting in the sand as he was tossed around.

With a swift movement of his hands, Kane grabbed the man's head and shoved him back, right hand reversed, its heel pushing against the man's forehead. With the fingers of his right hand, Kane dragged at the indentations below the man's eyebrows, forcing him to open his eyes. Kane remained there a moment, looking at the man's eyes as the Incarnate continued to howl in agony.

Kane's head turned to Decard, Brigid and the others as they moved closer. "Look," he instructed. "Look at his eyes."

Where the Incarnate's eyes had been a dark chocolate brown before, now they were a light tan. Their color was fading away.

Chapter 10

Damp with sweat, the wispy silk of her dancing costume clung to Rosalia's toned body as she ran across the desert. Her shapely tanned legs stretched out, eating into the distance with seeming effortlessness. Her right arm pumped back and forth, the hand held rigid, cutting the air like a blade, while her left hand clung to the handle of the little metallic carrying case of the interphaser unit. Her breathing came regularly, deep breaths drawn in by her nostrils, held in her lungs, released in a steady stream between her parted lips. Despite the hot afternoon sun, the sweat sheen glistening on her body, Rosalia showed no signs of tiring.

Her dark eyes were fixed ahead, looking for the signs that Señor Smarts had promised she would recognize. She had never been to this dugout before, at least not on foot, and she was certain that it would be easy to miss. Tom Carnack's gang knew the value of keeping things hidden from prying eyes, even out here in the middle of nowhere. When you were a trader, it didn't pay to advertise where you stored your goods.

As her long legs continued to kick forward, racing for the western horizon, she spotted the stump of a dead tree off to her right, barely poking from the ground. She angled her run toward it, slowing as she approached.

Rosalia put down the interphaser and stood there a moment, looking at the little stump. It rose just three inches above the sand, the bulk of the tree snapped off and long since removed. The brown bark had been blackened by smoke where someone had burned the tree's remains, and Rosalia knelt a moment, scrutinizing the burn marks carefully.

There, to one side, carved into the blackened stump so that it showed as a pale yellow streak, was a symbol. A circle, irregular in its hasty carving, with parallel lines scored across it at an angle. Carnack's symbol.

Rosalia glanced back to where she had come from, up at the sun shifting a little lower in the sky as the afternoon progressed. Then she looked back at the tiny carving and judged what direction it pointed. All she needed to do was head in the same direction as the carving indicated, a straight line all the way to the horizon until she found the hideout. But if she misjudged, deviated even a little from that route, she ran the risk of passing the base, never finding the hidden entrance.

Scanning the landscape to the west, where the carving indicated, Rosalia saw a low outcropping forming a muddy brown lump against the blue sky. She shielded her eyes from the sun, narrowing them to get a better look. Up there, circling overhead, she saw a family of buzzards, looking for scraps. That would be it, then—Carnack's base.

Picking up the carrying case by its handle once more, Rosalia resumed her jog toward the rocky outcropping. With no markers around, it was hard to guess how far away the rocks were, but she estimated it was perhaps a mile— five or six minutes, maybe.

GRANT URGED the solar-powered chariot to even greater speeds as the wind whipped into his face. "She can't have got much farther," he told himself as his vehicle roared over another dune, throwing up a cloud of dusty sand in its wake.

The chariot landed on the other side of the dune, the hard impact jarring through Grant's body, making his teeth clack together. As he landed, Grant spotted the tiny figure in the distance, just a speck amid the dirty yellow sands. He turned the chariot toward the dark speck, smiling as the dot became recognizable as a human form, the thin lines of the legs and arms protruding from the torso.

"Now I've got you." Grant grinned as he gunned the chariot's engine.

As Grant got closer, he confirmed that the figure was Rosalia. He saw then that she was holding a square case that glinted in the sun—the interphaser. Raising his head, Grant stared ahead, trying to discern where she was running to. There was nothing there, just a little outcropping, perhaps two stories high, and stretching maybe thirty feet along the sand. Hardly a great hiding place—at best the dancer might have hoped to use it for shade until the sun went down and she could travel more comfortably.

Of course, she had the interphaser, but Grant reassured himself that she couldn't have figured out the operating protocols involved from just a single observation of the unit in use. Smarts, he accepted, might just be wily enough to get the unit working by a process of trial and error, but he couldn't imagine Rosalia getting it operational by anything other than luck. Not that luck hadn't already played its part in her survival and escape to now, he reminded himself.

In short, all she could do now was run. And there was nowhere to hide; Grant knew it and she had to, as well.

SHE RAN, and the only sound in her ears was the rhythm of her body, the beating of her heart, the pulse throbbing below her ears. But as she neared the rocks, Rosalia heard another sound, a sound that didn't belong, an intrusion on her body's rhythm, and she glanced over her shoulder, quickening her pace automatically.

There, racing across the dry dirt, a plume of sand tossed up in his wake, was the dark-skinned Magistrate aboard one of the little electric chariots. He was a huge figure, standing erect over the low-set console of the twin-wheeled buggy.

The trace of a smile crossed Rosalia's lips for a moment, bunching the pleats of skin at the corners of her eyes. She spun back, standing still for several seconds as she let Grant get just a little bit closer. "Too late now, Magistrate man," she whispered. Then she blew Grant a kiss before turning once more.

A second later, she trotted into the shade of the outcropping and was lost to the solid black shadow that it cast.

Grant urged the chariot onward, all the more determined not to lose his quarry now that she was so close.

BACK AT THE settlement, Kane lifted his hand from the shrieking Incarnate's head and stepped slowly away from him. The wounded Incarnate continued to toss and turn, his head weaving backward and forward as though taking punches, his body writhing on the ground, tossing the fine grains of sand up into the air.

Kane turned to Decard, his face stern and impenetrable. "Well?"

Decard looked from Kane to his writhing guardsman and back, fear lining his youthful features. "What is it? What's going on?"

Kane glanced to Brigid and Keb before he uttered the word on his mind. "Virus," he stated.

"No, Kane," Brigid said thoughtfully. "No virus I know talks back. He called you an…ape-thing?"

"Yeah," Kane muttered as if to himself. "Sounds like the kind of bull Enlil and his cohorts spout."

"The Annunaki?" Brigid confirmed, and Kane nodded. "This doesn't look—" She stopped herself as she noticed the irritation on Kane's face.

"Nothing those lizards do ever looks like what we expect," he reminded her with irritation. "Nothing they do conforms to what we think they'll do. Every time we think we've beaten them down it turns out they've got another trick just waiting to be played."

Keb looked to Brigid for reassurance before he spoke. "Kane," the medic gently urged, "for those of us who came in late, perhaps…?"

Kane gestured to Keb's fallen colleague as the man bucked and writhed as though possessed. "I think this is an Annunaki virus that—" he hesitated, trying to find the right word "—overwhelms people's minds."

"A mind virus?" Decard asked. "Could such a thing exist? Keb? Brigid?"

"Hypothetically." Brigid nodded. "But how would such a thing be spread?"

"That creature touched him," Kane reminded them.

Brigid shook her head. "It touched you, too, Kane."

Kane disagreed. "No, it didn't," he told her. "I was damn close, but we never touched. You made sure of that, Baptiste. And thank you," he added after a moment.

Keb looked at his shrieking colleague. "With just the one host, and everyone who contacts it dying in a matter of hours, this would be a very slow way to intentionally spread a disease," he observed. "If it is intentional."

"He's right," Brigid agreed. "I touched the girl in the tent before she died. Nothing's happened to me."

"What about an incubation period?" Decard suggested. "Maybe, Brigid…" He stopped, clearly uncomfortable with speaking his thoughts aloud. "Maybe you're a carrier now?"

Brigid pointed to the suffering Incarnate who had worn the crocodile mask. "No," she said firmly. "It's affected your man here immediately, and the evidence we've seen is that that's true for everyone else who's come into contact with it. If I had it, you'd all know by now."

"You could be immune," Kane suggested, no cheer in his voice. "Back in Cobaltville, there was a program of immunization against a number of diseases. Since Baron Cobalt turned out to be an Annunaki in sleeper form, isn't it possible he'd have immunized his loyal subjects with whatever they needed to survive this virus?"

Brigid held her hands open in despair. "Anything's possible, Kane," she acknowledged, "but we left Cobaltville years ago. Why is this virus—if it is a virus—only showing up now? What held it back? Who's unleashed it and why?"

"By mistake maybe?" Decard postulated.

"Could be just to thin the herd in the Outlands, outside

of ville walls," Kane proposed. "The Annunaki are very into culling the herd, selective evolution or whatever you want to call it."

Brigid looked at the Incarnate as he writhed in the sand, his eyes now wide open and disturbingly colorless. He had stopped shrieking, but continued to mumble and mutter from deep in his throat, as though clearing phlegm.

"I don't see it," Brigid decided. "There are too many variables for it to ring true," she told Kane. "We're looking too deeply for an answer to something that's likely much more simple."

Slowly Kane nodded, accepting her point.

"The monster's the key, then," Keb said as the group stood, considering its next move.

The four of them stood there, watching in helpless silence as the wounded Incarnate who had worn the crocodile's face pounded at the ground, occasionally screaming at the top of his lungs before reverting to the mumbled patter of nonsense that they had seen in the other altered people.

Finally, Kane turned away and activated the Commtact hidden beneath his skin. "Kane to Cerberus. You there?"

A moment later, Brewster Philboyd's voice came over the Commtact receiver. "Yes, Kane."

"We've got us a creature of unknown origin," Kane explained, "approximately eight feet tall, jet-black skin, appears to be disintegrating with movement—"

As Kane spoke, Lakesh interrupted: "Kane, Lakesh here. Please describe again."

Kane gave a full description of the creature that they had faced less than an hour earlier. He concluded, with a request. "We think that this creature is the host for the virus or infection that Decard originally reported. Trouble is, we lost it after the battle—the thing retreated underground. Now, this creature moves like lightning, and it's a burrower, so it won't be easy for us to track from the ground. I'm wondering if we can employ the Vela satellite for some surveillance."

IN THE CONTROL ROOM of the Cerberus redoubt, Lakesh bent over a desk as he considered Kane's request. He looked across to where Brewster Philboyd sat at the communications relay desk, an unspoken query on his face.

Aged somewhere in his midforties, Philboyd wore black-rimmed glasses above his acne-scarred cheeks. His pale blond hair was swept back from a receding hairline, and his lanky six-foot frame seemed hunched as he sat at the computer terminal uplinked to the satellites and communications relay. Philboyd had joined the Cerberus team along with a number of other Moon exiles and had proved to be a valuable addition to the staff. His dogged determination to find the cause of a problem or uncover the basic workings of a system had assisted in refining the operation of the portable interphaser. While he wasn't a fighter, Philboyd was as determined as a dog with a bone when he addressed a scientific or engineering problem. Just now, the unvoiced problem was whether the Vela-class satellite could track a body underground.

Philboyd nodded after a moment, showing Lakesh a shaky hand that suggested that he would try but could not guarantee results.

"Kane," Lakesh replied, "we can try that, but no

promises. Do you know which direction the creature moved off in?"

"Hard to say," Kane answered. "Like I said, the thing spun itself a tunnel into the ground, disappeared inside. Maybe south, but I can't say for sure."

As the conversation continued, with Brewster Philboyd taking down details and coordinates, Mariah Falk and Clem Bryant entered the operations center, full of enthusiasm. Lakesh held his palm up to them as they approached, warning them to remain silent until the communication with Kane was over. He needed to concentrate on every word.

"One more thing," Brewster explained as he watched the satellite feed from California. "Grant's requested some monitoring assistance, too. I can't be watching two places at once, no matter how close you guys are. I'll see if anything leaps up from under the surface, but I'll need to keep with Grant for a while."

From the communications link, Kane voiced his assent. "Grant's out on his own," he said, "so I want you to stick with him, priority one."

With that, Kane signed off, and the conversation was over. Lakesh motioned Mariah and Clem over.

"Mariah believes that she's found something," Clem began as Mariah unfolded her map of Arizona onto Lakesh's desk.

THE CHARIOT PULLED to a stop beside the rocks, and Grant leaped from it, Sin Eater in hand, using the vehicle for cover as he surveyed the area.

Up close he saw that the outcropping was formed of two

strips of rocks. The right-hand set towered to about two stories while the others, to his left, were a little lower, just over eight feet. The strips of rocks formed a narrow corridor, locked in shadow, its floor carpeted by fine sand. Rosalia had disappeared between the two strips but, even from here, Grant could see that there was hardly anywhere to go. The shady corridor between the rocks ran no more than eighteen feet. At best, she might hope to ambush him if he entered, but she was unarmed, he knew, and Grant was confident he could take her.

Warily, his pistol pointed ahead of him, Grant made his way toward the narrow corridor formed by the rocks.

The outcropping cast shade across the landscape, thick black shadows, and Grant took a few moments as his eyes adjusted from the fierce sunlight. Slowly, the shadows of the corridor took on a familiar greenish hue as his eyes filtered out the sun, and he began to discern the details of the rocky walls. The little corridor was tight, not wide enough to take two men abreast, they would need to walk single file. Its depths seemed so dark after the harsh desert sun, and Grant stood near to the entrance, checking ahead with his gun raised, his eyes flicking left and right, up and down, trying to spy Rosalia.

Slowly, tentatively, Grant took a step forward, edging his back against the higher of the two walls. He couldn't see Rosalia, couldn't even sense her presence. He stilled himself, willing his heart to hush as he listened for her breathing.

Carefully, Grant continued down the short passageway between the rocks, his eyes flicking to and fro as he searched for the svelte woman.

By the time he reached the end of the shady passage, Grant wanted to punch something. She wasn't there, wasn't anywhere. She had ducked into this naturally made alleyway between the rocks. He had seen her blow him a kiss and step into the shade and then—nothing.

Grant stepped back into the sunlight and scanned the horizon, looking farther to the west to see if she had continued running while he was carrying out his methodical search. There was no one in sight.

Warily, his senses heightened and alert, he walked around the outside edge of the lower group of rocks, checking to see if Rosalia had doubled back and hidden here while he was searching the shadowy corridor. He paced back to the chariot, which remained where he had left it. There was no sign of her.

Think in three dimensions, Grant, he reminded himself as he reached for the top of the lower group of rocks and pulled himself up by the powerful muscles of his left arm. The surface of the low rocks was sprinkled with sand and spattered with the white residue of bird droppings, but there was no sign of the woman.

Grant took several steps backward until he reached the edge of the outcropping. Then he sheathed the Sin Eater and sprinted across the narrow expanse of rock before leaping into the air and grabbing the edge of the higher group of rocks. He grunted as his chest slapped against the hard rock wall, then clambered up using his hands and whatever toeholds he could find.

Atop the higher outcropping, Grant saw exactly the same thing as he had on the lower group. "A fat lot of nothing," he muttered, kicking at the flurries of shifting sand that spun about in the breeze. The circling buzzards squawked at his intrusion into their territory as he stood there.

Grant activated his Commtact and called to Brewster Philboyd at Cerberus headquarters. "I think I've lost my rabbit," he explained. "Are you able to give me a fix on her?"

Philboyd's voice came over the Commtact with crystal clarity. "No can do, Grant. I was watching the whole thing. She went in and you followed, then you came out. Wherever she is, she isn't running. Is there a cave or caves inside?"

"Not that I saw," Grant replied, an edge of irritation creeping into his voice.

WHEN DOMI RETURNED to the little desert hamlet, she felt the grim air that had settled over all of the personnel. Señor Smarts had been persuaded at gunpoint to drive one of the chariots back to the settlement, while Domi rode behind him in her own vehicle. They had abandoned the third chariot, trusting that Decard's men would be able to pick it up once Domi advised them of its location.

Smarts limped from the back of the chariot, gripping his leg wound and gritting his teeth against the pain, while Domi followed, twirling the stolen Incarnate staff in her left hand while she casually held the Detonics Combat Master to the brigand's back.

"Hurry, hurry," she urged Smarts as they walked toward the sole thoroughfare of the hamlet. "No time to waste."

Over his shoulder, Smarts glared back at her, his eyebrows knitted in annoyance. "I am wounded, you understand?" he spit.

"Yeah." Domi smiled. "I shot you good, you fink."

"Like all Magistrates, you have no honor, *señorita,*" Smarts snarled at her.

Domi stopped twirling the silver staff and took two steps forward, placing the muzzle of her pistol flush against Smarts's left cheek. "You bopped me in the back of the head with a case," she reminded him. "Twice."

The color drained from Smarts's face, and his eyes remained on hers as Domi pushed the gun forward. Finally, he staggered back, muttering, "My apologies, *señorita.*"

"Keep 'em," she told Smarts as he winced at the pain running through his leg. Domi held the gun on him, her fierce ruby orbs eyeing his body as though deciding where to place a bullet. Finally, she stepped back and pulled the gun away, holding it in a more casual grip but still glaring at the wounded man. "You maybe don't want to get on my wrong side anymore," she warned him. "I'm not like Kane and the others. I don't believe in all that honor shit. You play that card again and I'll likely put a bullet between your eyes, little man."

Smarts nodded warily. "I understand," he acknowledged.

Domi held his gaze a moment longer, until he finally looked away. "When Kane's done with you, you had better run. Or you had better have a damn good reason for why I don't carve a strip off you for blindsiding me."

With that, Domi urged the Mexican toward the buildings. A pair of Incarnates—eagle and jackal masks atop their heads—came over and spoke to Domi. She explained where the other chariot was, and she asked them to guard Smarts very carefully while she gave a full report to Kane.

Domi was directed to one of the shacks, where she found Kane, along with Brigid, Decard, Keb and two more Incarnates standing guard over a third Incarnate who had been strapped to a bed. Domi recognized the tied Incarnate as the one who had been wounded in the skirmish with the black-skinned monster. He lay on the bed, pulling at his bonds and writhing as though with fever, a stream of guttural sounds emerging from deep in his throat.

"What's been going on?" Domi asked with forced cheeriness.

Decard shot her an angry look but said nothing as Kane stepped forward and guided her through the door and into the next room where they could be alone.

"Just after you left, we made a discovery," Kane said. "The guardsman who got hit is now a carrier of the same thing that the pregnant girl had."

Domi swore, her eyes turning back to the bedroom door from which the man's moans could be heard. "What is it, do you know?"

"Not yet," Kane acknowledged, "but we've got theories." He told her about how the Incarnate had been the only person touched by the strange creature, the proposition of an Annunaki virus that overwhelms its host. Domi nodded in concerned silence the whole time.

Then Kane pushed the drapes back and looked out the window at the expanse of sand outside. "What about you and Grant?" he asked.

"I got the boy Smarts," Domi said, gesturing outside with her thumb, "but Grant had to chase Rosalia down. I've not heard anything since, but he had Philboyd tagging her the whole way. She won't get far."

Kane nodded. Grant could take care of himself, and the man would have been in touch via Commtact if anything were amiss.

GRANT HAD LOWERED himself from the tops of the outcropping and was carefully searching the naturally formed corridor that ran between the two stretches of rocks. When he had passed through here the first time, not ten minutes earlier, the rocks had seemed to soak up the light, casting the whole route into a midnight shadow. Now, confident that Rosalia wasn't about to leap out at him, he waited with his eyes closed until they had fully adjusted. Then, Sin Eater in hand, he checked every rocky jut and crevice.

He missed it the first time, but on his second sweep through the eighteen-foot-long passageway, left hand running along the lower rock wall, he found what his eyes had failed to see. There was a tunnel, a burrow, like something an animal would use, rising from the ground to the height of Grant's waist. It was easy to miss; the way that the rocks cascaded within the tunnel made it appear to be almost flat, disguising the tunnel by nothing more than a trick of the shadows.

"Hmm," Grant breathed. "Hidden in plain sight."

He knelt, looking into the little tunnel entrance. It hardly looked wide enough to accommodate his wide shoulders, but it would be a cinch for a smaller person—someone of Domi's stature, say, or the lithe Rosalia with her willowy figure—to slip through it in an instant. For a moment, Grant considered calling Domi in to assist him, eyed the hole again and decided he could make it. It was one woman, no matter how vicious, and he was an ex-Mag. She may have made a chase of it for a while, but she had just run out of track.

Grant ducked, crouch-walking to the tunnel entrance before leaning warily in. Inside, he saw, the tunnel sloped downward at a sharp angle. Getting down that slope would be more like falling than crawling, he decided. Flipping himself around, Grant leaned on his buttocks and let his feet dangle into the hole. Then, gritting his teeth, he pushed off, sliding down the rough surface of the tunnel, using his free hand to slow his descent.

More darkness for a few moments, then Grant's descent stopped as quickly as it had begun, and his feet slammed into a solid rock floor. Automatically, the ex-Mag bent his knees, absorbing the impact. He calculated that he had fallen no more than twelve feet below the surface.

Crouching instinctively, Grant looked around him. He was on a rocky ledge covered in sand and copper-colored dirt, within a large, underground cavern. The cool air of the cavern hit him with abruptness after the blazing heat of the desert sun on his face, and despite the carefully climate-controlled environment of the shadow suit, he felt a shiver run through his body.

He could hear noise coming from just below him, voices talking. Grant sank to his belly and pulled himself silently to the edge of the rock plinth he had landed on. Stilling his breath, Grant peered over the side of the ledge.

Beneath him he saw a string of lights, just naked bulbs, running around the cavern a few feet below his hiding place. Two men were down there, discussing some woman that they both knew—intimately—and Grant tuned out their sordid conversation as his gaze swept the expanse of cavern.

The underground cave was roughly circular in shape, and it stretched at least fifty feet from the wall where Grant was to its far side. It was hard to judge accurately as the string of lights had been used to illuminate the first two-thirds, but the last part had been left in darkness. Within the lit area, a number of people milled about, and many of them openly bore arms. They were a ragtag group, with no real uniformity to their clothes or weapons, but they were clearly acting together as somebody's handpicked militia. Grant estimated perhaps twenty-five guards in the cavern, along with a few others who appeared unarmed and busied themselves at errands of one kind or another. One girl in her early teens was pouring piping-hot water into mugs from a kettle over a small gas stove. As Grant watched, a man bearing three days of beard on his chin and a Ruger M-77 rifle across his back stomped over and muttered something to the girl. She physically cowered, handing the man a mug as she bowed her head, but it didn't help her. The man took the mug, then dealt her a heavy backhanded blow across the face before walking away, back to a game of dice he was playing with several other armed individuals.

Grant's gaze continued to work around the vast chamber until something significant caught his eye. Off to the far right, a bank of large, upright tubes bubbled with a blue-green liquid. Grant couldn't tell from here whether the liquid was luminous or if the tubes were illuminated, but it didn't matter—he knew what he was looking at. It was a laboratory of some sort, doubtless brewing up some new flavor of trouble.

As he watched the whitecoats in the lab work through their experiments, two familiar figures walked into the cordoned-off area of the lab: Rosalia, her silks now wrapped tightly around her and a man's camo jacket draped over her shoulders, and Tom Carnack, looking none the worse for wear after his ordeal in Hope, and now carrying the metallic case that contained the interphaser.

Carnack called one of the whitecoats aside and rested the carrying case on a worktable before cracking its seals.

Grant shifted his position, wishing he could somehow get closer. An instinct, a sixth sense, suddenly nudged him and he looked around him, certain he was being watched. There was no one there, no one to the sides or behind him. He rolled carefully away from the edge and looked down the sloped side that led down to the cavern floor—no one there, either.

Warily, his senses still on high alert, Grant turned back to the scene in the cavern. If Carnack was here, then that meant that this was his storage depot, or at least one of them. And with the laboratory, Grant deduced, this had to be the place that the brigand leader had alluded to when he had bragged of his experiments with hybrid DNA. As the thought struck him, Grant felt the weight of the Sin Eater pistol in his hand. Where a moment before it had been an irrelevance, no more noticeable than the clothes he wore, suddenly it felt like a coiled snake, waiting to strike. A well-placed shot in this enclosed area and those chemicals would go up in flames, Grant realized. Then it would be all over for Carnack's new baronies, aborted before they had even been born.

As he stretched the pistol toward the laboratory, sighting down the length of his right arm, a sudden noise caught Grant's attention from above. He glanced up automatically, and saw the boy, Benqhil, the guide who had taken them to Carnack's negotiating rooms back in Hope, sitting atop a higher ledge, his feet dangling casually over the side.

His lips were drawn back, his teeth clenched, and he let out
the strange penetrating sound again—part whistle, part
trilling.

The atmosphere in the cavern changed immediately.
Suddenly the bandit guards were alert, checking their
weapons as they rushed across the cave toward Grant's
hiding place as Benqhil pointed him out. Even as he began
to move, Grant saw the first flashes of gunfire from the
floor below as guards turned their pistols on him.

Chapter 11

Mariah Falk stared at the impressive view from the San Francisco mountain range as she followed Edwards along the thin trail leading to the summit of Humphreys Peak. It was so strange, she thought, to see how little it had changed since she was last here, more than two hundred years before.

Like a number of the Cerberus personnel, Falk had endured an extended period in cryogenic hibernation while the Russo-American conflict played out, and had missed the terrible years that had followed, when North America had been nothing more than aptly named Deathlands.

When Mariah had shown her findings to Lakesh earlier that day, he had immediately agreed that the triangulated epicenter of the quakes, here in Arizona, was worth checking, in case anything new was brought to light. Mariah formed one-third of an investigation team, along with Clem Bryant, for moral support, and Edwards, who was assigned to bodyguard duties. Together, the group had swiftly jumped to a nearby military redoubt, leaving them with a short hike to reach the mountain peak.

As she stood there, gazing at the reddish peaks that jutted around them, Clem Bryant's rich, soothing voice broke into her thoughts. "You seem pensive, Mariah. Is something wrong?"

Mariah slowly turned to look at Clem. He had been following a few paces behind her on the narrow path, showing no signs of exhaustion as he hefted a large backpack full of supplies.

"I was just remembering the last time I was here." Mariah smiled. "Must have been Christmas 1978, or maybe '79. I came here with a group of college friends, did some skiing at Coconino, probably hiked along this very trail."

"How was it?" Clem asked. "The skiing, I mean."

"Dreadful." Mariah laughed. "No sense of balance, scared of going fast, convinced I was going to break both legs. I was pitiful." Mariah stood wistfully, looking out at the snow-dappled peaks of the far mountains, and she giggled once more. "Just dreadful."

From a little higher up the path, Edwards cupped his hands to his mouth and called to them to hurry. The former Mag had shaved his hair to a severe crew cut that showed off his bullet-bitten right ear, and he wore an olive-drab undershirt that clung to his rippling muscles. "You two girls finish your slumber party and let's get moving!" he shouted.

Mariah turned back to the path, shaking her head and preparing herself for the last half-mile trek to the site she had identified, but Clem stopped her, brushing his hand lightly against her arm. She looked at him and he smiled.

"I miss 'dreadful,'" he told her.

"Me, too," she said, nodding before beginning along the trail once more.

"I DON'T KNOW WHAT it is you two girls find to dawdle over," Edwards growled as the three of them finally reached the epicenter of the quakes.

Clem raised his eyebrows in amusement.

"Something funny?" Edwards asked Clem, a threat in his tone.

"I detect an air of tension, Mr. Edwards," Clem replied after a moment's thought.

"And I wonder why that is?" Edwards growled as he stomped away to check their immediate surroundings. "Off on a wild-goose chase with a rock lover and a cook. Un-fucking-believable."

Clem watched as Edwards left the clearing and rustled through the undergrowth, checking for traps or watching eyes.

"That man certainly has a lot of anger," he said as he turned to Mariah. She was working at a sextant on a tripod, comparing its readings to the notations she had penciled onto her map.

"He's got a good point, though," Mariah observed, not bothering to look up from her work. "It could be a wild-goose chase, Clem."

"A walk in the fresh mountain air could never be anything less than a profitable use of one's time," Clem countered.

Mariah looked up at him then with her ingratiating smile. "You know what I mean."

"I do," Clem agreed, stretching his arms around and spinning slowing to absorb the wonderful scenery. "But just look around you, Mariah. Feel that cool air in your throat. It's all frightfully invigorating, isn't it?"

"We *live* on a mountain, Clem," Mariah reminded him.

"No, we live *in* a mountain," Clem responded. "And most of the time, we simply *work* in a mountain."

Mariah shook her head. "You love all this, don't you?"

"Me?" Clem said innocently. "I'm a diver—under the sea is my chosen habitat. This is about as far away from that as one's likely to find."

"Which doesn't answer my question," Mariah reminded him as she ticked off the readings and moved the sextant on its retracting tripod legs.

Clem laughed. "It's nice to get away from the office early once in a while," he admitted.

As Clem finished, Mariah raised a finger to get his attention, her nose buried in one of the maps she had brought with her. "We're about four hundred yards from where we need to be," she decided.

Clem stepped across, reaching for the sextant. "Then allow me to do the carrying," he insisted, "while you lead the way."

Mariah and Clem pushed through the rugged terrain, with Clem wielding the long-legged sextant like a staff.

"Do you realize that this was all a hot zone less than a century ago?" Mariah asked as she led the way.

"You wouldn't think it today," Clem replied. "It's remarkable the way that nature humbles even the most forceful of humankind's attempts to destroy her."

Once they had traveled a little way down the slope of Humphreys Peak, Mariah pointed to her left. "There—do you see it?"

Clem looked where she was indicating and saw a shadowy crack running across the surface of the mountain, cutting through the scrubby grass there. "That looks like our quake site, all right," he agreed.

The crack ran more than a quarter of a mile, and was wide enough to drive a tank through at its largest divide.

It looked ancient, as if it had always been a part of the mountain, but Mariah pointed to the striations in the visible rocks and a few other things, explaining that it had opened up very recently.

"There's shearing here," she explained to Clem and Edwards when the latter joined them from his patrol. "The quake literally pushed half the mountain up by perhaps five feet."

"Five feet isn't so much," Edwards argued.

Clem looked at the man, the tone of his voice never mocking as he asked, "For a mountain?"

Edwards looked to Mariah for confirmation. "Are you saying that the whole mountain has moved?"

Mariah nodded. "It's not so unusual," she said, trying to sound reassuring.

Clem looked at her. "I detect a 'but' coming along," he encouraged.

Mariah sighed, looking frustrated as she gazed at the crack in the earth. "Would you accept 'woman's intuition' as a good enough reason to explore this crevice?"

Edwards looked doubtful, but Clem just nodded and smiled. "I can't think of a single better reason," he assured Mariah as he reached for his backpack and began unloading climbing gear.

Edwards still looked uncomfortable. "I don't know, guys," he said, "I'm not real happy about going in there if we don't know—"

Clem slapped the well-muscled man amiably on the back. "Come on, Edwards, where's your sense of adventure?"

"At the rear of the queue behind my sense of caution and my sense of self-preservation," Edwards growled.

"I'll tell you what," Clem said. "I'll go in first, and if you hear me screaming you can all run for the hills." He looked around as though seeing the mountains for the first time. "Or, perhaps, *away* from the hills."

Edwards shook his head. "My orders are to keep you two safe, Bryant, and this isn't my idea of safe."

Clem looked up at Edwards and Mariah as he tightened the climber's harness around his waist. "If our parents had played it safe, we'd never have been born." He smiled. "Come on, let's see what's down there."

As Edwards stood there, feeding the climbing line slowly through his hands while Clem disappeared from view, Mariah considered what a strange contradiction Clem Bryant was. He was always urbane, never took offense, and he demonstrated a passing knowledge in every field. And yet, out here in the field, the man showed no fear and was certainly not the bookworm-cum-chef she had expected.

FOLLOWING DOMI'S DIRECTIONS, two of Decard's Incarnate warriors shared a solar-powered chariot to pick up its missing twin. All Domi had needed to do was point in its general direction—the landscape was so bleak that it would be easy to spot the discarded buggy even from a distance, a little square blot on the sand.

The Incarnate driving the chariot wore a stylized cat mask over his features, while his companion was the bug-faced man who had suffered a bloody nose in Rosalia's lightning-fast attack. The bug-masked man, whose name was Amun, had volunteered for the assignment, determined to regain some honor after his disastrous earlier performance.

They bumped over the dunes until Farouk, in the cat mask, pulled the two-wheeled vehicle to a stop a few feet from the unit that Smarts and Rosalia had abandoned. Farouk pointed to the discarded vehicle, and Amun stepped from the back plate and strolled across the sand to it. As he did so, he heard a strange humming in the air, like a million insect wings, and he looked up instinctively, the metallic blue paint on his bug mask catching the sun.

"Do you hear something?" Amun asked, turning to his colleague. "A whirring, buzzing sound?"

Farouk nodded. "I hear it."

The noise was faint, but it grew perceptibly louder as they listened. Farouk pointed with his staff toward the west, and Amun peered in the same direction. Out there, close to the horizon, a cloud of billowing sand was being tossed into the air. The plume of sand caught on the breeze, dragging like a mist toward the north.

As the two Incarnates watched, the cloud grew larger, the noise louder, and suddenly they saw figures in the cloud. A dozen vehicles raced across the dunes, motorbikes and quad bikes, with a bulky Sandcat bringing up the rear, their wheels churning the fine sand up in a frenzy. The Incarnates knew then what the humming noise was: twin-stroke engines.

"They're heading this way," Amun declared, "coming straight for us."

"Friends of the man Smarts?" Farouk suggested. "Reinforcements, come to collect their brother?"

Amun was already standing on the back plate of the abandoned chariot, running through the prep sequence and firing its engine. The chariot's wheels spun uselessly in the sand for a few seconds, then suddenly found a grip and the vehicle lurched forward. "Back to the others," he instructed his partner. "Quickly!"

With the approaching horde bearing down on them, the two Incarnates powered their chariots across the sand at maximum speed.

CLEM BRYANT CAREFULLY lowered himself through the crack in the mountain, swinging freely for a moment until the toes of his booted feet knocked against the rock face ahead of him. He let go of the climbing cable and stretched out one arm until he could feel the cold surface of the rock there. Gradually, swaying a little uneasily, Clem dropped into the hole.

"Everything okay, Clem?" Edwards's voice echoed from above.

Clem looked up, discerning the ex-Mag's head silhouetted against the bright sky. "Fine so far," he called back. "Just like diving," he added to himself.

As he lowered himself farther, Clem felt the sudden absence of the rock face against his toes, and he peered down into the darkness. Unable to make out anything in the shadowy depths below, Clem reached for the flashlight he had attached to his belt, shifting its beam as he did an ungainly pirouette at the end of the climbing cable. The bright xenon beam showed the rock face clearly, and he aimed it below him, past where his feet swung.

Edwards's voice came again from above. "You need more rope, Clem? You're not moving."

Clem nodded to himself, taking a slow, calming breath before he continued into the darkened area below. "Ready when you are," he called back to Edwards. From the beam of the flashlight, Clem could see that the crevice opened wider. As he lowered farther, he found himself dropping into a circular area. "A room," he muttered, his eyes sweeping over the cavern. "It's an honest-to-goodness room."

Excited now, Bryant lowered himself until his boots met with the rock floor. As he found his feet, Clem called up to Edwards, ordering him to let down more rope so that there was sufficient slack for him to operate.

"You found something, Clem?" Edwards called back.

Clem cupped his hand to his mouth and responded, "I'm not sure." His voice reverberated off the rock walls of the little, hidden room.

Edwards dropped another ten feet of rope, giving him plenty of slack, and Clem walked around, peering at things in the beam of the flashlight. It was a defined room, circular in construction with benches carved from rock lining the walls. There was a pit in the center, likely used for a fire, and a low wall beside it separated the pit from what appeared to be a ventilation shaft. Clem wandered over, holding his hand by the opening to confirm that a current of air was flowing from it.

"How delightful," he said aloud, marveling at the little room beneath the mountain.

The circular nature of the room suggested that this was artificial, probably man-made. The floor was a flattened expanse of the rock that made up the mountain, and the ceiling formed a simple dome overhead, with struts interrupting the side benches at regular intervals, presumably to ensure that the domed roof didn't collapse on its inhabitants. A few rocks littered the floor where the crack in the mountain had opened, but it was otherwise free from debris.

As Clem paced around the outside wall of the circular room, he noticed a low doorway cut into the rock. He stepped toward it and was abruptly halted by the rope attached to his waist. Clem looked longingly at the doorway for a moment, intrigued by what was on the other side, then he glanced down at the harness that attached him to the surface.

"Oh, well," he decided, "in for a penny and all that." Smiling, Clem reached for the buckles of his harness and detached it. Once he was free, he stepped briskly through the doorway and into the next room.

BACK ON THE SURFACE, Edwards was on his knees, calling to Clem down the dark rent in the ground. He received no answer and, after the third attempt, he gave up, exasperated.

Mariah turned to Edwards, concern marring her features. "What's he doing down there?" she asked. "He's been gone too long."

Edwards shook his head slowly. "I shouldn't have let him go down there," he decided. "Not alone." With that, he unclipped the catch on the paddle holster at his right hip and pulled out the Colt Government Model .45 he habitually wore there. With the swiftness of long-practiced routine, Edwards checked the chambers of the pistol were full before replacing it in his holster. Then he stepped over to his backpack and swiftly attached his own climbing rig around his waist and across his shoulders.

"You going to be okay, Mariah?" he asked.

She nodded, mouth closed tightly.

"There's no one about for miles," Edwards assured her. "Nearest mat-trans is downslope, the one we came here by. No one's going to sneak up on you without you seeing them coming."

She nodded again.

Edwards stood at the edge of the crevice and raised his voice once more. "Clem? I'm coming down to join you."

A few seconds passed, and Edwards and Mariah tensely listened as the ex-Mag's voice echoed from the walls. Then Clem's voice came back, tinged with excitement.

"Bring Mariah," he said. "She'll want to see this."

FOUR MINUTES LATER, Edwards and Mariah joined Clem in the second chamber. Like the first, this one was a simple circular room carved out of the solid rock of the mountain. The walls were lined with shelves, and each shelf held a tiny fetish, a little humanoid form no more than six inches in height. Each fetish appeared different, and the overriding feeling at looking at them was one of revulsion—every single one was an ugly caricature of a person or animal or hybrid of both.

The center of the room contained a dip, like a wide basin carved into the floor, almost eight feet across. The basin contained a cloudy liquid to a depth of roughly ankle height.

"I see you've found some dollies to play with," Edwards said, admiring the numerous fetishes that lined the walls.

Clem shot him a look, but the man was too busy chuckling at his own joke as he examined one of the little figurines.

"Do you have any idea where they came from?" Mariah asked Clem. "What any of this stuff is for?"

Clem shook his head. "Not really," he admitted. "There's a drainage system running beneath the paddling pool." He pointed at the cloudy liquid and Mariah leaned closer, trying to see through the gunk.

"What is this?" Mariah asked, indicating the liquid. "Stagnant water?"

Clem sniffed. "Doesn't smell like it to me. It smells like the sea, don't you think?"

Mariah nodded. "Now that you mention it..." she agreed.

Clem gestured around at the shelves that ran the length of the circular room. "These look like artifacts of a primitive culture," he postulated, "familiar and yet I can't place them."

Mariah looked at the little figurines for a moment, her brows furrowed in thought. "I've seen them before, back when I was here skiing. There was a museum in Phoenix, I don't recall its name. They had a display, just like this, and I remember my friend Sally calling them Barbie-steins. Like Frankenstein Barbies," she added after a moment.

"I followed." Clem nodded, indulging the geologist.

Mariah stood there, her tongue flicking as she tried to form the word she hadn't thought of in over two hundred years. "Kachina!" she said at last. "They were called kachinas. Kachina dolls. Cripes, the things you remember." She laughed.

"Kachina dolls," Clem repeated thoughtfully, rolling the word around his mouth. "Do you recall anything else?"

Mariah pushed a hand through her hair as she considered the question. "They had to do with the local religion. Tribal stuff, I don't really remember, Clem. I spent a lot of that holiday wondering if some guy in my group was ever going to notice me. Girl stuff, you know?"

Edwards picked up two of the little figurines and shoved them together into one of the deep hip pockets of his combat pants, clipping the fastening over it to make sure they remained secure. "Let's get out of here, people," he instructed. "Won't do to wake the dead."

Clem held up a hand to halt the man. "Look at this place, Edwards," he said. "This place was built, carved out of the solid rock of a mountain. Just imagine how much effort that would take, how much energy and organization."

Edwards shrugged. "They tell me that the ancients built pyramids that aligned with the stars, 'impossible' stone circles and other crap I've got zero interest in. I'm past being all amazed that they did it with a primitive pulley system and six thousand indentured slaves. Go tell it to someone who cares."

Clem smiled at the man's bluster. "A primitive pulley and six thousand slaves would do it, but where would they put the rocks they carved away, Mr. Edwards?"

Edwards gestured to the first room with his thumb. "Let's get topside," he instructed. "Time to clear out and go home. Anything else needs to be done here, someone can come back."

Clem took another look around the room before they left, then reached for the water bottle that he had attached to his climbing rig. "One moment," he told Edwards, who looked irritated as he waited in the doorway.

Unscrewing the cap of the bottle, Clem walked past him and tossed the contents into a corner of the circular room with the rock benches. Then he returned into the second chamber and knelt at the pool of liquid in its center, swishing a little of the contents into his emptied bottle. He held the bottle up to the flashlight, examining the cloudy contents. The bottle was about one-third full.

"There we are," Clem said, smiling. "A little something for the folks back home."

"That's great," Edwards growled. "Now let's get moving, huh? We've got a twenty-minute trek back to the mat-trans, and I've worked up an appetite with all this climbing."

Clem turned to Mariah as they followed Edwards back into the main room, where the climbing ropes dangled. "Even critical scientific exploration has to stop for lunch, it seems," he whispered.

She glared at him, then started to laugh.

Soon, the three of them were making their way back to the surface, ready to return to the Cerberus installation.

Chapter 12

Grant stepped out from the recess in the rock wall, retracting his Sin Eater into its hidden wrist holster and holding his now empty hands high above his head. "Don't shoot," he instructed, raising his voice to be heard above the footsteps of the approaching brigands.

Three armed men had reached his hiding place, and another half dozen hurried up the sand-dappled slope.

"Who are you?" the lead man demanded, shoving the long barrel of a Colt Anaconda pistol toward Grant's face.

Grant looked past the pistol at the man who held it. He wore a dirty red bandanna across his forehead, dusty, unwashed clothes with a belt of bullets around his waist. The other men and women who had chased up here upon Benqhil's whistled command were dressed in similarly grimy, sweat-stained clothing.

"Speak," the bandanna-wearing man urged, shoving with the pistol until it was just a few inches from Grant's forehead.

"I'm an old acquaintance of Tom Carnack's," Grant explained, watching the man's eyes for the telltale flinch of recognition at the name. "That name mean something to you, or do I gotta point him out?"

Still holding the pistol at Grant's head, the bandanna-wearing man glanced across the cavern and called for Carnack. "Tom? Got someone here claims to be a friend of yours."

From the corner of his eye, Grant saw Carnack's head look up, then the sharp-featured young man started making his way across the floor of the cavern toward the slope. The brigands who had rushed up the slope made way deferentially for Carnack and Rosalia, who strode beside him.

"Mr. Grant," Carnack said as he looked the Cerberus warrior up and down. "Didn't expect to see you again. How you been? My man here treating you all right?"

In a flash of movement, Grant's right hand slashed across and down, grabbing the bandanna-wearing man's pistol by the barrel, plucking it from his hand. Before the astonished brigand could react, Grant drove his knee into the man's solar plexus, knocking the wind out of him. As the brigand staggered backward and fell to the ground at Carnack's feet, Grant raised one corner of his mouth in a smile.

"Not so bad, Tom," he said, "but a little light on the hospitality." Grant flipped the Anaconda in his hand and offered the weapon, butt first, to Carnack.

Carnack smiled as he took it, his teeth gleaming from the lights beneath. "You keep that up, and someone's liable to put a bullet in your head," he said ominously.

"Well," Grant said, shrugging, "that's a pretty big risk anyway, far as I can see."

Carnack stood there for a moment, studying the pistol in his hands as his men waited, their own guns aimed at the interloper. Then, almost casually, he raised the gun and sighted down its length, pointing it at Grant's head. "So," he said, smiling amiably, "I can't think of any reason to let you live."

Grant nodded in agreement. "I can appreciate that," he replied. "For one thing I know where your hidden base is now. I'll be honest and say, if our positions were swapped, I'd sure as hell shoot you."

Carnack cocked the hammer on the .44 and offered Grant a look that oozed sincerity. "Well, it's nice that we could agree on something in the end," he stated. "I wouldn't say it was nice knowing you, Grant, but at least it didn't last long, eh?"

Standing with his hands raised again, Grant lowered them just a little, one finger extended as though to make one more point. "I don't see Señor Smarts here," Grant said. "He get lost?"

"I've got men on it," Carnack responded coolly. "Sent them the very second Rosie here came back to the fold."

Grant nodded. "Yeah. See, I knew you were clever. I'll just bet that, given a few weeks, maybe a month or two, you'll have that interphaser up and running, too."

Carnack's smile turned to a sneer as the realization dawned on him. "You know how to work it, don't you?"

Grant nodded. "But you'll figure it out," he said. "Maybe even before my team use the reverse function to, you know, pop up here out of nowhere."

"You're joshing," Carnack blustered, but he was clearly worried at the prospect.

"You'll be fine," Grant assured him. "Just switch it off until you're ready to use it. Blocks anything coming in or out." He raised his arms high once more, watching as Carnack considered his options. "You do know how to switch it off, don't you?" Grant prodded.

With a curse under his breath, Tom Carnack lowered the

pistol and carefully replaced the hammer. Then he looked Grant in the eyes, a snarl across his lips. "You're going to show us how to use this interphaser thing, Grant, and maybe I'm going to let you live. But you try anything—anything at all—and there's thirty men here armed for bear who'll make sure you walk on stumps for the rest of your very short life. Get me?"

Grant nodded, slowly lowering his hands. "Not really into the stumps-for-legs look," he uttered.

"Come on," Carnack urged, leading the way back down the slope and into the main area of the cavern.

Of course, Grant had been bluffing; there was no reverse function to the interphaser, nor was there any way to block an incoming or outgoing transit. But that nasty little possibility was just enough to give Grant necessary breathing space. A good lie was better than a hundred bullets, he reminded himself, a thin smile crossing his lips and raising the edges of his gunslinger's mustache.

Grant took three steps after Carnack, passing Rosalia, who stood waiting impatiently against the rock wall. She gave Grant a look of contempt through slitted eyes and, once he had passed, she grabbed his arm and, with a swift movement of her feet behind him, flipped the big man onto his back. Then she crouched over Grant, unbuckling the holster of the Sin Eater he wore at his wrist.

"You could have just asked," Grant told her.

"Shut up, Magistrate man," she responded, spitting in his face before she let go of him and stood up once more.

KANE, BRIGID AND DOMI were preparing to leave Decard and his Incarnates at the little desert settlement when Domi suddenly turned her head, as though listening to far-off voices. "Roamers," she said after a moment, turning to Kane and Decard as they settled on a contingency plan should they not return with Grant inside of two hours.

Kane's eyes flicked to her as the albino woman walked across to the window of the shack and stared out at the bleak terrain beyond.

"Domi, what do you see?" he asked. Kane knew that Domi had survived life in the harsh Outlands; he trusted her instincts implicitly.

"Didn't see," she told him, still peering through the window. "Heard. Engines coming. Lots of them."

Decard looked at Kane and Brigid where they stood in the little room. "It could be my men returning," he proposed.

"More than that," Domi said. "Combustion engines, old-school tech."

Kane shook his head. "Coming here? But that makes no sense—who's out here?"

Brigid looked at him with her vibrant green eyes, her face emotionless. "Carnack's men," she said.

Kane cursed. "We've covered a lot of territory," he agreed. "Entirely possible we've hit close to one of that snake's outposts."

Domi turned from the window, mouth downcast. "We've got their man—Smarts. Bet you they're coming for him."

The whining noise of the engines was louder now, loud enough for them all to hear, and as the four of them stood in the little shack, out of the sun, they heard one of the Incarnates calling to Decard. "Incoming!"

"Damn," Kane spit, running to the doorway and outside. "This is high on the list of shit I don't need right now."

"Agreed," Decard said, his Sin Eater dropping from its holster into the palm of his hand.

Outside the shack, the remaining Incarnates were taking up positions around and on top of the buildings, facing out toward a cloud of dust that was kicking up on the western horizon. Brigid and Domi fanned out to take up defensive positions as Decard and Kane got a full report from the watch. The report was brief and to the point—hostiles were approaching, no demands, no warning.

"How can we be sure they're hostiles?" Decard asked.

An Incarnate in a mask that resembled a stylized chimpanzee handed Kane a set of binoculars, while Decard engaged the targeting system in his Magistrate helmet. In unison, they studied the area where the dust cloud billowed.

"You got 'em, Decard?" Kane asked.

"Seven bikes, four quads and what looks like a—damn—is that a Sandcat?" Decard asked, studying the approaching group through the helmet's sensors.

Kane ignored his question and posed one of his own instead. "Two bikers off to the left, you see them?"

Decard's head made a minuscule movement beneath the intimidating faceplate of the helmet. "Got them. What's that between—?" He stopped, realizing what the bikers were dragging.

It was an Incarnate, his mask lost, his powerful, sun-bronzed body covered in sand and stained with blood.

"Farouk," Decard stated somberly.

"Oh, now we got worry," Kane muttered, passing the binoculars back to the Incarnate in the chimpanzee helmet.

Then he raised his voice. "This is an organized group,

people," he explained, "which means they made the decision to come here together. My partner thinks they're here for our guest, Señor Smarts, and I'm inclined to agree."

One of the Incarnates hissed, muttering about the barrage of trouble that Kane and his people had brought down on the squad, until Decard held a warning finger in the man's face, instructing him to silence.

"I brought Kane's team into this operation," Decard stated. "I'll take full responsibility when I make my report."

"You'll be lucky if you're still alive," the jackal-masked Incarnate retorted.

Just then, the eagle-masked Incarnate came out of one of the shacks, shoving Smarts before him. The fey Mexican was wrapped in a cord that held his arms tight to his sides, and he seemed to be having trouble keeping his balance. His leg wound had been bandaged, but the material was darkening with blood as he took successive steps. Behind the pair, Keb came from the shack, his medical kit in hand.

Kane pointed to the cloud of sand on the horizon. "Friends of yours, I think," he told Smarts.

Smarts smiled, despite the obvious pain that he was in. "You should never have tried to hold us, Señor Magistrate." He laughed. "You shouldn't have even stepped into our world."

Kane held the man's gaze with his blue-gray eyes. "I like poking my nose where it's not wanted," he said.

"Do you have any idea what we do to Magistrates we find roaming outside of their safe little villes?" Smarts hissed.

"Run away from them in terror?" Kane suggested.

"And, anyway, I'm not a Mag. Now, I think you're going to call your friends off, don't you?"

"And why would I do that?" Smarts asked.

"Because I'm all done with playing around," Kane spit, flicking his Sin Eater from its holster and into the palm of his hand.

Smarts's eyes widened as he looked at the weapon in the man's hand.

Brigid's voice came urgently to Kane's ear as he locked gazes with the little Mexican.

"Kane," she said. "They're here."

Kane looked back and saw the bikes pulling up about twenty feet from the shacks that his group sheltered around. Beside him, Brigid spoke quietly once more.

"Looks like negotiations are open," she said.

Beside her, Decard grunted. "Look at what they've done to Farouk," he said, unable to take his eyes from the Incarnate's bloody, broken body. "And where is Amun?"

Kane glanced from Decard to Smarts, looking at the little man's self-satisfied smile. In an instant, Kane's left fist shot out, clipping Smarts across the jaw and knocking him, unconscious, to the ground.

"Including Grant, we're down four men, Decard," Kane said, turning back to the man from Aten. "We've got the goon squad out there and a tunneling monster at our backs. How do you want to play this?"

Decard just stood there, watching the crowd of brigands through the emotionless faceplate of his magistrate's helmet.

"Decard?" Kane urged. "Dec?"

"I'm going to bow to your greater experience on this

one, Kane," Decard finally stated. "You run the show and I'll back your plays."

Kane acknowledged Decard's decision with a single wordless grunt, then, senses alert, walked carefully between the two shacks before him, heading toward the gang waiting beyond the settlement limits.

Pushing his back against the side of one of the buildings, giving himself as much cover as he could, Kane raised his Sin Eater and aimed it at the centermost biker. Raising his voice, he called out to the group. "Good afternoon, gentlemen," Kane began. "You seem to have something there that's ours."

A bike rider off to the right of the group pulled down the kerchief that masked his mouth, and called back. "An' you have somethin' of ours," he said, his voice going hoarse almost immediately thanks to the swirling dust in the air.

"Then perhaps we ought to open negotiations," Kane responded from his shadowy hiding place, moving his aim across to target the speaker.

"You don't take what's ours," the biker replied. "End of negotiations." Even as he spoke, the biker was reaching into the large saddlebags at the back of his motorcycle, pulling out a long-barreled shotgun in a matte-black finish.

"That's a hell of a shame," Kane replied. "See, I'd have been pleased as punch to get rid of this worthless sack of shit we've been hauling around with us."

As he watched from concealment, Kane saw the biker snap open the shotgun and place two rounds in the breech. As he cracked it shut, Kane was aware that his companions were similarly readying themselves.

"Decard," Kane called without turning his head.

Instantaneously, Decard's voice responded. "What is it, Kane?"

"These punks want to play a little game of Last Man Standing. You think your troops can handle that?"

Behind Kane, hidden by the shacks, Decard began giving silent instructions to his Incarnates, using hand gestures to tell them to take up offensive positions.

"Ready when they are, Kane," he called back.

Kane's eyes flicked across the other members of the group of brigands, subconsciously taking in their weapons as they readied themselves to attack the little settlement. Mostly they carried revolvers and single shooters, but a woman to the left had loaded up a grenade launcher. Seeing that, Kane wondered if these people even hoped to bring back Smarts alive.

"I'm obliged to ask you," Kane said, his voice carrying across the sand-swept plain, "to reconsider this course of action. I don't want to see anyone get hurt."

The spokesman for the group spit sandy debris from his mouth before he spoke. "Too bad," he said, revving his throttle as he rested the massive shotgun across the handlebars of his bike. Suddenly, the bike lurched forward, and his teammates followed his lead, rushing toward Kane and the desert hamlet.

Without conscious thinking, Kane's index finger squeezed the trigger of the Sin Eater, unleashing a stream of 9 mm bullets at the lead biker. The bullets ripped into the man's throat and face in a line of red-rimmed holes, and he fell backward as the bike continued to speed ahead, his shotgun blasting as he toppled from the saddle, discharged buckshot clouding the air above.

WITH THE EYES of every brigand in the cavern watching him, Grant followed Tom Carnack to the little, marked-off laboratory area of the underground hideout.

"Nice place you've got here," Grant said flippantly, looking around at the high stalactites and the jagged rock walls.

As soon as he said it, Grant felt Rosalia rabbit-punch him in the kidneys, and he staggered forward under the blow.

"Shut up and keep moving," she told him.

Carnack gestured to the laboratory area where three whitecoats worked at the bubbling tubes while a fourth examined the interphaser under an illuminated magnifying plate.

"Right, then," Carnack said, gesturing to the interphaser. "How's it work?"

Grant looked at him contemptuously for a moment. "Just like that? You expect me to give up the information just…" He snapped his fingers.

"You doing that is the only thing that's keeping you alive, friend," Carnack said, a reptilian smile crossing his lips.

Grant nodded. "Which means that, once I tell you…"

Carnack laughed. "Oh, I see now. You think I'm going to get the information, then blow your brains out? Is that it?"

Grinning, Grant winked at the man. "Something like that."

"So, what kind of reassurance would you like that I'll let you live," Carnack asked, "assuming I *do* let you live?"

"Put down your little hand cannon there and tell your associates to back off," Grant said. "And then we can go from there."

Carnack looked at the Colt Anaconda in his hand for a

moment, then called "Rosie!" before tossing it over Grant's head into Rosalia's outstretched hand.

The dark-haired woman took the weapon and shoved it into the waistband of her silk pantaloons at the small of her back.

"Everyone else," Carnack shouted, "back off and give us some space."

The other brigands stepped away, watching warily from just outside the edges of the cordoned-off laboratory.

Carnack stepped forward, and his hot breath played across Grant's face as he spoke, just inches from the ex-Mag. "Anything else?"

"Yeah." Grant smiled. "Use mouthwash." Even as the words were leaving his lips, Grant swung his huge right fist into Carnack's belly in a solid haymaker.

The brigand leader doubled over at the end of Grant's fist as the ex-Mag followed through with a left cross, cracking Carnack across the jaw and slamming him back into one of the wide tubes full of bubbling liquid the color of seawater. Carnack howled in pain, his arms windmilling as he crashed against the thick tube and keeled sideways.

Grant was already in motion. Before Carnack had even hit the large tubes, Grant swung his elbow backward, sensing intuitively where Rosalia was standing. His elbow smashed into her breastbone with a solid thud, knocking her off her feet with a gasp of expended breath. Pivoting on his right foot, Grunt swung out with his left until it connected with the woman as she dropped to the ground like so much deadweight.

Still turning, Grant slapped his palm against the work surface before him, using it as a prop to reach for Rosalia as she slumped to the ground. The fingers of his left hand probed around her waistband ungently, pulling the Colt Anaconda from where she had tucked it just moments before. As he did so, the whitecoats who had been working in the area rushed past, terrified, determined to get out of the way, blocking the potential attacks of the other brigands as they hurried away.

Guns were being raised all around him, Grant knew, the confusion dissipating, replaced with thoughts of retaliation by Carnack's foot soldiers. But as they raised their weapons, Grant heard Carnack gasping, struggling to raise his voice.

"Nobody shoot," he cried. "You'll hit the equipment!"

"That go for me, too?" Grant asked as he crouched beneath the worktable, using it for cover as he pointed the long-barreled, stainless-steel revolver at the nearest of the bubbling tanks.

"Careful, man," Carnack shrieked. "You have no idea what you're about to—"

"Then enlighten me," Grant cut him short, cocking the hammer of his gun.

SIX MOTORCYCLES and four quad bikes roared across the sandy expanse to the little desert settlement, while the driver of the Sandcat held back, waiting beyond the main area of the fray, ready to mop up the survivors. From their hiding places on the roofs of the shacks, Incarnates stood up and fired the translucent energy beams from their staffs, while Brigid, Domi, Kane and Decard picked off riders with their handguns.

The biker with the grenade launcher pumped two grens

into the air before Kane's bullets caught up with her, driving straight through the gas tank of her vehicle. The bike was turned into a hurtling inferno, its rider shrieking in agony as her skin charred and she lost control. Even as the bike exploded, Kane was running back between the shacks, his head low.

Instructing everyone to get down, Kane dived to the sandy ground in the main thoroughfare. Behind him, he heard the twin grenades slap against the shacks, exploding in a cacophony of fury and shaking the flimsy single-story buildings where they stood.

The Incarnates on the left-hand building had moved quickly enough, leaping from the low roof of the shack before the grenades hit. Only one of those on the right building had moved in time, and his partner howled as flames licked the walls and the whole structure began to collapse.

Just ten feet away, Domi sprang from her position on the ground like a puma after its prey, leaping toward the Incarnate as the building beneath him sagged. She shoulder-slammed into his body, knocking him from the roof, clear of the flames.

"You okay?" she asked, breathless.

The Incarnate in the chimpanzee mask nodded, his body trembling with adrenaline.

Across from the explosions, Brigid's arms cut the air as she ran past the other shacks and headed away from the settlement. She glanced over her shoulder as she heard the second explosion, and saw the shack crumble to the ground in a burst of dust and splintering wood. TP-9 in hand, she continued to sprint, turning to her right in a long arc around the hamlet. While all eyes were on the main fray, Brigid had decided to take the chance to secure a decisive victory.

She rushed in a long ellipse, far from the bikers speeding between the shacks to engage the Incarnates in battle. But Brigid's eyes were on just one target—the heavy-duty Sandcat.

Head down and keeping her body low, Brigid kept herself in the driver's blind spot before running the last few yards and leaping atop the little tanklike vehicle's roof. She clambered across the armored bubble that contained a pair of USMG-73 heavy machine guns, even as their operator was spinning them toward her, reacting to her surprise attack. Without turning back, Brigid tossed what appeared to be a little ball-bearing behind her, straight at the armored dome. As it hit, the silver ball cracked open, and a light-ning-bright flash of light was emitted, right into the gunner's field of vision. Brigid knew she couldn't take out the gunner from outside, but the flash-bang would be enough to put him temporarily out of commission until she had gained entry.

The gunner reacted, pulling the twin triggers of the USMG-73s, launching two long streams of bullets over the length of the vehicle. Yet Brigid had already dropped from the roof, crouching across from the driver's door, grinning as the man looked at her in astonishment.

Silently, Brigid gave him the come-on, her index finger curling to draw him nearer. She saw the man shout some-thing angrily before reaching for the pistol he kept on the dashboard and flinging the door open.

As the door opened, the man was leaping from his seat, swinging his pistol around and spitting a curse at Brigid.

"I'll do you, Red…" he began, as Brigid revealed the TP-9 in her other hand, blasting a bullet straight into the man's forehead.

"Whatever," she answered, leaping past the falling figure and clambering inside the Sandcat as bullets from the heavy machine guns streaked past overhead.

Within, Brigid headed for the machine gunner's installation. Inside, it looked to Brigid that the Sandcat had been rebuilt. Whole panels were missing, and there were a number of rusty welding spots across the bare metal floor, the upholstery stripped away.

The gunner in the dome was screaming. "I can't see, man, I can't see. My eyes are freakin' burnin'," he howled.

Raising her TP-9 once more, Brigid put the man out of his misery. "Didn't even see what hit him," Brigid muttered as she activated her Commtact. "Kane," she called as the Commtact came to life, "I've secured the Sandcat, but I'm going to need someone to operate the top gun."

"Little busy," Kane's reply came back, his voice breathless.

BACK AT THE DESERT settlement, Kane was scrambling away as a quad rider and a motorcyclist barreled toward him along the sandy thoroughfare. As the biker blasted bullets from a Ruger single-action revolver, Kane ducked between two of the remaining shacks. The bullets drilled into the wall behind him, and the biker skidded to a halt, glancing down the tight passageway that separated the shacks. Kane wasn't there.

As the quad rider pulled his vehicle to a halt, churning up the sand, Kane reappeared on the roof, spraying his attackers with bullets from his Sin Eater before they even had time to react. "Turkey shoot," he muttered, holding the trigger down until he was sure both men were dead.

Nearby, Domi and Decard caught another biker in their cross fire, while beams from the Incarnates' weapons shunted the attacking riders from their saddles.

It was all over in less than three minutes. The brigands had been ill-prepared for a trained military force led by Magistrate minds.

As they were mopping up the final stragglers, Kane spotted the low-slung form of the Sandcat approaching them. Still woozy from being knocked senseless, Smarts gasped when he saw the wag approaching, wondering for a moment if it might be his salvation. That was until the driver's door opened, and Brigid's red mop of hair poked out.

"I have a corpse in back," she said, sighing, "if there's a gentleman among you who might care to give me a hand."

Decard and one of the Incarnates made their way over to the large, blocky vehicle while Brigid sat sideways in the driver's seat, her booted feet resting on the sand.

Just then, there was a familiar vibration in Kane's skull, and he activated his Commtact. "Kane here, go ahead."

Brewster Philboyd's voice responded. "Kane, I think I've found your bogey. Still underground, traveling west-southwest at a leisurely pace. I guess the tunneling slows it down."

"Yeah," Kane agreed, his mind thinking fast. "West-southwest...? How close would this be to Grant's current location, Brewster?"

"Less than a mile," Brewster replied. "It's pretty much on a collision course. What's out there?"

"Hidden base, I think," Kane told him. "Tell me when it gets to a quarter mile, or if it veers off. We're on our way."

Concluding the communication, Kane turned to Decard as the young ex-Mag carried the gunner's corpse from the Sandcat. "Decard, we're moving out," Kane told him.

"We or you?" Decard asked, indicating his Incarnates.

"I've got a partner to protect," Kane told him, "and I think we have a lead on the creature. Your crew has taken a lot of hits today, shown bravery in the face of danger. I think it's time you took them back home."

Decard looked about to object, but he stopped himself at Kane's unflinching gaze. "Thanks for coming out here, Kane, you and your people. We'll stay on here for a few hours, tend to the wounded, see how the infection plays out in the locals. I'll report in to Cerberus as soon as I can."

Kane held his hand out to the man. "You're doing a good job out here, Decard," Kane assured him. "I'm proud to have been a part of it."

Domi walked past, preceded by Smarts, her Detonics Combat Master pointing at the latter's back. "Been good seeing you, Decard," she said as she shoved Smarts through one of the Sandcat's open doors.

"You, too," he agreed.

A moment later, Kane hopped into the Sandcat beside Brigid, pulling the door closed behind him. Brigid fed power to the engine and the Sandcat began a long, slow turn before heading off into the west where the sun was beginning to sink.

As the Sandcat drove away, Decard held his fist to his chest in salute, watching the Cerberus warriors depart.

Chapter 13

With a trickle of blood running from his scalp, brigand leader Tom Carnack gazed at his adversary in astonishment as Grant sighted down the length of the Colt revolver at one of the three tall tubes of bubbling liquid.

"Are you insane? You have to realize that you're outnumbered," Carnack said after a moment, a little of the old cockiness returning to his voice. "There's no chance of you getting out of here alive if you do something stupid now."

From his position of concealment beneath the worktable, Grant's dark eyes flicked to Carnack for a moment before returning to the bubbling tubes. "Let me worry about that," he instructed. "What's in the tubes?"

"Nothing important," Carnack lied.

"So if I put a hole in them, it won't matter, right?" Grant prompted.

"Okay, man, okay," Carnack said in pacification. "Let's not do anything rash here."

"What?" Grant asked. "Is it explosive?"

"No," Carnack replied, sounding a little downcast now. "Just…"

"Just what?" Grant urged.

"Irreplaceable." Carnack bit at the word.

"I'll go out on a limb and say these are cloning tanks," Grant stated, looking them up and down. "Nutrient baths. You've got yourselves a portable womb here. Am I close?"

Carnack sneered, irritation sweeping over him now as his head recovered from the recent trauma it had suffered. "This stuff is priceless, you half-wit."

"This is the little project you were telling us about back in Hope," Grant concluded. "The baron kindergarten."

"Why don't you put the gun down, and we'll figure ourselves some way that we can all get out of this intact," Carnack suggested, taking a step toward Grant.

From the corner of his eye, Grant saw another brigand enter the open laboratory area, sneaking in with the obvious intention of flushing him out.

Grant squeezed the trigger of the Colt Anaconda once, feeling the recoil as the large-bore bullet blasted from the chamber.

Carnack ducked instinctively as the bullet raced past him, over his head, before it smashed into one of the bubbling tubes, spilling splinters of glass and greenish liquid all over the floor. Carnack looked behind him, then back at Grant, horrified.

"Gun pulls a little to the right," Grant told him. "Now, you tell your boy there to back the hell off before I shoot another hole in your precious stock."

Carnack turned and instructed the sneaking brigand with a quick, hushed phrase. Grant watched as the man stepped backward, anger on his features, leaving him alone with Carnack in the laboratory area along with the unconscious form of Rosalia.

"You said that you haven't cracked the birthing process yet," Grant stated calmly. "That changed since I last saw you?"

Carnack shook his head. "No."

"And how much of this genetic material do you have left to experiment with?"

"Once we get it right, as much as we want," Carnack assured him. "We can just pluck it right out of the ugly little bastards."

"What about right now?" Grant asked.

Carnack looked shiftily around. "What you see here, man, two canisters of the goo and two nutrient stacks. Was three until you went cowboy. Whitecoats already got through five of them," he added. "But this'll be enough— just got to find the right, bloody expertise."

"DNA experts are hard to find," Grant lamented. "Especially outside of ville walls."

"Tell me about it." Carnack nodded thoughtfully, smearing back the trickle of blood from the side of his face. "Didn't your lady friend, the pretty redhead, say she was a gene scientist?" he remembered.

"Why? You thinking of cutting a deal?"

Carnack looked at Grant as the Cerberus warrior crouched beneath the worktable, the gun in his hand leveled at this most precious of treasures, and he seemed apologetic. "I think we got off on the wrong foot," he said. "There's a ton of money to be made from this little enterprise if we just pool our talents. You with that lanky geneticist woman, me with the gunk she needs to work with. What say you, Grant, my boy?"

"A partnership?" Grant asked.

Carnack held his open hand in Grant's direction. "Yeah, that'll work. We break this DNA sequencing code and, well, there'll be plenty of riches to go round, eh?"

Grant edged warily out of his hiding place and stood before Carnack, eyeing the brigands who stood all around, just beyond the perimeter of the lab itself. "Yeah," he said, taking Carnack's extended hand in his left.

Grant pulled the brigand leader close, aware that this was the only shield he had, out here in the open, under the scrutiny of the other bandits in the cavern. The deal would go sour, he knew; it was simply a way for Carnack to keep his little project—and himself—alive until he could stab Grant and his crew in the back.

"We have to get up aboveground so I can radio my friends," Grant said to Carnack.

Carnack looked at Grant for a moment, weighing his options, before he nodded and led the way up the tunnel.

RACING ACROSS the desert in the Sandcat, Kane watched the horizon as Brigid Baptiste spun the steering wheel, pulling around a clump of towering cacti.

"Come in, Grant. You're about to have some company," Kane said into his Commtact, "of the big, black-skinned and mean-spirited variety."

"Got me a monster coming to crash my party?" Grant asked over the Commtact.

"Brewster managed to tag the thing, and he tells me it's headed in your direction," Kane explained. "ETA—two minutes."

"That close?" Grant said, clearly astonished.

"We'll be there as soon as we can," Kane reassured his

partner. "We've got your coordinates, and Brewster will guide us to your exact location."

"There's a hidden entrance," Grant replied thoughtfully. "Tiny little rabbit hole. If you're not careful, you'll walk straight past it."

"We're in a Sandcat," Kane explained. "How small is this rabbit hole?"

GRANT SNAPPED his fingers to get Carnack's attention. "Carnack? What other entrances are there to this place? Can we get a Sandcat in here?"

Carnack looked annoyed. "You what?" he said. "Partnership or no, do you honestly think I'm going to just let your friends drive in here armed to the effing teeth and steal my gear?"

"Now," Grant told him steadily, "new agenda, and it's called survival. We have got something very big and very mean and a damn sight more alien than I want to get into right now heading this way. You and your men are in trouble like you would not believe unless you wise the hell up."

Rosalia's voice came from behind Grant's shoulder, and he spun to train the gun on her, holding both of the brigands in its sights. "He's right, Tom," she said firmly. "I saw it."

"Welcome to the party," Grant said quietly. "Been awake long?"

"I heard what you said about that creature coming here," she replied. "I hate to admit it, but you and your Magistrate friends may be our only hope of surviving."

Carnack looked at her, an unspoken query in his expression, and Rosalia nodded solemnly, long lashes closing over her eyes in resignation.

"It's like nothing you can imagine, Tom," she said. "A force of nature, an engine of destruction. Anger taken form and substance."

"ETA—one minute." Kane's voice updated his friend.

"Time to do or die," Grant told them.

"I'll have you shot for what you've brought here," Carnack barked at Grant.

"Yeah," Grant agreed, "but do it after I've saved your butt."

"Deal," Carnack replied before turning to issue orders to his men.

WITH THE SUN sinking toward the western horizon, Decard stood beside the tunnel entrance that the monster had created at the edge of the little desert hamlet, his lengthening shadow stretching out behind him, across the blood-soaked sand. The tunnel was caving in on itself now, and this evidence would soon disappear as the sands were shifted by the restless desert winds.

The youthful ex-Mag looked up at a noise from the main street and, as he watched, Keb the field medic walked out of one of the three standing shacks left in the wake of the brigands' attack, his head held low in disappointment.

"What happened?" Decard asked, walking across to speak with the physician.

Keb gestured behind him, not bothering to turn. "Died," was all he said.

The shack that Keb had exited held the remaining settlers, Decard knew. "What? All of them?" he asked.

Keb nodded. "The woman held on for a while, drooling, not making any sense," he said. "She was as strong as I've ever seen, fighting against this thing as it took her over, used her up. A hardy farming woman. But there wasn't anything I could do there, not in the end."

"Where does that leave us with Isha?" Decard asked, referring to the infected Incarnate who had worn the crocodile mask.

Keb looked at him as they stood in the open street amid the wreckage of motorcycles and quad bikes. "He's got perhaps two hours," Keb admitted darkly. "Unless we...quicken it for him."

Decard looked away, the phrase echoing through his mind as he watched the wisps of cloud float languidly overhead. Finally, irritation marring his features, Decard turned back to Keb. "And there's nothing else we can do?" he demanded.

"If there's a cure to this thing," Keb proposed solemnly, "I'm not going to find it in the next two hours. Not under these conditions."

Decard nodded, taking in the information and hating every word.

Keb spoke quietly, not looking Decard in the eye. "I don't like to see a friend suffer."

"Me either," Decard agreed, flinching his wrist tendons to bring the Sin Eater pistol back into his hand. He stood outside the shack that held his loyal Incarnate, looking at the pistol in his hand for a long time.

"It can run its course," Keb reminded him as he stood at his elbow, "if you prefer."

Decard shook his head, pushing open the door to the shack. "If it comes for me, attaches itself to my brain, my body, I want you to do the same," he said. Then he instructed the Incarnate guards to depart, leaving him alone with the altered warrior strapped to the bed.

CARNACK HAD LED Grant to the shadowy section of the cavern, farther than the hanging lightbulbs reached. Grant followed, strapping on his Sin Eater and the wrist holster once more, after Rosalia had handed them back to him in preparation for the forthcoming battle. Standing beside Carnack, Grant peered into the darkness and saw metal highlights glinting from several vehicles that were stored in the shadows.

"It's a little hangar," Carnack explained, "just land vehicles. The Sandcat can come in through the entrance there." He pointed.

Grant could see a winding tunnel that disappeared around a sharp bend. "What's it look like outside?" he asked.

"Camo netting. You'd never see it." Carnack smiled. "But my guys will open it up," he added, instructing two of the brigands to do just that.

Even as he spoke, one of the cavern walls, just eight feet from where he stood with the brigand leader, crumbled inward as a mighty black claw smashed through it. As the talons burst through the wall, the brigands took aim and began unleashing a wealth of gunfire at the intruder, Rosalia among them, armed with a little 15-round pistol— a Smith & Wesson Sigma. She had found herself something larger, too, Grant observed, a compact submachine gun based on the old Heckler & Koch MP-5 K design. The submachine gun was shoved into her waistband, its abbreviated nose creating a square lump along her hip, bulging beneath the silk pants.

With a loud crash, the rock wall fell in and the hideous monster stood there as the wreckage of the wall showered the ground. The gauzelike material that had covered the creature before appeared to have been sloughed off, and Grant watched as the hideous thing surveyed the cavern, ignoring the bullets that slapped against its coal-black carapace. The green smoke continued to billow from its eyes, and Grant wondered how such a creature could see. How *would* it see?

Head low, the creature stepped tentatively into the cavern, a stream of bullets smacking off its armorlike body. And then, like a flash of lightning, it was in motion, its speed uncanny on those strange, reversed knees, a hand covered in bony protrusions snapping out and grabbing one of the brigands by his head, picking him up like a doll.

Grant held his fire, watching the magnificent creature move, seeing those strange, ashlike flecks pouring from its body with each motion.

INSIDE THE SANDCAT, Kane, Brigid, Domi and their prisoner, Señor Smarts, were still over a minute from Grant's location. As Brigid pumped the accelerator, urging more speed from the heavy wag, Smarts raged at Kane from the seating behind him. "Am I to understand that we are to go into the belly of the beast? You are crazy, Señor Kane," he cried.

Kane glanced back at the tied man sitting in back of the wag. "My partner's in there," he said, "and so are yours."

Smarts nodded his acknowledgment, looking annoyed. "I do not like to do this," he said. "I have seen this monstrosity in action once. I have no desire to do so again."

Brigid pulled the Sandcat around as they shot into the tunnel, taking the narrow, rock-walled passageway at high speed, flipping on the bright headlights automatically.

"You'd rather let your friends die?" Domi asked, reloading her pistol as they raced down the tunnel. "Nice."

Smarts looked pensive. "No, of course not. In my experience there is always an easier solution than guns. You just need to consider what that solution might be."

"Got to tell you, Mr. Smarts," Brigid called over from her seat at the steering wheel as she raced around the sharp corner in the tunnel, "I don't believe that this creature is going to be dissuaded from its rampage by any amount of smooth talking."

Smarts looked aimlessly around at the interior of the Sandcat, considering everything he saw and everything that he had seen in the past couple of days.

Brigid's foot slammed on the brake, pulling the Sandcat to a screeching halt at the end of the tunnel. She and Kane flung open the doors before dashing past the other parked vehicles and into the main area of the hidden cavern.

Sitting in the back of the Sandcat, Domi looked at Smarts with her strange, red eyes. "If I untie you, do you think you can play nice?" she asked.

Smarts nodded, but he appeared deep in thought. "What about the mat-trans?" he suggested, continuing the conversation with Brigid as though she had never left the vehicle. "Your portable mat-trans would be able to send the creature away, to an island. To…under the sea or into space," he postulated.

Domi looked at him as she untied his bonds, and a wide smile crossed her white lips. "That may just be brilliant, you sly old fox," she said.

"Ah." Smarts nodded. "You like my idea?"

"If it can work," Domi told him, running it over in her mind.

HER NAME WAS Nicola and she was fourteen years old, but small for her age. Nicola served Carnack's gang, fetching them drinks and making them hot meals, and when she wasn't quick enough or if she didn't smile enough or, well, sometimes for no reason, one of the gang would beat her so that she might learn to do better.

Nicola never learned.

She was what her grandmother used to called "filled with skydark." The radiation had gotten to her in her mommy's belly and it had messed up her brain. Years earlier, they would have said she had learning difficulties, and before then, they would just have called her "slow" or—that beautifully poetic euphemism—"touched."

Nicola had lived with her family, mother, father, an older brother and a younger sister, for a long time in Hope, back before the refugees had swarmed into the little fishing town like locusts, eating and destroying everything in sight. She had gone to church and she had gone to school and she had tried very hard to be good in the eyes of the Lord. One day, while she was out collecting groceries for her mother—Nicola loved to help—a pretty lady had come over to speak with her. Nicola knew better than to talk to strangers, but the lady was so pretty she looked a lot like a princess from a picture book. The lady had said that her name was Rosalia, and she had asked Nicola if she liked dancing.

"I love to dance," Nicola said, nodding so much that it seemed her head might be shaken from her neck.

Somehow, Nicola had ended up going home with the beautiful princess lady instead, her mother's groceries forgotten.

Rosalia had led Nicola through the shantytown on the outskirts of Hope, all the while promising to teach the young girl how to dance as she never had before. "I love to dance, just like you," Rosalia had explained. "I'll show you how to dance properly, so that you are graceful and beautiful and so that everyone in a room cannot help but watch you."

When they reached Rosalia's home, Nicola had been introduced to the beautiful lady's friends, men who scared Nicola a little at first but seemed friendly enough. The men clearly approved of Rosalia's protégée. She was pretty, her toothsome smile wide and bright, and she seemed compliant enough.

But when Rosalia showed Nicola how to dance, with beautiful, swirling moves like autumn leaves floating on the breeze, Nicola had stumbled and tripped and slipped and fallen and not really been much of a dancer at all, despite her passion to try. Somehow, in spite of these short-comings, pretty Nicola had remained with the gang, helping them as best she could, but she would only dance when they asked, and then only when the gang members were drunk, and they would belittle her efforts and try to trip her as she listened to the music in her mind.

Rosalia had never spoken to her again, had not even smiled at her.

A nice man called Tom had befriended Nicola one day. She liked Tom. He was funny and he had a nice smile and he always seemed to be listening to what she told him, even though what she told him wasn't always that interesting. His friend, the clever man with the olive skin, Señor Smarts, had once told Nicola that Tom was "a people person," whatever that meant.

Tom had traveled with her when they moved to the cavern, and he gave her instructions about serving the men here while they worked at their special project. He had told her that her project was special, too, and that it involved fetching them meals and drinks and anything else they asked for.

There had been times, Nicola knew, when the men had wanted more than just food. One night, three of them had come to her, smelling of beer, and one had grabbed her and they had all done things, terrible things. She remembered lying there, among the crates where she liked to sleep, wondering what she had done to deserve that. She had turned her head away from each man as his body pounded at hers, and she read the writing on the crate beside her head a thousand times. Paquerette Dresses. She had never looked inside.

The first man's name, the one who had grabbed her by the hair and held her down, was Barry or Barney, she thought, but most of his friends seemed to call him "Wretched," a funny kind of nickname that she didn't understand. She had seen him around the cavern after that night, and she had tried to keep out of his way.

Now, wide-eyed, Nicola observed as the tall, jet-black monster strode across the cavern, flicking bullets aside the way a normal person might flick aside insects. She watched as the huge creature stood before a group of brigands, blasting their rifles and pistols at it to no effect. One of the group was Wretched Barry. Nicola watched, a wide smile across her face, as the creature's powerfully muscled arm darted out and shoved against Barry's chest. The movement was so fast, so powerful, that the monstrous hand didn't push Barry out of the way—no, it went clean through his chest, the clawed hand poking through the far side, wrapped in bloody gobs of Wretched Barry's inner flesh and the bent remnants of his spine.

Nicola remembered, then, the sermons that the minister had given in church every Sunday, about the wrath of a furious God, and she knew what the creature was, at last.

Arms outstretched, Nicola walked forward, stepping ever closer to the imposing, coal-black giant. She closed her eyes as tears streamed down her cheeks, and the smile on her face was so wide, her beautiful white teeth glittering in the flashes of gunfire from all around.

"Nearer my God to thee," she murmured as she placed her arms around the creature's huge torso, pulling herself close and hugging it tight.

She felt it then, a beautiful enlightenment, dazzling in her brain, opening like the petals of a flower, filling her mind with such wonderment. As she felt the thing unfurling and squirming inside her head, pretty Nicola slumped to the floor. And in her mind, at last, she was dancing with such grace, such beauty that she would have made her mother weep with joy.

In an instant, the girl that had been Nicola was no more.

TOM CARNACK HELD the recovered Colt Anaconda, pointing it at the behemoth as it tossed the stupid backward girl aside, and he wondered what to do. All around, his men were unleashing salvos of ammunition at the great creature as it stalked across the cavern, but it didn't seem to notice them, just occasionally flicking at the bullets that struck it.

"What the hell is this thing?" Carnack shouted, looking to Grant as if the ex-Mag held the answer.

Grant was studying the brutish thing from a distance, walking slowly around the outer edge of the cavern, keeping as much space between himself and the monster as he examined it from different angles, his Sin Eater raised by not firing. "I'm not sure," he admitted, as Carnack chased to keep up with him.

"Well, it damn well followed you here, didn't it?" Carnack screamed. "You brought this here—you must have done something to tick it off."

"I don't even think that it has a coherent thought process," Grant said, watching as the creature speared one of the brigands with the sharp claw of its foot, tossing the man in the air with a kick.

"Eh?" Carnack asked, confused.

"Coherent thought process," Grant repeated. "I think it just follows instincts, and its primary instinct is to…kill?" he finished, as though trying the final word on for size. "No, it's not killing," he realized. "It's something more subtle than that—it just looks like it's killing."

DOMI RAN INTO THE MAIN area of the cavern, seeing the towering creature making its way across the far side, swatting bandits aside like snowflakes. She had the Detonics Combat Master in her hand, but she knew that it wouldn't do her any good. This monster was absorbing and dismissing the impact of far more impressive ordnance than her little pistol; it seemed a pointless exercise to even try.

Still, with a gun in her hand she had a chance, at least,

and they had come here primarily to save Grant and stop Tom Carnack's insane plan to repopulate America with barons, not to go toe-to-toe with that monstrosity.

She kept her head low as she rushed through a series of cots and sleeping equipment, spotting a couple who incredibly had managed to sleep through the whole fracas.

Domi stopped beside them, crouching on her haunches and speaking in an urgent voice. "Wake up, sleepyheads. Going to get yourselves killed if you're not careful."

The woman, straggly blond hair sagging across her face, looked at Domi through heavily lidded eyes. "Wha—?" she asked, confused. "Who are you?"

Domi smiled, trying her best to be ingratiating despite her fierce appearance. "You have company," she explained, "and me and my buddies are here to help you out."

The man who had, until that moment, appeared to be sleeping beside the blonde, suddenly moved into action, producing a large-bore handgun from beneath the covers. "You want to run that by me again, freak?" he snarled, pointing the weapon at Domi's face.

Domi's hand moved like lightning, a blurred white streak in the air as she knocked the man's pistol aside. "Here to help," she told the couple, glaring at the man. "Get up, get dressed and either get in the fight or get out of here."

Domi stood and moved on, her gaze sweeping the room as she tried to locate Grant, Kane and Brigid among the melee.

CHASING ALONG A LITTLE way behind Domi, his left leg dragging a little with the pain of the bullet wound, Señor Smarts watched the albino woman go about her work. As

she exited the open sleeping quarters, Smarts made his
way forward, his eyes on the gun that Domi had slapped
from the man's hand.

Smarts leaned down and picked up the weapon as the
couple hurriedly dressed beside him. "I'll need this," was
all he said before moving on.

As he followed Domi through the cavern, always
keeping his distance lest she realize he was trailing her,
Smarts checked that the gun was loaded. It was a King
Cobra, six rounds and a short barrel, but it seemed to be in
good working order, oiled and well maintained. A full
complement of bullets resided in its chambers, waiting for
the order to do their murderous work. This would do it.
This would do the job. Head low, Smarts continued through
the cavern, determined to finish the albino freak who had
caused him so much pain and suffering.

As GRANT considered the implications of his statement,
that the monster wasn't trying to kill at all, Domi's voice
was patched through the Commtact, directly into his head.
"Señor Smart Mouth here has had an idea," she explained.

On THE OPPOSITE side of the cavern, running over heaps of
boxes and canned food, Kane and Brigid made their way
around the back of the monster. As he ran, Kane engaged
his Commtact.

"Kane here. What's the idea, Domi?"

"He says we could use the interphaser to trap the
creature, move it to who knows where, somewhere it won't
be able to cause any more damage," Domi explained.

Brigid Baptiste took up the conversation, her words

piping through to the field team over their Commtacts. "Flawed," she said. "We'd need a parallax point and someone to activate the interphaser unit. That's something that couldn't be done remotely."

"Which would mean someone getting hairbreadth close to that thing," Kane added, frustration in his tone.

"Plus," Brigid pointed out, "we'd lose the interphaser. Not something I'd want to do if I could avoid it." Brigid had spent many months, along with astrophysicist Brewster Philboyd, perfecting the operation of the mysterious technology of the interphaser. She wouldn't relinquish the profits of all that hard work in a hurry.

AS THE CREATURE swayed under the impact of simultaneous fire from three shotguns, Domi saw Brigid's red hair pop up from behind some crates, just twenty feet from her. From their Commtact conversation, it seemed that Kane was with her, so all it needed now was to find Grant and they could be on their way.

Domi looked around her, trying to locate the ex-Mag. As her head turned, she spied the glint of metal off to her left, and something instinctive was tripped in her brain, urging her to drop to the floor. Even as she was dropping, she heard the recoil of a pistol as someone began shooting at her.

"Die, you bitch *conchita!*" she heard, heavy footsteps running through the cavern. That was Smarts, come for revenge, no doubt.

Bullets were spraying everywhere, and off to Domi's right the monster was howling in rage, that terrible, painful screech, and yet, despite all this, for an instant all Domi seemed to hear was Smarts as he ran toward her, his left leg dragging a little with the wound, the little handgun pointed at her.

He fired again, another shot from the snub-nosed little Colt that he clasped in his bunched fist, the flare of propellant as the bullet left the barrel. He was panicking, Domi could see, and he didn't have enough bullets in the little gun to do a whole lot of that. She held her place on the rough ground as the bullet raced overhead, missing her by feet rather than inches.

As Smarts swung the Colt pistol around, trying to find his target, his teeth locked in a savage grimace, Domi kicked herself off from the ground and leaped at him, the Combat Master clutched in her right hand.

It would take a moment, that was all, less than a second to shoot the man in the head, put a bullet through his skull and finish him. But it would just have been a wasted bullet.

Smarts fired again, the shot going wild as the chalk-white woman leaped from the floor and plowed into him, her head and shoulders slamming into his chest, knocking the breath out of him in an awful spasm of pain. He tried to turn the gun on her as he felt himself falling backward, and agony fired through his leg where he had taken a bullet from her earlier that day. Suddenly, something hit the side of his head, crashing violently into his skull and making him see sparks before his eyes.

Atop the fallen Mexican, Domi bashed the butt of her Combat Master into his head a second time, putting all her strength into the blow. She felt the man's body sag, and he lay there on the sandy ground, his eyes rolling back in his head, unconscious.

Domi reached across and plucked the Colt pistol from

the man's limp hand before standing up and skirting around the laboratory area as she continued her journey toward her friends. As she ran she glanced at the Colt King Cobra. One bullet left—not even worth hanging on to, she decided, tossing it to one side.

ROSALIA HANDLED the knockoff Heckler & Koch submachine gun the same way she handled a sword, spraying the approaching creature with bullets in a graceful swing of movement. She cursed as she watched the bullets impact against the creature's hard skin, having no effect whatsoever.

This was a hopeless battle, and she knew it. Yes, Rosalia was a dancing girl, but the ability to dance—to cloud men's minds with their own hormones, as her teacher had explained it—was but one of the talents she had learned from a young age. She was a sword mistress par excellence, an expert in knife combat, both thrown and wielded, and a crack shot, too. On top of that, she was versatile in the use of bow and arrow, bo-staff and lance, and she had even had some training in basic diplomacy before she had graduated from the never advertised school close to the Mexican border.

Tom Carnack had paid the school a small fortune to acquire Rosalia's services and to keep her on retainer as personal bodyguard, assassin and companion.

Right now, Rosalia was recalling the words of Mother Superior about facing the most powerful of foes. "If a foe appears unstoppable, bat your eyes prettily and let others do the work, Sweet Rose. Your body is your weapon, but it need not engage in the battle to defeat your foe."

Rosalia checked behind her as the creature took another

step closer across the vast cavern, and she called to a group of armed brigands there. "Flank me and stay close," she instructed.

They foolishly believed that she would lead a victorious attack, little realizing that all they were now were human shields to protect her from the unstoppable creature's rampage.

IN THE CENTER of the cavern, the creature staggered under a grenade attack. The grenade slapped against its chest, blossoming in an explosion of red-and-gold flames, dark smoke pluming up toward the ceiling. When the smoke cleared the monster was still standing, and it tossed its head back, almost as if to laugh, before unleashing another of those uncanny alien shrieks.

"Could there be another way to use the interphaser idea?" Grant's voice piped through the Commtact loop.

"Such as?" Brigid urged.

"Take, drag, pull, push this creature to a parallax point," Grant suggested rapidly.

"And then what?" Kane asked.

He saw that Rosalia was leading a charge at the huge creature, flanked by two bandits holding flamethrowers. The flamethrowers spit at the dark-skinned monster, riddling its body with fire, slowing it for a few moments. Then it stepped forward once more, a flaming arm reaching for the nearest of its attackers, pushing him backward by the face until he crashed to the floor, screaming as Rosalia ducked the thing's other swinging arm, leaping to one side and rolling across the floor. Kane knew what would happen next—the man's eyes would begin to lose their color and he would start to babble that hideous, nonsensical torrent of words before expiring.

"I've got it," Brigid said, realization in her tone.

Kane spun, looking at her as they crouched by the crates, close to the high ledge that Grant had originally landed upon when he had entered the cavern almost an hour before. "What is it, Baptiste?" he asked.

"Cerberus," Brigid said, a playful smile on her lips. "We'll take it with us to Cerberus."

"So that it can kill everyone there?" Kane asked.

Over the Commtact, Domi's voice said something similar, only more specifically referring to her lover Lakesh's ultimate fate at the creature's hands.

"We won't give it a chance to attack anyone," Brigid explained. "We'll knock it out first."

"Baptiste," Kane wailed, "bullets are having zero effect on that thing—nothing seems to be able to stop it. How the devil are you planning on knocking it out?"

"You've forgotten about Domi's attack with the chariot," Brigid chided him. "It ran after she hit it with that—ran away from us."

"So, what did you have in mind?" Kane urged.

"Sandcat," Brigid told him. "We'll drive that freak to wherever we need it." And then she showed Kane what she meant, miming by using the TP-9 handgun as a projectile, pushing at her open palm.

"You are utterly insane," Kane told her.

Grant's voice piped over the Commtact then, as he tried to make sense of the conversation as best he could. "What's her plan, Kane?" he asked. "I'm not seeing a lot of other options open to us just—" He stopped in midsentence, and

Kane saw Grant appear from across the cavern, unleashing a stream of bullets at the creature as he ducked its swinging clawed arms.

One arm slashed through the air, just sweeping over Grant's head, missing him by a fraction of a inch before it drove onward and into a crate marked Paquerette Dresses in military-styled lettering. The crate collapsed in on itself as the monster's arm slashed through it, and a cloud of white powder burst forth.

The creature bellowed its angry wolf-parrot howl and turned its head slowly, smoldering eyes searching for a target.

As Kane watched from across the cavern, Tom Carnack's head popped up from behind another crate, and the man began shooting at the creature from a long-barreled revolver.

"No, Tom," Kane muttered under his breath. "Just run. You won't…"

Even as he said it, Kane saw the inevitable. The creature lunged ahead, its mighty arms sweeping forward, grabbing the brigand leader by head and leg and pulling him from the ground as he continued to shoot the blaster.

"Let go of me, you ugly bastard," Carnack yelled, pumping shot after shot into the monster's face until his gun clicked on empty.

The creature lifted him higher, and then everyone in the cavern heard Carnack's rising shriek, a tortured, hideous sound. Having caught up with Grant, Kane and Brigid watched as the monster twisted Carnack, bending his body in two directions until, finally, the brigand's body tore apart at the waist, a fountain of blood spewing forth. And, through it all, Carnack continued to scream until his voice gave up.

Brigid looked away, biting her lip as the screams echoed through the cavern, and she heard Grant mutter something beneath his breath.

"And now, we are in trouble," he said.

As the creature continued its rampage, tossing the few remaining brigands aside with mighty sweeps of its arms, Brigid turned to Kane, her voice taut with emotion. "Nobody deserved that," she said. "Not even a murderous piece of crap like Tom Carnack."

Kane nodded, his eyes watching the monster as it darted toward the center of the cavern, where the thick pipes bubbled.

"Damn," Grant said, tracking the thing with his Sin Eater.

"What is it?" Kane asked.

"It's heading for the lab," Grant told them.

Chapter 14

The boy, Benqhil, sprinted across the desert, kicking up plumes of sand in his wake. He had watched from his high perch as the massive creature came bursting through the cavern wall, seemingly oblivious to the hail of bullets launched at its body, and brushing aside the heavier artillery like so much dust. When he saw it do that, Benqhil had chosen to retreat. Tom would not expect him to stay and fight; Benqhil was a messenger and lookout, not a warrior. One day, yes, a brave in Carnack's brotherhood, a man. But not this day.

Becoming a man was important to Benqhil, and he had learned much from observing the older members of the gang. They had shown him how to load and fire guns, how to stand up for himself, how to knife fight and how to walk tall through the shadow-filled alleyways of Hope. But, he realized as he ran from the hidden cavern, having wormed his way up the incline and through the tiny aperture that ran between the two strips of rock like an island amid the sand of the desert, the thing that really turned a boy into a man was the simple act of surviving long enough to become one.

KANE TURNED to Grant as the creature continued its journey toward the bubbling pipes and cluttered worktables of the fenced-off laboratory.

"Is that stuff explosive?" Kane asked.

"Not sure, but I do know that the interphaser's there," his partner growled.

At his side, Kane looked all around, trying to see an opening in the furious attack on the creature that he might use to reach the laboratory area. Even as he looked, the monster lurched into one of the tall columns of luminous fluid, toppling the pillar with a slashing arm, bony protrusions scraping across the glass until it broke. The creature stood there, blocking the route for either Kane or Grant. Kane cursed as Rosalia and a group of the remaining brigands took up positions, blasting their weapons at the brute, hemming it in.

Engaging his subdermal Commtact once more, Kane sent an order to Domi. "Domi, are you able to reach the lab area, close to the hostile?"

"What's on your mind, Kane?" Domi's bright voice asked.

"Interphaser's there," Kane explained.

"So is the hybrid DNA," Grant added. "Two small metal flasks."

Even as Grant said it, the petite albino woman was leaping across the cavern through the hail of bullets, ducking and weaving as the brigands continued to swarm at the monstrous figure in the center of the underground cave.

"I'll get it," she promised over the Commtact, her lithe form an alabaster blur as she sprinted and leaped to the laboratory section like a bouncing ball of white lightning.

A moment later, the albino warrior was within the cordoned-off lab, barely six feet from the dark skin of the monster's back as she searched the work surfaces for the interphaser and its carrying case. The monster spun, howling at her as it swung its mighty arms, and Domi veered to one side, leaping from the path that the creature's limbs slashed through the air. Bullets ricocheted from its hard carapace as it observed Domi's swiftly moving white form, and it flicked them aside as it howled at her, that awful, low-note caterwauling.

Grant looked across to Kane and Brigid as the three of them walked in unison, reeling off shot after shot at the monster alongside the brigands.

"Domi's too close—she's going to need a distraction," Brigid told Kane.

Kane's eyes flicked around him until he spotted a fallen brigand who was howling mumbo-jumbo in a strained voice. The brigand still held a flamethrower, the gasoline pack strapped to his back.

Kane sprinted across the cavern, pumping a single shot into the brigand's forehead. He was dead anyway; this was nothing more than a mercy killing now, Kane knew. Swiftly, he pulled the fuel cylinder from the dead brigand's back, standing it on the uneven, rocky ground as he hefted the lance of the flamethrower itself in both hands, his Sin Eater resheathed in its wrist holster. With a low thrum, the flamethrower kicked into life in Kane's hands, and he dowsed the creature and the worktables around it with fire.

The monster turned to Kane, its head held low. The flames danced around it, and for a moment it seemed stunned. Then it moved, swishing its huge arms outward as it moved with incredible speed, knocking into six of the remaining brigands, toppling them over like tenpins.

Across from Kane, Grant and Brigid split up and fired continuously at the hulking brute as it surged forward, their bullets hitting its armored body before zipping off in all directions.

Kane held down the activation stud on the flamethrower, playing the jet of flame over the creature and the closest edge of the lab. "You found them yet, Domi?" he said into the Commtact.

Domi stood in the laboratory, her feet splashing in the pools of spilled liquid where the great tubes had been destroyed. The liquid at her feet was catching fire now, a wavering trickle of flames playing across its reflective surface the way that flame will run across the surface of alcohol in a glass. She had found the familiar triangular unit of the interphaser, knocked over but otherwise undamaged, tucked beneath a large glass magnifying plate that had obviously been used to study it prior to the creature's arrival. Domi searched around for the metal carrying case, finding it in a cupboard below the worktable, the cupboard door snapped from its hinge. Carefully, Domi replaced the precious device in its padded carrying case, snapping the locks shut.

"Got it," she assured Kane over the Commtact. "Just gift wrapping it now."

As Domi spoke, there was a burst of flame across the other side of the lab, and she automatically leaped to the side. A metal canister popped open where Kane's flamethrower attack played over its surface, firing gunk everywhere.

"I think you just found one of the flasks of soup," Domi added as she made her way from the burning laboratory.

As Kane let go of the flamethrower's activation stud, allowing the unit to cool for a moment before he continued the attack, he saw the monster's fist shoot out, caving the skull of a bandit who was trying to hold it off with a shotgun. At the man's side, Rosalia fell to avoid the creature's next attack.

Engaging the flamethrower's activation stud once more, Kane played the flames over the creature again, waving the wand up and down, left to right, keeping the steady stream of fire spitting forth. As he did so, he spoke into the Commtact. "Grant, I need you to start the Sandcat," he explained. "It's our best chance."

"Acknowledged," Grant said, running across the cavern toward the shadowy area that led to the wide exit tunnel.

"Everyone to the 'cat," Kane added after a moment. "Maybe we can drive the hostile where we need it."

Brigid Baptiste was at his side now, reeling off shots from her TP-9 pistol as he held the creature back with the stream of fire. "I thought you said this plan was utterly crazed," she reminded him.

The flamethrower in Kane's hands sputtered and died, and he tossed it aside as he spoke to her. "It is, but I trust the planner, Baptiste."

Smiling, she shook her head, her red tresses swinging to and fro as she laid down covering fire while Kane recalled his Sin Eater instantaneously to his hand.

They were close to the far wall now, where Grant had first entered the cavern, and Brigid pointed to the high ledge. "Higher ground?" she asked, raising an eyebrow at Kane.

"Read my mind," he agreed, covering her as she ascended the slope.

DOMI LEAPED over the blood-spattered bodies of dead brigands as she dashed across the cavern, carrying the interphaser in its protective metal case. As she ran, she noticed Smarts lying there, his face drenched in scarlet, a vicious wound across his skull. The man looked dead—had to have got caught in the cross fire. Shame, Domi thought.

Even as she thought it, Smarts's arm snaked out and his hand clutched Domi's ankle as she was running past, pulling her down to the ground with him.

Domi kicked behind her like a mule, an automatic reaction to being caught, but Smarts avoided her swift attack. As their eyes met, the wily Mexican produced a tiny blade, perhaps three inches in length, from his sleeve and jabbed it at her.

Domi kicked out again, her foot connecting with the man's wrist, throwing his aim. She scrambled ahead, getting out of reach of Smarts as his blade swished through the air once more.

Ahead of her, Domi saw the door of the Sandcat open, and Grant's huge form leaped inside. She turned back in time to see the next attack from Smarts, the knife swinging close to her face. Domi swung upward with the metal box that held the interphaser, regretting doing it with such a delicate piece of equipment even as she realized it was her primary defense.

The thin blade batted against the metal carrying case and, when Smarts pulled it back, it was bent halfway to the tip. He looked at it a second before tossing the weapon aside.

"Then I'll finish you with my hands, you little white-skinned freak," he snarled, his left fist jabbing at her face.

Domi dropped below his swinging punch, feeling the passage of air as it rushed over her head. Then she swung with her free hand, a ram's-head fist straight into Smarts's gut.

The man yelped in pain, but he stood his ground, glaring evilly at her.

Head down, Smarts charged at her across the sandy ground, determined to knock the petite woman from her feet by weight alone. Like a matador, Domi sidestepped at the last instant, pulling her body backward as Smarts rushed past, his fists swinging. As he passed, Domi's leg swept out, clipping the man's ankles and forcing him to lose his balance. Smarts toppled forward, slamming into the ground—hard—with his jaw and chest.

Standing over him, Domi eyed the Mexican warily, her lips pulled back in a savage smile, her breathing coming heavy now. He was down but, she wondered, was he out?

In the second that she pondered it, Domi saw the man move again, trying to roll himself over despite the wound in his leg. She put the carrying case on the ground and reached for the knife that was held in a leather sheath at her ankle. Then Domi's knife was in her hand and she pounced on the man's back, holding him down.

"I asked you to play nice," she growled close to Smarts's ear, letting him see the knife she habitually wore on or off mission.

"Then you are a fool, *señorita*," he hissed, trying in vain to shrug her from his body.

"You either stay down or I will put you down," Domi told him, "once and for all."

Smarts ignored her, and the sharp point of his elbow

swung back, catching her high in the breast. Domi fell backward, just barely retaining her position atop the man's legs. The huge knife slashed down, a streak of metal through the air as Domi cut into the tender area at the base of Smarts's spine. Smarts howled, a terrible cry from deep in his chest, as Domi's knife dug into him, and he struggled once more to shake her weight to no avail.

Domi leaped back suddenly, the bloody knife held in her hand, her face now an emotionless mask. She stood there, poised over Smarts as the man tried to turn to look at her. He struggled, but his body wouldn't react to his demands; his legs would no longer move.

"My legs," he howled. "What have you done to my legs?"

"You got me all wrong, right from the get-go," Domi told him. "I'm not like Kane and Grant. I'm not a Magistrate by trade or blood. I'm from the Outlands."

With those words, Domi grabbed the handle of the interphaser's carrying case and jogged away, leaving the wily little Mexican man howling his rage at the ground as he lay there, paralyzed.

A moment later Domi was beside the vehicle, scrambling in through the passenger's door.

"What kept you?" Grant asked as he fed power to the engine.

"A little bit of unfinished business," Domi said as she wiped the bloodied knife on her sweat-stained top.

Swiftly, Domi placed the carrying case containing the interphaser to one side of the storage area in the rear of the Sandcat before climbing into the raised seat to operate the machine guns in the armored turret, her knife now back in its sheath at her ankle.

"All set," Grant acknowledged over his Commtact as he fed power to the engine of the wag.

Domi turned the twin USMG-73 heavy machine guns and began firing a continuous hail of bullets at the coal-skinned creature. Grant wrestled with the steering wheel of the Sandcat, its heavy treads whirring to gain traction across the rocky surface of the cavern. He kept the monster framed within the rectangle of the windshield the whole time, working the wheels to pull the vehicle around to where Brigid and Kane held their ground while Domi's attack forced the hideous creature back.

As Grant pulled close to the raised ledge, he slapped the door release, and the passenger's door swung open.

"Get in," he shouted through the open door, simultaneously transmitting the command to his partners via Commtact.

Standing amid the wrecked laboratory in the center of the cavern, the hulking creature struggled against the barrage of bullets that Domi was blasting into its chest from the twin machine guns. It bellowed in rage, perhaps even pain, and flicked at the bullets as though they were fireflies. Then, head down as if to charge, it strode three swift paces forward on its strange, reverse-hinged legs.

Standing atop the ledge, Kane turned to Brigid, emptying another clip from his Sin Eater into the creature's torso, dead center, to little effect. "You first, Baptiste," he instructed.

Brigid looked over the side of the ledge, slipping her TP-9 pistol into its holster as she prepared to jump the ten-foot drop to the roof of the Sandcat. "First step's a killer, Kane," she told him with a smile, before leaping from the rocky edge.

Kane covered her exit with his Sin Eater, burning through another clip in next to no time as he held the trigger down, unleashing a stream of 9 mm slugs at the rampaging creature as it took another ponderous step toward the ledge. Kane was one of its last remaining attackers now; most of the brigands had either been killed, wounded or they had run. Even Rosalia was nowhere to be seen, Kane realized, wondering what had happened to the alluring dancer.

Brigid landed in a crouch on the roof of the Sandcat, just behind where Domi was firing twin ribbons of death at the monstrous brute. Brigid flipped herself off the roof and sprinted the last few feet to the open door, then ducked inside. Grant acknowledged her with a curt nod before turning back to watch their hideous attacker through the windshield. "Think this'll work?" he asked.

Brigid rushed into the body of the armored vehicle and reached for the blocky carrying case of the interphaser. The metal case had taken a few dents, but the unit inside looked to be in fine working order.

"The interphaser itself looks fine," Brigid confirmed, shouting to be heard over the firefight outside, "but I wouldn't like to second-guess whether this plan will actually work."

Overhead, Kane leaped from the high ledge, still blasting with his Sin Eater as he dropped to the cavern floor. The monster was glaring at him, its furious green eyes smoldering their putrid mist into the air.

"Come on, you ugly son of a bitch," Kane muttered under his breath, standing to the side of the Sandcat, his pistol raised.

Grant looked at the monster through the windshield, then at Kane, who stood beside the open passenger's door. "Get in, Kane," he shouted.

Kane just waited, holding the pistol in a steady two-handed grip as streams of bullets blasted from the Sandcat's USMGs beside his head. "Tell Domi to shut off the attack," he shouted, not bothering to take his eyes from the monster watching him just fifteen feet away.

Grant passed on the order, shouting to be heard within the confines of the Sandcat.

"Are you loopy?" Domi asked, her fingers still depressed on the firing studs of the heavy weapons.

"Kane knows what he's doing," Grant told her. "At least, I hope he does," he muttered to himself as he heard the barrage of gunfire from the heavy machine guns come to a sudden halt.

Through the windshield, Grant watched as the huge creature swept aside the last of the bullets from Domi's attack. Two surviving brigands fired occasional blasts from their hiding places within the cavern, but the monster just ignored them, its eyes fixed on Kane, that billowing green smoke pouring into the air above.

Suddenly the Sandcat rocked, and Grant and Brigid heard something heavy clomping across the roof of the vehicle.

"Kane's on the roof," Domi explained as her hands worked quickly, reloading the twin guns with new strips of ammo that she had found in the storage locker beside the armored bubble.

"What the fuck is he doing?" Grant muttered to himself, his foot pressing at the accelerator pedal, revving the engine while he held the emergency brake, locking the low wag in place as its engine roared.

Then they heard the recoil of Kane's gun above them, followed by another shot, and then another.

On the roof of the Sandcat, Kane staggered his shots as he fired at the hulking brute before him. "Come on," he muttered, "come to Daddy."

The monster watched him, shrugging and flinching as the 9 mm slugs pinged against its hard carapace.

"Yeah, that's right," Kane whispered. "I'm an annoying little bug and you're going to come right over here and squash me, aren't you, big fella?"

Suddenly the jet-black monster tossed its head in the air, opening its mouth and unleashing that awful shriek that was part wolf howl, part parrot's caw, a mist of boiling saliva thrown before it. Then its head dipped and its smoking, green eyes zeroed in on Kane where the ex-Mag stood on the roof of the Sandcat.

"Well, come on, then!" Kane shouted. "I'm right here!"

A blur, and the creature was in motion, arms back, head ducked, charging toward the Sandcat and the annoying little human thing that stood atop it. Kane had almost forgotten about its speed, felt sure that he had underestimated as he dived flat on the roof and swung himself into the vehicle by the open door. As he did so, Domi took her lead and depressed the twin studs of the heavy machine guns once more, loosing streams of steel-jacketed death at the charging behemoth.

In the driver's seat, Grant watched Kane almost fall into the Sandcat, his arms splayed out and his legs tangled behind him.

"Floor it," Kane instructed, flipping over and reaching for the large door handle with his extended leg, pulling it closed with the toe of his boot.

Grant didn't need the instruction. His hand was already releasing the emergency brake by the time Kane fell into the passenger's seat, and the Sandcat hurtled forward as Grant fed full power to its engine. The tanklike vehicle collided with the monster with a bone-jarring impact, and Grant felt his teeth clack together as he continued powering the Sandcat forward.

The massive creature lay across the nose of the wag now, its legs bent and being driven across the rock floor ahead of it, its arms reaching for the windshield, slapping at the streams of bullets that came from the twin machine guns atop the vehicle.

"We've got it," Grant confirmed, his eyes narrowed in intense concentration as he tried to see past the obstruction of the unwilling passenger on the hood. He turned the wheel in a languid arc, wary that he not shake the monster loose as he pulled into the low-roofed exit tunnel.

From the raised dome, Domi's urgent voice shouted down to the main body of the vehicle. "Grant, you're too close to the wall!"

They all felt the right-hand side of the Sandcat scrape along the rough rock walls, a shower of sparks playing up and down its metal flank like witch fire. Grant tugged at the wheel, correcting their course as he powered the Sandcat down the narrow tunnel toward the exit.

"I'm blind on my starboard side," Grant explained. "Any advice gratefully received, but make sure it's in enough time that I can react, okay?"

Even as he said it, Domi's voice shouted again. "Pull left! Pull left!"

Grant spun the wheel, looking through the clear window to his left to assure himself that he had room to maneuver. As he did so, the monster's huge arm slapped against the windshield, jarring the strengthened plastic in place. "Brigid," he shouted, eyes fixed straight ahead. "How far to the nearest parallax point?"

"Less than two klicks," Brigid responded from the back of the Sandcat, as she examined the interphaser. "Bear south."

"What the hell way is south?" Grant yelled as he wrestled with the wheel, trying desperately to see past the huge creature as it secured itself to the Sandcat's hood and began pulling itself toward him.

"Right," Brigid shouted back, "go right!"

The Sandcat rocketed out of the tunnel and bumped over the dunes as the sinking sun painted the whole desert a rich vermilion.

Still catching his breath, Kane brought himself up into a sitting position and searched his pockets for a new ammo clip for the Sin Eater. As he reloaded by touch, he looked back at Domi manning the turret, ignoring the beast barely a foot before him, pounding its jet-black fist against the re-inforced plastic of the windshield.

"Did you find the hybrid DNA?" Kane asked, raising his voice to be heard over the straining engine and the pummeling of bullets outside.

"I couldn't see it," Domi admitted, "but I'm pretty sure you hit one flask with the flamethrower."

"What about the other one?" Kane demanded.

"The whole lab was up in flames, Kane," Domi reminded him. "No way I was standing around there a moment longer."

"It's probably incinerated," Brigid pointed out hopefully.

"'Probably' isn't enough," Kane growled. "I don't like loose ends."

Grant's irritation came through clearly in his sarcastic response as he fought with the wheel of the heavy vehicle. "You want to go back?"

Kane turned to look through the windshield once more, an angry scowl crossing his features. "No, you're right. It has to have been incinerated."

In the raised turret, Domi turned her head back, looking for the hidden entrance to the underground lair behind them. Smoke billowed from it now, marking it clearly on the landscape. "The whole place has gone up in smoke," she told everyone, her voice quavering a little from the recoil of the heavy machine guns that she operated.

The Sandcat bucked and writhed as it leaped over the sand dunes with the heavy weight of the monster dragging it down, and the engine roared louder as Grant pumped his foot against the accelerator, urging even more speed from the vehicle.

Grant pulled at the wheel, struggling to make it turn as the creature's arms pulled around the chassis and its clawed hand reached down into the spinning wheels that drove the treads. "Getting hard to turn," he admitted, straining against the steering wheel.

Kane leaned across and clasped the wheel from where he sat, pulling it toward him with all his strength. As they struggled together, Grant and Kane saw the creature pull itself up, its head passing over the view window of the windshield, its thick torso dragging past them. Then, all they saw were the creature's legs as it pulled itself to the roof by its mighty arms.

Suddenly Domi let out a shriek and, when Kane looked down the length of the wag, he saw her swinging back and forth in the swivel chair of the raised turret. "It's got the guns," she cried as an all-powerful fist slammed against the strengthened glass of the bubble.

The armaglass bubble shook along with the rest of the Sandcat, but it held firm.

Domi ducked out of her seat and dropped into the main body of the Sandcat as the mighty fist pounded against the armaglass a second time.

"ETA, Baptiste?" Kane urged, his voice strangely calm, the eye of the furious storm.

"Almost there," she promised.

"This had better work," Grant growled, fighting with the steering wheel as he tried to keep on a straight path.

They rushed across the dunes, a cloud of sand kicked up in their wake, the engine of the Sandcat screaming in protest at the demands being made on it as they headed farther to the south.

"Brake!" Brigid shouted suddenly, glancing up toward the dashboard.

Grant slammed his foot against the brake pedal, spinning the wheel rapidly with one hand as his other engaged the emergency brake. The Sandcat spun into a skid and then, as the weight of the hulking passenger shifted above their heads, the Cerberus warriors felt the wag begin to roll. Sand was kicked up as the Sandcat toppled onto its side, and the monstrous creature flew from the roof as the wag continued to roll, first upside down, then over onto its side.

BEFORE HIS SQUAD left the little settlement, Decard made a final report to Lakesh at Cerberus redoubt. The report was short and to the point.

"Conclusion—everyone infected dies."

Lakesh's voice came through over the portable radio equipment that Decard's team had used to contact the Cerberus redoubt.

As they spoke, several of Decard's Incarnates were busy burying their dead comrades—three in all, including the man who had been infected by the strange virus, a single bullet wound now visible dead center between his eyes. They had found Amun's body in an even worse state than Farouk's, where the bikers had torn him to pieces. This would go down as a black day for the brave Incarnates of the city-kingdom of Aten.

"Thank you for the report," Lakesh responded. "Do you have any further idea of what it is?"

"Theories, but nothing we could prove," Decard replied sadly, watching his men dig shallow graves for their colleagues. "The whole thing is over in a few hours. It just moves too quickly to study."

Lakesh thanked him once again, then broke contact. In the silence that followed, Decard watched the sun as it finally disappeared below the western horizon.

BRIGID LAY THERE, clutching the interphaser close to her body, holding it protectively, like a baby, as she struggled to keep her grip on consciousness. Something had hit her across the top of the head, probably the roof or side wall as the vehicle rolled. She looked around, but her eyes were blurred with tears. She blinked the tears away, shaking her head and feeling the pain there, running along her scalp and clawing down to her eyeteeth, making her feel she was about to sneeze. "Kane?" she asked. "Grant? Domi?"

Grant's voice was the first to respond. "Present," he said. "Kane? You want to wake up, buddy?"

Kane had toppled into Grant with the rolling of the vehicle, and his weight was pushing Grant down against the side door.

"What was…?" Kane muttered, his eyelids fluttering as he came back to consciousness. "How long was I out?"

"Seconds," Brigid confirmed, carefully making her way to the front of the rolled wag. "We need to keep moving. It's outside."

Kane grunted something unintelligible, feeling beaten and bruised where the vehicle had flipped. Behind him, Domi was grasping at the back of his seat, trying to pull herself up.

"Everyone in one piece?" Kane asked as he wedged his feet in a recess and pushed at the door that was now above him.

"Let's just finish this," Grant responded, a weary edge to his voice.

Kane flipped the door open, and the Sandcat rocked in place with the movement. He tensed his forearm, drawing the Sin Eater into his palm as he prepared to exit the vehicle.

Swiftly, Kane dragged himself up and leaped clear of

the toppled wag, scouring the area with his eyes, his Sin
Eater in the ready position. Grant was just behind him,
backing Kane up as he climbed from the Sandcat. There
was a ridge of churned-up sand where they had rolled, a
little clump beside a flattened, compacted streak across the
fine grains.

Brigid and Domi followed a moment later, keeping pace
as Kane and Grant led the way toward the fallen beast that
lay ten feet from the felled Sandcat.

"Looks dead," Grant said, keeping his voice low.

"It isn't," Kane assured him. "Look at its chest—it's still
breathing. Baptiste? Do you have your parallax point?"

Brigid searched the terrain with her eyes until she saw
a circular indentation in the sand, roughly six feet across.
She rushed over to it and began brushing sand away until
she saw the cuneiform markings that surrounded a circular
stone base. She had no idea what it was, some kind of
Pueblo artifact maybe, but it didn't matter. The interphaser's
sensor was registering this as a viable parallax point.

Brigid leaned down, swiftly setting up the interphaser.
Domi stood beside her checking all around, her Detonics
Combat Master in her right hand and her recovered
backpack slung over her shoulder.

"Where are you planning on sending the big bad?"
Domi inquired.

Without looking up, Brigid instructed Domi to call
Cerberus. "Tell them we'll need to use the mat-trans
chamber. Tell them to fill it with anaesthetic gas."

The idea had come to Brigid when she had realized that
the mat-trans chamber could be used as a temporary prison.

"That's insane," Domi cried.

Brigid glanced up at her for a moment, her emerald eyes burning with determination. "The interphaser would disappear with the creature," she explained, "and that's too big a risk and too high a cost. It's breathing, which means it needs air the same as the rest of us. Now, call Cerberus and tell them we're coming home. Tell them we'll need to be pulled out of the jump chamber as soon as we arrive. Tell them no one is to touch the creature."

Nodding, Domi acknowledged Brigid's instructions and engaged her Commtact, passing on the requests while Brigid finished programming the interphaser for the jump.

Kane and Grant circled warily around the monstrous creature as it began to shake itself back to full awareness. Its long arms stretched out ahead of it, its claws and bone protrusions dragging through the fine sand, and ponderously it began to raise its torso off the ground.

"Baptiste," Kane called loudly, his eyes and blaster trained firmly on the monster as it pulled itself up. "Do you have us that jump point ready?"

Brigid punched in the code and glanced over at the monster. "Ready when you are," she called back.

Stirring to wakefulness, the creature moved slowly as it struggled to its feet, assuming its full, majestic height once more.

"We're bringing it over," Kane shouted to Brigid. "Engage the interphaser in ten seconds."

"Ten seconds?" Grant spit, incredulous. "Are you nuts? How are we supposed to—?" His words dried in his throat as Kane pulled the trigger of his Sin Eater and held it down, blasting a stream of bullets into the creature's face.

"Come on, ugly," Kane growled, "time to play ball."

The coal-skinned creature tossed its head, its green eyes billowing smoke as the bullets slapped against its armored skin. And then, with no warning, it leaped, eight feet of taut muscle hurtling toward Kane and Grant as they turned and ran.

"Well, you sure got its attention," Grant shouted as they ran across the sand toward the interphaser.

Ahead of them, the blossoming flower of the interphaser had emerged from the little metal pyramid, tip and base, a swirling cone of colors and lightning streaks.

Kane looked over his shoulder, blasting shot after shot at the creature as its powerful legs pounded against the ground. "It's all in the subtle planning," he told Grant as they leaped into the blossoming flower of the interphaser, with Brigid and Domi accompanying them.

The monster followed, its huge feet slapping against the sand, its massive weight barreling ever onward, reaching into the cone of color as its prey disappeared from sight.

In a moment, the monster, the interphaser and the four Cerberus warriors were gone, and the only evidence of their passing was the overturned Sandcat they left behind.

Chapter 15

The familiar armaglass walls of the Cerberus mat-trans chamber appeared before Kane's eyes and, for a moment, he could see the silhouettes of figures moving about beyond, within the confines of the control room. He looked around as he recovered from the jump. Beside him, Domi was slumped against the armaglass wall.

Grant was in a ready crouch, his Sin Eater poised, but he looked unsteady, swaying a little where he was poised. Brigid Baptiste was beside the interphaser, the little pyramid having traveled through the quantum slipway with them.

And then, still running, the creature, its mouth open in an appalling shriek, rushed out of nonspace into the reality of the room, literally forming before Kane's bewildered eyes. He tried to raise his own pistol and to shout a warning to Grant, but his arm felt heavy and his voice wouldn't come. As the creature continued its charge, Kane felt himself toppling forward, that feeling of tripping in a dream, when you shock yourself awake.

But he didn't awaken. Indeed, Kane fell to the tiled floor of the room in an inglorious heap, his fist still tightly clutching the pistol, but his finger never receiving the impulse to twitch against the trigger.

The others were falling around him, sinking to their

knees, toppling over; even the hideous creature that had come through with them seemed to lose its momentum, its legs crossing beneath it, tripping over itself. There was something in the air, Kane realized, as his thoughts slowed to a crawl.

THE PUNGENT SCENT of burning chemicals came to Rosalia as she struggled to escape the heavy, dreamless sleep. She was lying on the hard ground, sharp rocks pressing against her.

Immediately alert, she pushed herself up from the ground, struggling to free her leg where a heavy weight rested over it. She looked down at her leg and saw Wils, one of the gang members, lying there, mouth and eyes wide open, blood streaking across his face. Dead, she realized.

Ahead of her she could see the flames, tinted blue and green with the chemicals that burned within them, where the laboratory was being reduced to ash. Thick, dark smoke poured from the lab area, funneling up into the air, and already the highest of the stalactites were lost to the black fug.

All around, men were howling, screaming, nonsensical words emanating from their throats. Others were dead, lying in their own blood. Looking across the cavern, Rosalia spotted two brigands making their way into the exit tunnel, holding kerchiefs over their mouths and nostrils so as not to breathe in the awful fumes of the burning laboratory.

She struggled up, wary of further attacks. Something had happened, but she hadn't seen what. The monster was gone; that was for certain. She paced through the moaning bodies, considering the true value of helping any of these people. There wasn't time—the smoke from the lab was polluting the air in the cavern, and soon no one would be able to breathe in here.

She stopped for a moment close to the lab and peered across at it as the thick, black smoke rushed upward from its center. The interphaser was gone but there, on one of the work surfaces, she could make out one of Carnack's precious flasks, the gunmetal tubes that contained the genetic material he had had his men working on night and day. She leaned over, weaving her hands between the chartreuse-tinted flames, struggling to grasp it. She pulled her hand back in a sudden jerk as a flame licked at her arm. It was no use—the flask was too far away, impossible to reach.

Time to go, she realized, running toward the tunnel. Above all else, Rosalia would always be a survivor.

"KANE," THE VOICE URGED beside his ear. "Come on, Kane, I know you're awake. Quit pretending."

His eyes flickered open and, for a moment, he was dazzled by the bright lights of the Cerberus medical bay. He turned his head, feeling sore and drained and empty inside, and saw Reba DeFore standing over him, her blond hair tied back in an elaborate braid over her shoulder, her stocky body sheathed in a white jumpsuit.

"Reba," he muttered, feeling the word scratch against his throat. "What happened?"

"You took a lung full of anaesthetic gas. Domi instructed us to fill the mat-trans chamber with it before you made your jump, 'enough to knock out an angry elephant,' were apparently her exact words."

"No, I said 'a horny elephant,'" Domi corrected from the next bed over to where Kane lay. She looked awake, fresh-faced and full of life, despite the trauma that they had suffered on returning to the Cerberus installation.

Kane became aware then of other people in the room, two more beds where Grant's and Baptiste's familiar forms lay.

Something about Baptiste...

The thought wouldn't hold; Kane lost it almost before he had time to even acknowledge it.

"Whoa," Grant muttered, sitting up on the bed he had been laid out on. "I can't remember shit and my head is pounding."

Standing in the center of the room, DeFore addressed them all in her clear voice. "You all imbibed quite a heavy dose of anaesthetic gas," she explained, "so you may feel some aftereffects for a while—wooziness, nausea, a general inability to concentrate."

"I feel hungry," Domi piped up, and Kane and Grant agreed.

"The effects will wear off in a few hours," DeFore continued. "If you need anything at all, I'll be right here."

They thanked her as she scribbled something in her patient notes.

"Canteen," Grant said, pointing to the door. "Who's with me?"

Domi nodded eagerly, but Kane looked across to the bed beside Grant's and realized then that Brigid hadn't said anything. The redheaded woman just lay there, her eyes closed, a blissful smile on her lips.

"Is she okay?" Kane asked, turning to DeFore. "She's not waking up."

"You all took different doses and you all have different constitutions," the redoubt medic reassured him. "Domi was awake for five minutes before you joined us."

"Yeah." Domi chuckled. "I've been sitting here the whole time watching you drool, Sleeping Beauty."

"Nice," Grant agreed with a smile.

DeFore addressed Kane as she checked the monitoring link to Brigid's vital signs. "She's fine," she said, "just needs to sleep it off a little longer. I'll let you know if there's any change."

Kane ran a hand through his dark hair. "Thanks, Reba. I'll pop back later."

Kane joined Grant and Domi as they made their way to the canteen, leaving Brigid Baptiste under DeFore's watchful eye.

AFTER KANE and his field team had been pulled out of the mat-trans area, Lakesh oversaw the removal of the monster that they had brought with them. The adjacent operations room had been evacuated of all but the most necessary personnel, and those who remained wore hazmat suits and gas mask rebreathers. As one team continued to douse the area with anaesthetic gas from huge hoses, the remainder carefully wrapped the creature in tarpaulin, heeding Domi's instructions that no one touch it. The whole operation, with the smoking lances of anaesthetic gas and the wide-brimmed masks of the hazmat suits, reminded Lakesh of old-fashioned beekeepers with their smoke guns, suited up and collecting honey from the hive. But this wasn't a bee— more like a hornet caught in a jar. A very, very angry hornet.

Once the sleeping creature had been wrapped up, its limp body was rolled onto a wheeled flatbed that was normally used to move crates around in the storage area of

the redoubt. Under Donald Bry's instruction, a path was
cleared of all personnel and the flatbed carrying the monstrous body was slowly wheeled out of the control room.
The masked men with the anaesthetic hoses kept pace, as
they proceeded down the wide main corridor that was
carved directly into the rock of the mountain.

Wearing his gas mask, Lakesh hung back, watching
warily, wishing he knew what it was that they were handling.
Decard's reports had not boded well, and he feared that the
monster might reawaken at any moment. If he understood
correctly, its very touch burned into an individual, mind
and body, eating the victim up from within. Lakesh shivered
at the thought, crossing his arms over his chest.

As soon as he had received Domi's instructions, he had
planned the next stage. If anaesthetic gas might be used to
hold the creature, then a continuous supply piped into a
room could be used to quell it until they could find a more
permanent way to deal with it. Reports from the field team
had been sketchy, but as he understood it, the creature was
apparently impervious to bullets and other attacks. Something immensely powerful was driving it, an internal
engine that stopped at nothing to reach its goal. The real
question, then, was just what that goal was.

Creature and flatbed were loaded onto an elevator and
a small squad squeezed inside, anaesthetic lances piping
more mist into the air. The doors closed and Lakesh stood
in the corridor with Donald Bry, watching the indicator
lights of the elevator as it dropped to a lower level. The
team down there already had clear instructions of what to
do, and they were all prepared with their own lances of
smoky, anaesthetic gas.

Under heavy sedation, the monster was wheeled into a midsized storage room where its limbs were chained. Six portable air recyclers had been brought to the room, and they had been converted to feed anaesthetic gas from large, free-standing cylinders. "I just hope it's enough," Lakesh said as he and Donald Bry came down the stairs to observe the final part of the pivotal operation.

Still slumbering, the black-skinned creature was left alone in the emptied storage room, feeds of anaesthetic pumping through the air in vaporous clouds, sequenced so that at least four units would be pumping at any one time. The door was locked, leaving only a small window of glass within the door itself through which to observe the behemoth. Lakesh had considered using a windowed observation room, but the glass would always pose a weak point, no matter how strong it was, compared to the solid concrete walls of the storage room.

As the door was secured, Lakesh and the others breathed a long sigh of relief inside their gas masks. The portable hoses were switched off, and the extractor fans for the corridor were engaged so that the guards wouldn't need to remain masked the whole time.

"What happens next?" Bry asked, his voice muffled through the mask.

"Perhaps Kane or Brigid will enlighten us," Lakesh suggested, "once they wake up."

"Let's hope that they wake up before *it* does," Bry said with deep concern.

IN THE MEDICAL BAY, Reba DeFore watched the indicators as they reported Brigid Baptiste's condition. Heart rate and breathing seemed normal, and nothing was untoward in her blood pressure level. Brain-wave activity seemed a little more rapid than normal, but that was only to be expected, DeFore considered. Brigid was an honest-to-goodness brainiac with a high IQ and an astonishing faculty for mental recall—her hallucinatory nightmares would surely be something to behold.

Chapter 16

Kane returned to find Reba DeFore sitting at her desk, working at a series of charts beneath her desk lamp.

"Any word on Baptiste?" he asked, leaning against the door frame and instinctively keeping his voice to a low whisper.

"There's nothing to worry about, Kane," DeFore assured him. "She was hit with a strong dose of that knockout gas, but she'll sleep it off. Her breathing's normal. No use hurrying her."

Kane gritted his teeth, biting back his concern. "You mind if I wait?" he asked.

The blond-haired physician gestured toward one of the chairs in her immaculate office. "Be my guest," she encouraged. "You can tell me all about what happened out in California."

Pulling a chair across from the corner of the room, Kane sat and began to relate events to the medic while they waited for Brigid to awaken.

BRIGID WOKE SLOWLY and with great effort, as though clawing her way from a pool of quicksand. Her head felt muzzy, and her senses came back to her very slowly, one by one, as though being overwhelmed with heady incense.

Her eyes opened and she tried to focus on the expanse of white before her. With an effort of will, she brought the white into sharp focus, dappled white squares a few feet before her. Tiles, she remembered. Ceiling tiles. It was strange, as if she had forgotten what ceiling tiles were for just a moment.

She blinked, holding her eyes scrunched closed for a slow count to five as she held a deep breath. Then she opened her eyes again and looked around her. She was lying on something horizontal and cushioned—a bed. Her head turned to her right and she saw a transparent cylinder there, the tiny bubbles clinging to its side. Liquid, water—in a glass.

And past that, the off-white walls, a tower of black blocks on a pedestal in one corner. Crash cart.

She knew where she was then. The Cerberus medical bay, lying in bed. Alone in the recovery room.

The room was silent, but, just barely she could hear the low murmur of voices coming from nearby.

Slowly, warily, Brigid raised herself until she was sitting on the bed. She wiggled her toes, feeling the sensation slowly return, the little tiny fireworks of pins and needles as they came back to life.

With one hand resting on the bed beneath her, Brigid pulled herself around until her feet swung over the edge. Her long hair flopped over her face, tickling at her nose, as she tried to steady herself, feeling like a passenger aboard a ship in a storm, her insides roiling. She sat there for a moment, head bowed, red-gold hair over her eyes like a curtain, taking in deep breaths. Something had really affected her there, making her head feel so clouded, but it was going now, dissipating.

Carefully, Brigid stretched her right foot down until it touched the cold tiles of the flooring. She felt the cold seep into her, feeling the goose bumps rising up her ankle, along her leg. Grunting with the effort of pulling her other leg from the bed, Brigid forced herself to stand, swaying a little as she stood in place, arms outstretched for balance, to protect her should she fall.

She looked around once more, gazing at the long, white oblong before her. *Bed.* The square block beside it. *Cabinet.* The tower of shiny black things. *Crash cart.*

This was weird, she realized. As if her memory was slowed down. No, not her memory. It was something more fundamental than that, something more akin to understanding.

Seeing the glass of water atop the cabinet once more, Brigid reached forward and picked it up with a shaking hand, bringing it to her lips. Slowly, she sipped at the water, feeling its coolness wash into her mouth, trickle down her throat.

Suddenly, the glass slipped from her hand, falling to the tiled floor where it shattered into a puddle of water and glass shards.

"Baptiste?" a man's voice called from the next room.

She felt him enter the room, pushing through the door behind her, his steps light despite his large and imposing presence.

"Baptiste? Are you okay?" the man was saying.

Brigid turned to face him, saw the large figure there, another behind him, this one with long blond fur atop its head, weaved into tresses, a female. Apes.

No, not apes. People. She knew they were people. She knew who they were. But for a moment, the names wouldn't come.

The male was stepping forward, his hands grasping her by the shoulders, pulling her toward him, into him, holding her steady.

"Careful now," the male was saying. "Careful. Broken glass and bare feet—not a good mix."

Her lethelogica passed in a flash, and, like a spiritual revelation, she remembered who he was. "Kane," she mumbled as the tall man guided her away from the puddle on the floor, holding her tightly in his arms.

"Yeah," he replied soothingly. "It's okay now, Baptiste. You're okay."

"My head feels all messed up."

The female with the ash-blond tresses—Reba, Brigid remembered suddenly, like a light being switched on in her head—spoke quietly as she bent to clear away the shattered glass. "You took a big dose of tranquilizer gas," she said. "You've been asleep for almost four hours."

Brigid looked at the physician as she wrapped the glass carefully in a paper hand towel she had pulled from a dispenser on the wall. "Thank you, Reba," she said, barely any sound to her voice.

Kane helped Brigid from the recovery room, letting her rest her weight against him as they slowly exited into the little office where DeFore had been working at her charts. He sat her down in one of the empty chairs that ran along the side wall and crouched before her, his blue-gray eyes looking into hers.

"Are you okay, Baptiste?" he asked.

Brigid began to nod, then stopped as she felt the heaviness still in her head, that awful, roiling feeling once more.

"I think so," she told him, her voice pathetic, little more than a whisper. "Feel kind of…hungover."

"Well, it was a heck of a party," Kane assured her. "Got a bit rowdy there at the end."

Brigid smiled, knowing that Kane was making fun of her, just a little. "Tell me all about it," she said, reaching forward and placing a hand on his face for reassurance, feeling the warmth of his cheek.

Moving backward, Kane reached for the wheeled chair at DeFore's desk, sat and began to relate the events of the last hour or so that they had spent in California. Brigid's recollections were faint, but gradually, with Kane's help, she started to piece it all together.

DOWN IN THE BASEMENT, Grant stood outside the storage room that had been converted into a prison cell for the captured monster, looking at its imposing form through the three-inch square of reinforced glass in the door. The hulking creature was slumped across the floor, its chest moving slowly, rising and falling as it breathed in the anaesthetic mist that clouded the room. Wisps of green smoke from the creature's strange eyes mixed with the white of the anaesthetic, even though its eyes were now closed as if in slumber.

As he stood there, watching through the little window, Grant heard the footsteps on the concrete floor of someone approaching down the long corridor. He looked up and saw Domi walking toward him, a tight smile on her face. She had changed her clothes since they had got back to the redoubt, and now wore an abbreviated vest top in wine-red over her tiny, pert breasts, with a pair of cut-off denim shorts, leaving her bone white legs and feet bare.

"How's the prisoner?" Domi asked.

"Seems restful," Grant told her, stepping away from the little square of glass. "You want to look?"

"Uh-uh." Domi shook her head. "Seen enough of that ugly mug for a long time, thank you oh so much."

Grant glanced back to the window for a second, before chuckling quietly. "Yeah, I guess we all feel a little like that," he admitted.

"Any more clues as to what it is," Domi asked, "or where it came from?"

Grant shrugged. "Nobody's told me anything so far."

Domi smiled at him. "Tough being the hero sometimes, isn't it?"

Grant laughed at that. "You're mistaking me for someone else," he told her. "Hey, have you eaten?" he added, and Domi shook her head. "Let's go see what's in the canteen. Ever since I got hit by that knockout gas I've been starving."

Domi accompanied Grant down the long length of corridor, past the twin guardsmen who stood by the stairwell, there to ensure that the creature didn't break out.

"What happens if it wakes up?" Domi asked Grant as they climbed the stairs together.

"Lakesh has got six tanks of anaesthetic rigged up, feeding that room twenty-four hours a day," Grant assured her. "It isn't waking up any time soon."

Domi ran a hand through her short, pixie-style haircut. "I hope you're right," she stated ominously, her discomfort obvious.

BRIGID WAS GREETED with a round of applause as she walked through the wide doors into the Cerberus control center. She was feeling much better now—a shower and a change of clothes had done wonders for her temperament, and the muzzy feeling in her head had all but gone.

"Thank you," she said as the applause died down.

Brewster Philboyd waved to her from his place at the communications terminal. "Welcome back, Brigid," he said as she sat at the desk next to his and powered up the computer there. The two of them had worked closely on getting the interphaser operational about a year ago, and Philboyd had always had a lot of time for Brigid.

"Thanks for your help out there," Brigid said, placing her spectacles on her nose as her computer ran through its boot-up protocols. "We would never have tracked the creature without you watching our backs and fronts and every other part of us."

Brewster blanched, looking at the stunning figure before him, dressed in a tightly fitted white jumpsuit, the standard wear for Cerberus staff. On Brigid's rounded, athletic figure, the formfitting suit left little to the imagination.

Seeing his embarrassment, Brigid leaned forward and whispered in Brewster's ear, "You can stop watching now, Brewster. I think I'm safe."

Brewster blushed, turning back to his computer, his eyes glazed. Brigid sniggered as she ran through the password screens and accessed the shared mission report files. It came as little surprise to see that both Kane and Grant had neglected to file a report on the field mission in California, and Brigid knew that there was little hope that Domi would ever concern herself with such "boring paperwork."

Brigid tapped at the keys and added the next case number to her report before filling in the basic details of locations with map references, personnel involved and basic weapons inventory data. An archivist from Cobaltville, Brigid knew the value of keeping accurate records that others might refer to in future—if a Cerberus field team came across another of the black-skinned creatures, her report might be the only information that kept them alive.

She looked at the screen, adjusting her glasses as she ordered her thoughts. Her hand reached across and she plucked a pen from a tub to the side of the little desk. Reaching down to her side, she pulled open the drawers until she found a little notepad, its top page dotted with her familiar, precise handwriting. She placed the notepad on the desk, flipping it to a blank page, and began writing a few key words to get her thoughts together.

MARIAH FALK SAT at one of the plastic-topped tables in the Cerberus canteen, enjoying a late snack, having missed dinner thanks to her brief excursion to Humphreys Peak. She sat there, letting her mind wander as she thought back to the strange little underground rooms that she had been exploring with Bryant and Edwards just a few hours before. As she broke off a corner of the pastry on her plate, Lakesh came walking over with Cerberus physician Reba DeFore in tow, rustling a file of printouts in his hand.

"Hello, Mariah," Lakesh said. "We've just had the results back on that liquid you and Clem brought from your excursion. May we join you?"

"Be my guest," Mariah said, looking around for Clem. The canteen was his domain, and she knew he'd appear from the kitchens before too long, hurrying to wipe down a table or to check that someone was enjoying a meal.

Lakesh sat, checking through his paperwork for a few seconds, until Mariah caught Clem's eye and called him over.

While they waited for Clem to join them, Domi spotted Lakesh and came rushing over from where she sat with Grant.

"Hello, lover," she whispered, draping her arms around Lakesh's shoulders and pulling him close.

Lakesh turned, a bright smile crossing his face. "Dearest," he said apologetically, "I'm sorry that we've hardly had a chance to speak since your return. I seem to be juggling an alarming variety of pressing matters today."

Domi stroked Lakesh's nose, looking him in the eye from just a few inches away. "You'll make it up to me," she said quietly. Lakesh wasn't quite sure if that was an assumption or an order from his dearest companion.

Once Clem joined them, Domi went back to her table and Lakesh turned the papers around to show to Clem and Mariah while he used his pen to point at certain figures printed there.

"What we're looking at," Lakesh explained, "is an analysis of the contents of the bottle you brought back from Humphreys Peak. The lab boys are still doing a full battery of tests at the moment, but this is their preliminary report."

Clem looked at Mariah, then—apologetically—at Lakesh and DeFore. "You'll have to forgive my ignorance, Dr. Singh, but perhaps if you could talk me through these findings."

"Of course." Lakesh nodded, pointing to each value in turn. "What we have here are proteins, carbohydrates, lipids and phospholipids, electrolytes and urea, with a significant amount of water as the base within which it's all swimming around."

Mariah looked mystified, but Clem smiled and nodded as though he had rumbled a great secret. "Basic building blocks," he said, when he saw Mariah's confusion.

"I'm a geologist," Mariah reminded him. "When you say 'building blocks' I hear 'column and strata.'"

Clem looked to Lakesh and Reba for confirmation as he continued. "Proteins, carbohydrates, electrolytes—these are the building blocks of life."

"Clem's right," Reba DeFore agreed when Mariah looked to the ash-blond physician for confirmation. "The makeup of this pool you found is very similar to amniotic fluid. Allowing for the contamination of the vessel used, it's a very good fit for amnion."

"A...birthing pool?" Mariah said tentatively.

"More like a womb," DeFore said, "or the discharge of one."

Clem looked up and smiled. "I don't think I'll be needing my bottle back, Doctors." He laughed.

Lakesh flicked through his papers until he found a sheet covered in architectural diagrams. "I've also looked into this kachina that you mentioned, Mariah," he stated. "You may very well be onto something. The little figurines that Edwards brought back certainly look like kachina, which formed fetishes of many of the strands of Pueblo religion. The kachina were believed to be supernatural entities, spirits that could influence the natural world. Each one was designed to look unique, each with its own significance. Even the colors mean something to the people who made them."

"What are they made of?" Clem asked.

"The ones you found were constructed from cotton-

wood root," Lakesh replied. "The room that you found
yourselves in, the first one that you described to me, I
believe that that was a kiva, a room used for religious
rituals by the Hopi and other Pueblo people. Evidence of
these rooms goes back centuries, although there has never
been a consensus as to their original designation or
purpose."

"And are these kivas all accessed through a fault line in
a mountain?" Clem asked. "It seems rather an impractical
way to carry on your worship."

Lakesh pushed the paperwork across the table to where
Mariah and Clem could study it more closely. There were
two line illustrations on the top sheet that showed overhead
and side views of a circular room very much like the one
that they had found in Arizona. The designs showed a
single opening at the top of the room, through which a
ladder poked, allowing access from aboveground.

"Roof access?" Clem said after he'd looked at the
designs. "Very clever."

Lakesh indicated the drawings. "I'd suggest that the
rooms that you found originally had the same type of
access, but over the years it's been sealed off. Whether intentionally or not, we'll probably never know."

"You should consider yourself honored," Clem said,
turning to Mariah. "According to these notes, women aren't
generally welcomed in the kiva."

Mariah laughed before she turned to Lakesh and DeFore
across the table, all seriousness once more. "What does this
all mean, Lakesh?"

"Hidden rooms," Lakesh said, ticking off items on his
fingers, "evidence of a recent birth, a religion that worships

supernatural entities capable of influencing the world. I'd say it means that something was in there and, whatever it was, it's out."

"The earthquake freed it," Mariah realized. "I'm so dumb, why didn't I realize that from the start?"

"I think you did," Clem said, placing a reassuring hand on her arm. "Otherwise you wouldn't have insisted that we investigate the site."

Lakesh nodded in agreement, as did DeFore a moment later.

"We couldn't have got anyone there any sooner, Mariah," Lakesh assured her. "Your instincts were right on the money."

"Could this have anything to do with," DeFore began, considering carefully how to end her sentence without alarming Clem and Mariah, "the item that Kane's team brought back from California?"

Lakesh looked thoughtful as he considered the likelihood. "Geographically, the two were found relatively close to each other." He nodded. "It's a distinct possibility."

IN THE CONTROL CENTER ROOM, Donald Bry had resumed his post at the communications terminal beside Brigid Baptiste, while Brewster Philboyd took some time to himself. Bry's ever nervous face turned to Brigid as she scribbled reams of notes on the pad, seemingly faster than the ink of her pen could flow. She tore off another sheet, placing it before her on the desk, where it sat between seven other sheets that were arrayed in a spread like a fan of cards.

"You're looking busy, Brigid," Bry said when he saw her

finally stop for a moment, tapping the pen against her teeth in concentration.

She ignored him, clearly deep in thought.

Bry turned back to his terminal, then stopped. Something was nagging at him, and he looked back at the notes now covering Brigid's desk. Slowly, Bry peered at the notes, standing and walking the two paces between the desks to get a better look. There were drawings, diagrams really, of plant life and of little figures. There were words written beside the images, long streams of words, paragraph upon paragraph of tiny, neatly written characters.

As Bry looked at them, reading the notes on the sheet that Brigid had just placed in the center of the array, he shook his head and rubbed his eyes. He couldn't make sense of it, not at all. The notes were written in letters, in words, but not letters or words that he recognized. They weren't English, that was for sure, but nor did they look Cyrillic or the graceful, sweeping swirls of Arabic, the stern, blocky characters of Chinese.

Finally, Bry spoke quietly to Brigid. "What are you writing, Brigid? It looks...fascinating."

The beautiful redhead turned at his words, looking at him and yet, somehow, through him.

"Brigid?" Bry prompted again.

"Donald..." The word came breathlessly from Brigid's lips. "I was... I didn't realize that you were there."

Bry pointed to the notes on the desk. "What are you writing? I don't recognize some of these characters."

"The words," Brigid began slowly, as though teasing the sentence from her mind, "are all in my head. I can see them."

Donald leaned forward, reaching out to Brigid then. "Are you all right, Brigid?"

She looked at him, but her eyes seemed unfocused, the pupils wide as though they couldn't get enough light. "I can see you," she said.

"I'm right here," Bry assured her.

"I can see you all," Brigid said, ignoring him.

Bry stepped back then, a shiver running down his spine. He turned, looking around the busy room at the other staff as they worked quietly at their terminals. Lakesh's seat was empty, but Bry had known that when he came back on shift.

"Where's Lakesh?" he asked urgently, raising his voice for attention.

Over by the mat-trans anteroom, wiping the walls down, Farrell looked up and pointed to the doors. "He went to the canteen about five minutes before you arrived," he told Bry. "Lab results came in and he was hoping to catch Clem and Mariah, I think."

Bry stepped over to Lakesh's terminal, flipping on the trans-comm as he held the communications rig to his ear. A green light winked on on the desk and Bry spoke into the microphone, his voice echoing through the rooms and corridors of the vast redoubt.

"Paging Lakesh and DeFore. This is Donald Bry in the control room. Please could you come here urgently. I repeat, Lakesh and Reba—to the control room, ASAP."

Farrell's brows knitted in worry as he looked at Bry, and a number of the other personnel in the room looked similarly perplexed. "What's going on, Donald?" Farrell asked.

"I'm not sure," he admitted, looking at Brigid as she sat there, eyes wide, staring into nothingness as her hand scribbled out more of the strange notations like a thing possessed, "but I think we need to evacuate this room until we find out."

Voiced dissent went up almost immediately from the staff, but Bry held up his hands to calm everyone. "I'm ordering everyone out of this room. Please proceed to the exit in a calm and orderly manner."

"But what about the feeds?" the scientist at the satellite backup monitoring terminal asked.

"I'll monitor them," Bry assured him. "If everyone can wait outside this room, I'm sure this will all be over in a few minutes. Thank you."

It wasn't often that Donald Bry had to show his leadership skills, but his utter calm in the face of the unknown reassured the other members of staff. They proceeded to follow his orders, lining up in the corridor outside while he and Brigid Baptiste remained within.

Two minutes later, Lakesh arrived with Reba DeFore in tow. "What's going on?" he asked Donald urgently as they rushed through the double doors into the room.

Behind Lakesh, Reba closed the doors, drowning out the hubbub of urgent conversation from the impatient staff.

"Something's happened to Brigid," Donald explained, his voice low. "She's been writing nonsensical notes, presumably all afternoon, and she seems to be mentally altered."

The worry was clear on Lakesh's features, and he dashed across the room to where Brigid sat at her desk, scratching out more of the strange illustrated notes.

"Brigid?" he asked. "Brigid, dearest, can you hear me?"

Slowly, languidly, Brigid turned to face him, her pen still working at the notepad. "Dr.... Lakesh?" she muttered.

"Okay, dear," Lakesh urged, "keep calm. Stay with it. Stay with us."

Reba DeFore was already at their side, turning Brigid's free hand over and timing the pulse there against her pocket chron. "Pulse seems normal," she said. "Temperature feels fine, but I'll need my medicine bag to do a proper examination."

"Then get it," Lakesh instructed her. "We'll remain here. And tell everyone outside to wait."

Brigid's eyes widened as she looked at Lakesh and Bry, dropping the pen from her hand. When her speech came, it was slurred. "S'funny, Lakesh. I can see two of you," she explained.

"That's Donald," Lakesh told her, looking into her wide eyes. Where he could still see it around the widened pupils, the vibrant emerald-green of Brigid's eyes seemed to be losing its luster, fading to the yellow of dried straw.

"No," Brigid said finally. "That's not Donnie. I can see him, too, by your shoulder. Him...and him. Two by two, like on the ark. All those animals. Poor Noah—God's stable boy."

Instinctively, both Lakesh and Bry looked over their shoulders, checking behind them, all around the room. They were alone, just the three of them in all, including Brigid sitting at her desk.

"What are these notes?" Lakesh asked, turning to Bry.

"Like I said, they're just nonsense," Bry explained. "Look here," he added, holding up one of the lavishly illustrated sheets of notepaper.

Lakesh looked at it, saw the strange writing scrawled across the page. The characters seemed familiar and yet different, the way that Russian looks familiar to an English-reader. Much as he tried, Lakesh could make no sense of the curling letters, the bunched words. Beside the tightly packed writing was an illustration of a fat figure, reminiscent of a cherub, sliding down what appeared to be the inside of a plant stalk, a flowering bud sitting atop the hand-drawn sketch.

"This reminds me of something," Lakesh said finally, wincing as he tried to place the memory. "Voynich," he said after a long pause. "Look up Voynich."

Bry looked mystified. "What is Voynich?" he asked. "Is that the language she's writing in?"

"No," Lakesh told him, "Voynich was a mysterious book that was discovered at the start of the twentieth century, named after the book collector who initially acquired it. Assumed to be at least four hundred years older, the artifact is a book written in an unknown language that no one has ever been able to decode. I saw an article on this somewhere, *Scientific American* maybe, back before skydark. The pictures, they're what made me think of it. I think that Brigid is writing in, well, in Voynich. Whatever Voynich is."

As Lakesh explained it, Bry was already working the keys of one of the computer terminals, dragging all the information he could about the Voynich manuscript.

"According to this, the Voynich book baffled all attempts by cryptanalysts and was widely considered to be a hoax, although the true nature of that hoax, the why and wherefore, was never established," he paraphrased, skimming the information. "You're right, though, the pictures bear a striking resemblance to Brigid's, as does the script that she is using."

"The crucial point of the Voynich analysis," Lakesh recalled, "is that no one could ever work out how the hoax worked. It seemed too elaborate, somehow."

"It says here," Bry continued, "that some inroads were made in decrypting the manuscript when a version of Ukrainian was applied to it. John Stojko made some translations using a coded version of Ukrainian that dropped all vowels and replaced the letters with secret characters. But these findings—my goodness, Dr. Singh—this is the language of nightmares. Listen—

"'Eye of God, you are measuring empty religion for the world. Your aim, not religion, is living in you.'

"And—

"'Why are you measuring the measure? The measure is the same? Even after Great One, the bones will be broken. I am telling you.'" Donald shook his head, exhaling a long stream of breath.

"It has the illusion of making sense, yet never does," Lakesh agreed, turning his attention back to Brigid. She was still sitting there, rocking back and forth in her seat, the pen clutched in her hand. As Lakesh watched, he saw her lips moving, speaking words in a mumbled track that he could not quite decipher. "Hang in there, Brigid," he told her firmly. "Stay with us."

DOWN IN THE BASEMENT corridor, the two guards heard a sudden crashing coming from the converted storage room. The man on the left pulled his MP-9 subgun around and rushed down the corridor while his partner waited by the stairs.

When he reached the storage room, the guard stepped

warily forward, peering through the little square of reinforced glass. The smoky gas of the anaesthetic filled his
vision and, for a moment, the guard could not make out
anything at all. Then, as the fog cleared, he saw the monstrous form of the creature.

It was still lying there, held by restraints at ankles, wrists
and neck, the chains bolted to the floor with the same huge
rivets that had been used to reinforce the Cerberus redoubt
itself after attacks by the Annunaki. But it was moving now,
legs and arms twitching, its head rolling this way and that.
It was still asleep, but it looked to be struggling back to
wakefulness, trying to shake itself out of a bad dream.

Disturbed, the guard turned back down the corridor and
called to his partner. "I think we need more anaesthetic,"
he reasoned.

"You're kidding," his partner called from the stairwell.
"They're pumping enough crap in there to fell a grizzly."

"Well, that isn't a grizzly," the guard told his colleague.
"Maybe it's building up an immunity to the knockout
juice."

"I'll alert the brainiacs," his partner decided.

REBA DEFORE RAN back along the corridor from her
medical bay, carrying her black bag of instruments. As she
turned the corner, she very nearly ran into Kane.

"Sorry, Kane," DeFore apologized, "kind of in a rush."

"I can see that," he said, keeping pace with her as she
hurried along the long, wide corridor back to the control
room. "What's going on?"

"It's Brigid," DeFore told him. "She's taken a turn for
the worse."

"What?" Kane cried. "She was fine, absolutely fine. That anaesthetic can't still be in her system, can it?"

As DeFore reached the high double doors to the control room she turned back, shaking her head. "I don't think this is the anaesthetic, Kane. Let me work—I'll come tell you as soon as I know anything."

With that, the blond-haired medic slipped through the doors, closing them behind her and leaving Kane with the massing crowd of staff who had been evacuated from the room.

INSIDE THE CONTROL ROOM, DeFore rushed across to Brigid's desk and began attaching a monitor unit that could provide more information than her subcutaneous transponder alone. As she pumped air into the blood pressure hose, DeFore turned to Lakesh.

"Kane's waiting outside," she told him.

"Not good," Bry said quietly, as if to himself. When he realized the querulous looks that DeFore and Lakesh were giving him, he elaborated. "Once Kane's involved, trouble always follows," he said.

"Respectfully, I think trouble's already here," Lakesh chastised him.

"My instruments would tend to disagree," DeFore said, confused. "Brigid is a little hotter than normal, but she seems to be in basically good health."

Brigid seemed to be oblivious to the conversation. She gazed around the room as though seeing it for the first time. Suddenly, she stood, the blood pressure sleeve still attached to her arm, and wandered away from her desk.

"Brigid?" Lakesh called. "Brigid, where are you...?"

"Lakesh," Brigid slurred, smiling and turning to him. "It's so strange, I forgot you were here for a moment." Her eyes seemed to be looking through him, their color now washing away, a light, sandy yellow where they had once been green.

Lakesh strode over to her and placed his arms firmly on her shoulders. "Brigid, I need you to sit still," he told her. "I need you to explain what it is that you can see."

"See?" she asked, baffled. "You're just..." Her voice trailed off and she shook her head in confusion.

"Just what?" Lakesh encouraged her.

Brigid looked at him, trying to remember what the question was.

THERE WERE TWO of them where Lakesh stood. In Brigid's eyes, there were two people, two living, breathing creatures.

Lakesh was one. She knew Lakesh, her old friend and confidant. It was as if there were a tag, a label in her mind that read Lakesh—Friend when she looked at him. Brigid supposed that was how she saw everyone, how everyone saw everyone else, really, when you got down to it. We weren't really people at all, she realized, we were just the labels that people assigned to us.

Everything else in the familiar room was the same. The desks, the monitors, the keyboards, the huge, beautiful map that ran across the length of one wall of the room, its twinkling lights showing all the different ways to Sante Fe.

But there was something else, and she felt it, in her eyes, in her mind, as she looked at the living creature designated Mohandas Lakesh Singh.

Ape-thing. Primitive. Irrelevant. Dangerous. Survival

dictated that this thing die. Survival for her, and for all of her people.

And the desks were just hunks carved from the trees, and the computer monitors were just smoothed glass like ice, and the keyboards were blocks of shining solid and the map on the wall just a splash of colors and lights with no meaning, no discernible pattern.

Brigid turned to Lakesh, to the ape-thing that held her, and she urged her voice to speak, to tell him what it was.

"It's nice," she began, her head swirling with the other's thoughts, eating into her very identity, her very soul itself.

LAKESH PULLED Brigid closer as she whispered two words: "It's nice."

"What is?" he asked. "What is nice, Brigid? Tell me."

Her pale yellow cat's eyes locked with his for a moment, and a silly, girlish smile crossed her lips as her head began to loll back.

"It's nice…to forget…who you are…sometimes."

And then she dropped, all the strength leaving her muscles, and Lakesh grabbed her in an automatic reaction before she fell to the floor.

"What's happened to her?" Bry asked, with DeFore beside him clearly hanging on Lakesh's answer, as well.

"Unconscious," Lakesh decided. "But I don't think that that's all it is."

Chapter 17

The doors to the control room burst open and Lakesh and DeFore rushed out, clearing a path through the crowd of waiting staff as Donald Bry followed, struggling with Brigid's weight draped in his arms. When Kane saw them, he pushed the staff members aside and demanded to know what was going on.

"Brigid fainted," Lakesh told him, concern etched on his brow. "We're taking her to the med bay so that everyone can get back to work," he added, raising his voice midsentence for the benefit of the other personnel waiting with Kane.

Kane turned to Bry. "I'll carry her," he told the smaller man, and when Bry looked at Kane he saw something almost territorial in the ex-Mag's expression.

Bry rolled Brigid into Kane's waiting arms. "Thanks, Kane," he said, his breathing heavy. "Not really my thing, fetching and carrying."

Kane ignored him. He was already turned, jogging down the corridor with Brigid in his arms, making it look effortless. Donald Bry remained behind to ease the other staff members back to their tasks.

When they reached the medical bay, Kane was ahead of DeFore and Lakesh.

"Come on, people," Kane said, swinging the limp body

around as he backed through the doorway. "Let's pick up the pace."

DeFore followed a moment later, still clutching her medical bag. "Just put her down on the couch and I'll start an IV to raise her blood sugar," she told Kane.

Lakesh was breathing heavily by the time he came into the little warren of rooms, and he apologized, explaining how he wasn't as young as he used to be.

Kane glared at him, anger seething just below the surface.

"Just a joke, Kane," Lakesh told him apologetically. "Brave heart now. Dearest Brigid will be fine."

"No, she won't," Kane muttered as he watched DeFore roll Brigid's sleeve and tap for a vein to insert the IV.

"It's probably just an aftereffect of the anaesthetic," DeFore explained. "It hits people differently, delayed reaction. That's all."

"And her eyes?" Kane inquired. "Did you see her eyes?"

DeFore didn't answer. Instead, she kept her head down as she worked the IV drip.

"Lakesh?" Kane asked, turning to the Cerberus leader.

"Yes, Kane, I saw her eyes," Lakesh admitted. "They're gradually bleaching of their color."

The three of them waited in silence, as DeFore adjusted the IV line that fed solution into Brigid's vein. The quiet humming of the air-conditioning suddenly seemed very loud, the whirring fans and clanking parts like an orchestra tuning up.

Then Kane spoke, breaking the horrible silence. "It's my fault," was all he said.

"No," DeFore said, turning to the ex-Mag. "No, Kane, don't say that. It's not—"

"I saw it," Kane admitted. "I saw it touch her and I said nothing. I pretended it hadn't happened. I told *myself* that I hadn't seen it."

"Seen what?" Lakesh asked gently.

Kane's eyes looked off into the middle distance as the images replayed in his mind's eye. "When we used the interphaser to bring the creature back, landing in the mat-trans chamber where you could pump the sealed room with knockout gas, I saw it move. I saw it reach for her, just before I went under. Two breaths, that's all it took until we were all unconscious. But I saw it twitch, I saw its hand stretch out. Its knuckle brushed her bare hand, just for an instant, not even a second."

Lakesh and Reba were standing stock-still, hanging on every word of Kane's admission.

"And when I woke up I told myself I hadn't seen it," Kane continued. "That I had imagined the whole damn thing. Because I didn't want it to be real. I lied to myself about what I saw because I didn't want it to be real, you understand?"

Lakesh looked Kane squarely in the eye, and all traces of his usual good humor had left his voice when he spoke. "Kane," he began, "this isn't your fault. The anaesthetic knocked you out, the same as it did Brigid and Grant and Domi and that terrible, awful thing that we have penned downstairs. You could not be expected to trust your senses during those last instants before you sank into unconsciousness."

"I know what I saw," Kane told him.

"No," Lakesh assured the tortured warrior. "You've pieced together what you think you saw, because you have the evidence now. You couldn't have known what had really happened given the condition you were in at the time."

Kane's gaze swept the floor for a few moments before he muttered his assent.

"Now," Lakesh told him, "let's work on your information and see if we can't reverse whatever it is that's affected her."

Kane looked at him then, his gray-blue eyes touched with sadness. "It can't be reversed," he said quietly. "You had our reports, and you heard what Decard said about his Incarnates. They all died. Every last one of its victims died. Baptiste is dead, Lakesh. She's breathing just now, sure, but she won't be. Not for much longer. First it takes your mind, then it takes your body, eating away at you from the inside. Baptiste told me, when we first saw its effects, that it was using up people's energy at a fantastic rate. It was that use that was killing its victims."

"Thus, we need only find another energy source for it to feed on," Lakesh stated matter-of-factly.

"Can't be done," Kane stated.

"Has it been tried?" Lakesh asked.

Kane shook his head, teeth gritted in annoyance. "How would you do it? What do you plan to do? Plug her into a battery? A jenny?"

"Trial and error, Kane," Lakesh assured him. "Scientific method until we find what works."

Kane bunched his fists in his frustration, looking around the little room as though for something to hit. "She'll be dead inside of five hours, Lakesh. There's no time for trial and error. There's no time for anything."

The two men stood at the side of the couch where Brigid lay, deep in their own thoughts, puzzling their own conundrums, when suddenly, almost magically, Brigid's voice came faintly from where she lay.

"Keep the noise down, guys," she muttered. "I'm having enough trouble concentrating already."

Lakesh, Kane and DeFore all turned, leaning down to hear Brigid.

"What did you say?" Lakesh asked. "Brigid, are you... Is that you?"

Her eyelids fluttered a moment, and her pale, washed-out yellow irises looked eerily out from her skull. "I remember who I am," she said, "but it's hard. It's so hard. Like I'm not me anymore, like I'm not one but two."

"Who's the other?" Kane urged, his deep concern clear in his tone.

"I don't know its name," Brigid admitted. "I think there may be more than one here, inside me. Igigi. They're called Igigi."

Lakesh's eyes flicked to Kane, seeing if the man showed any recognition for the word, but Kane was focused utterly on Brigid Baptiste as she spoke in halting, strained tones.

"They were slaves, Kane," Brigid mumbled, her voice low. "They were Enlil's slaves, back when the Annunaki first walked the Earth, millennia ago. The Igigi were the royal family's treasured slaves."

"I remember Lilitu telling us about them now," Kane stated, recalling the alien woman who had brought them so much knowledge after the Annunaki had finally revealed themselves from the chrysalis state of their hybrid baron bodies.

"They knew about the Flood beforehand," Brigid breathed the words. "The knew about Enlil's plans to destroy humankind, to start afresh. Oh, it hurts so much now, Kane, it hurts so much," she said, her washed-out eyes tightly closed against the pain.

"I'm here," Kane assured her, his hand cupping over hers. "We're all here, Baptiste."

"They're in me, Kane," Brigid explained. "They're in me and they don't want to die. They didn't want to die."

Lakesh leaned forward, transfixed by the revelations that Brigid Baptiste was bringing them. The slave caste of the Annunaki were still here and somehow inside Brigid?

"A group of them hid," Brigid said, the words strained in her throat, "protected themselves using the same Magan technology that the Annunaki accessed in times of death and rebirth. I think that they died so that they could live, Kane. I think they died to live again." Brigid's head tossed backward, pushing into the cushions of the couch, and she let out a strained howl from deep in her throat.

"Come on, Baptiste," Kane instructed, "stay with us. Don't lose it now."

"Th-the upload went wrong," Brigid whispered. "The bodies never materialized. The Shadow Box broke but there was nothing for them to inhabit, no bodies waiting for them so that they might live again. Oh, Kane, help me, please, I can't do this anymore. It burns. It burns inside."

"You show me what I've got to fight and I'll fight it," Kane told her. "Just point me at it, Baptiste. I'll go through Hell and back if that's what it takes. We're *anam-charas*, remember. Our souls are entwined. There is nothing I won't do to make this right."

"The ville," Brigid muttered, "the city. It's too full. There are too many of them fighting for control, for domination. No, not a ville. A uni-mind. A prison. It's a prison, Kane, a prison where you are absorbed if you don't escape. And it's breaking apart. Oh, help me. Help me now."

Suddenly, Brigid's eyes snapped open and Kane saw that they were pure white orbs now, no color left. Even the sickly yellow had dissipated, washed away with her tears.

Kane's hand tightened on Brigid's as he knelt there, looking into those featureless, terrifying eyes. "Be strong, Baptiste, be strong," he encouraged.

Her voice came back strained, scratching at her throat, a hoarse, guttural sound. "Get off me, ape-thing."

Kane looked at Brigid as she writhed on the couch, her hair now damp with sweat. "We're losing her," he said to no one in particular.

"No, we're not," Lakesh insisted, standing and looking around the room for what he knew not.

Kane's eyes stayed on Brigid as she tossed and turned on the couch. "This is how they all went," he said bitterly. "Baptiste is strong. Her will's as stubborn as a mule, but it's overwhelming her now. I can tell."

"It's not her willpower," Lakesh said, speaking the words aloud before he had even acknowledged his own revelation. "It's her memory. Her photographic memory is keeping her from being completely overwhelmed."

"Say again?" Kane and DeFore asked in unison.

"She said it earlier and I just dismissed it for rambling," Lakesh told them. "Our memory of self is all that we have, but Brigid's memory is so accurate that this thing, this Igigi, cannot overwhelm it. At least, not immediately. It's like trying to paint over a huge mural—details keep popping out through the new layer."

Kane looked up from his position beside the couch. "So we have longer," he stated, "but we don't have an answer."

Lakesh turned to the physician DeFore, a plan forming in his head. "Reba, make her stable."

"Dr. Singh," the medic complained, "I don't think that I can."

"I need her to remain herself for a matter of ten, perhaps fifteen minutes," Lakesh instructed. "Increase the IV, pump her with adrenaline, whatever you feel you need to do."

DeFore didn't question anymore; she just began sorting through a cupboard for a glucose pack to add to the drip feed.

"And we'll need to move her," Lakesh stated, instructing Kane. "A stretcher, a gurney, a wheelchair. Find me something."

"Where are we going?" Kane asked.

"Basement," Lakesh told him, a wicked gleam in his eye. "It's time to enter the prison city of the Igigi."

WITH BRIGID laid out on a gurney, Kane, Lakesh and DeFore made their way down to the basement of the Cerberus facility. An IV drip on a wheeled pole was dragged along beside the gurney, the feed attached to Brigid's arm as she lay on the stretcher, her eyes bunched tight, her muscles tense with struggle.

DeFore stood next to the IV, monitoring its output nervously. She had brought replacement bags for the feed, including some adenosine in an effort to keep Brigid's racing heart rhythm regular.

As they descended, Kane spoke to Lakesh. "What do you plan on doing?" he asked.

"The only thing that we can do, I think," Lakesh told him as the elevator pulled to a halt on its whining hydraulics.

When the elevator doors opened, the group was greeted by an unexpected scene. A dozen guards stood in the wide corridor, including Grant and Domi, all of them heavily armed with their weapons trained on the door to the storage room that had been transformed into a cell for their monstrous captive. Donald Bry was giving orders to a handful of scientists who were rushing pressurized canisters of anaesthetic to the scene and swiftly attaching hoses to the canisters.

Lakesh caught Bry's attention as the elevator doors locked open at their widest point. "What's going on, Donald?" he asked.

Bry walked across to him, a grim expression on his face. "The creature's waking up," he explained. "It seems that it's building up a resistance to the anaesthetic. Gil called it in just after you left to tend to Brigid, but I didn't want to alert you—I knew you had your hands full."

"That's fine, Donald," Lakesh assured him.

Bry looked at the strange party with their sick colleague lying on the wheeled stretcher. "What *are* you doing down here, sir?" he asked finally.

"Keep pumping anaesthetic into the room," Lakesh told him, "and get me four gas masks, plus as many as everyone else here needs for when we open the door."

"Excuse me?" Bry said in astonishment.

"We're going in," Lakesh told him with a grim smile.

"Are you mad?" Bry responded. "You're hardly in a fit state to... And that monster will kill you if it wakes up. And Brigid's certainly in no condition to—"

Lakesh held up his hand to hush Bry's stream of complaints. "True, true and true," he said. "But I'll still need the gas masks, Donald. It's the only way."

Bry turned to the group in the corridor and began giving out instructions. In a few moments, Kane and the team had been handed gas masks and rebreathers. Kane slipped his over his head and let it hang by its strap around his neck. Beside him, DeFore looked at her own rubber mask with discomfort, handling it as though it were an alien object.

"It'll be fine," Kane assured her.

"This isn't my territory, Kane," she admitted. "I'm a medic, not a...a warrior."

"And what we need in there is a medic," Kane said reassuringly.

As they spoke, Donald Bry's voice called out instructions, advising everyone in the corridor that they had thirty seconds. "I want this corridor clear of nonessential personnel now, and I want all remaining guards to get as far back as possible, masks on," he explained.

DeFore worked another rebreather mask over Brigid's face, lifting her head gently as though bathing a baby.

With his own gas mask hanging beneath his chin, a heavy rifle clenched in his hands, Grant stepped over and spoke with Kane. "You need any backup in there, pal?" he asked.

"We'll be fine," Kane assured him.

"I'll go in with you if you want me to. We've been through a lot together," Grant began.

"No," Kane corrected, "we've been through *everything* together, and we survived it all. This won't be any different. And it will be a lot easier knowing you're just outside, in case anything does go wrong."

Grant shifted his Copperhead rifle to his left hand and held his right out for Kane to shake. Kane grasped his partner's hand, clenching it tightly for a long moment—no further words were needed.

Bry was counting down from ten at the top of his voice, and the last few people in the corridor rushed for the stairwell, the guards backing away from the door to the cell.

Lakesh leaned close, his voice emotionless as he spoke to Kane. "It's time," he said.

Gas masks over their faces, the four-strong team entered the open door to the cell, with Lakesh pushing Brigid's gurney while Kane went ahead to guide it inside. Wisps of foglike anaesthetic gas drifted from the doorway, reminding Lakesh once again of an apiarist's smoke around a beehive.

Kane looked firmly ahead, his eyes locked on the now still form of the hulking, black-skinned humanoid figure that they had brought back from California. Although still, the monster's chest continued to rise and fall slowly as it breathed, and wisps of green smoke were emitted in puffs from its closed eyes.

Behind them, guards began to take up positions, gas masks over their faces, their weapons trained on the door as DeFore pushed it closed behind her, the last to enter. His own mask in place, Bry stepped forward and locked the door. He had agreed with Lakesh that if the monster broke free, a locked door might make all the difference in such a scenario—and that it was provident to lose the four of them than to have it escape from the cell.

As they listened to the heavy bar being dropped across the outside of the door, Kane and Lakesh positioned the gurney close to the unconscious, hulking figure, close enough that Brigid might reach out and touch the foul, alien thing.

Applying the gurney's wheel brake, Kane looked at the monster, slumbering just two feet away from him. "So, what now?" he asked, not bothering to look up. His voice came muffled through the gas mask rebreather over the lower half of his face.

"As we discussed upstairs," Lakesh stated, "you need to touch it—together."

Kane's glance shifted to Brigid's strained form on the stretcher, and then he looked at Lakesh with mournful eyes. "You think she's up to this?" he demanded.

Lakesh shook his head. "No, I don't," he admitted, "but that's neither here nor there now. This needs to be done, Kane, if Brigid is to live."

"Can I get a guarantee on that, old man?" Kane asked, adjusting the straps on Brigid's gas mask.

"You're venturing into the unknown here," Lakesh advised him, "and, if I'm right, it's only your bond as *anam-charas* that will keep you from being utterly overwhelmed."

Looking up from her work securing an IV line to Kane's arm, DeFore voiced her own concern. "This *anam-chara* thing is what we used to call 'New Age nonsense,' Lakesh," she said. "Are you sure you want to stake two people's lives on it?"

"Kane's words back in the medical bay reminded me of the soul bond that he shares with Brigid," Lakesh said. "Their souls are forever locked, a friendship that transcends mere physical reality. If I'm right, they will act together, bolster each other as they go through the final phase of the process with the Igigi."

"The process?" Brigid repeated quietly, her blank eyes looking around the room in confusion. "Where are we?"

Kane leaned close to her, brushing her sweat-damp hair from her forehead and speaking as reassuringly as he could through the medium of the gas mask. "Lakesh has got some crazy plan," he told her, "to fix everything. You need to touch the creature."

"No, Kane," Brigid said, her voice barely audible through her own gas mask.

"I'll be right there with you, right at your side the whole way," Kane assured her.

"You don't know what it's like," she told him. "It's like there's two of me now. I don't even know who I am anymore."

"Sure, you do," Kane told her firmly, placing his hand over hers. "Now, we can do this."

"I'm scared," Brigid whispered, barely audible through the mask.

"Bullshit," Kane told her. "You're never scared, Baptiste, never for as long as I've known you."

With those words, Kane guided her hand over the side of the gurney, entwining his fingers in hers and pushing them both, together, until they teetered over the shiny black carapace of the hideous, terrifying creature sprawled out on the floor.

Lakesh and DeFore both stepped back, not intentionally, just an instinctive desire to get away, as they watched Kane's and Brigid's entwined hands touch the dark, armored skin of the monster in unison.

Suddenly, Kane's body shook, and he seemed to dance

on the spot where he knelt as though some kind of current was passing through him. Lying on the gurney, Brigid's form shook, too, and she let out a whine from beneath the gas mask before falling quiet once more.

Lakesh's voice cut into the silence of the room. "That's it," he said. "They're in. All we can do now is wait."

DeFore stepped back to her position beside the two warriors, assuring herself that the drip feeds were working. "I hope," she began, then stopped, trying to find the right words.

Lakesh looked at her, holding her gaze with his own. "We all do, Reba," he told her solemnly. "It's all we have."

IT WAS LIKE DIVING into a swimming pool, Kane thought, cutting through the stillness of the surface and feeling the surge of water rush all around, pressing against the ears. But it was more sinister than that. The water wanted to hold you, to keep you beneath the surface forever. He was choking, unable to catch his breath, and when he did breathe, his nasal passages, his mouth, his lungs filled with the inky blackness, the swarming, dark-hued insects that attached themselves to his insides.

Distantly, as though looking the wrong way through a telescope, Kane could see his hand over Baptiste's, the two of them touching the black, chitinous carapace of the mysterious creature.

Baptiste.

She was there, of course; he had almost forgotten, just for a moment. Brigid Baptiste, that tiny part of his very being, that precious splinter embedded within his soul, within the very core of his self.

Kane turned, and, as he did so, a multitude of images overlaid one another, vying for attention in his eyes. It wasn't the converted storage room, and yet he knew that that was here, too, all around him. It was something bigger, something more. A field. No, not a field. A landscape, no markings, just rolling hills of lush green grass, its rich smell filling his nostrils.

Brigid Baptiste was there, beside him, smiling as she always had, her hair radiant, her eyes that bright, wonderful green that he knew by heart.

"Kane." Her voice came like a breath.

"Where are we?" he asked, gazing into the depths of her beautiful emerald eyes, so pleased to see them filled with color once more.

"This is memory." She swept her arm out, taking in everything around them. Her arm was covered now in the black body stocking of the shadow suit, although Kane was sure she hadn't been wearing that when they had left the storage room. Had they even left?

Kane felt the pressure of the air around him, cloying, enveloping, and he shook his head like a dog shaking itself after a dip in the sea.

But Brigid didn't seem to mind at all. She stood before him, stretching her arms out straight from her shoulders, laughing in utter, total joy. "We're inside their memories, do you see?" she told Kane through her joyful laughter.

As Kane watched, Brigid began to spin, her feet dancing on the spot, head in the air, a child once again playing silly summer games, turning and turning until she fell down in the grass with dizziness. And still, Brigid laughed, laughed until it hurt, until her stomach cramped and she groaned with the delightful pain.

Kane bent, reaching for her. "Baptiste," he said solemnly, "you have to snap out of it. This place is doing something to you."

She just laughed and snorted as though being tickled by unseen hands. "Pish-posh, Kane," she said through her guffaws, "we're inside memory, you understand? This is a memory playground, everything I've always known but somehow made real." Slowly, her laughing abated and she just lay there, gazing into nothingness. "I see things," she told him as he crouched beside her on the fragrant grass. "I see things in my mind's eye, perfect re-creations of the things I've seen before, and that's how my memory is. But this place, this is like…like the difference between a sketch and a…a movie image. The difference between hearing a story and being there."

"Whose memories are these?" Kane asked, looking warily around.

"These are the Igigi," Brigid said. "They hid here, inside the creature that we tackled. They didn't mean to—it was all a mistake, a miscalculation. So they're all here, vying for space, desperate to be free."

Kane shook his head, trying to absorb her words. "I don't understand," he admitted. "How can they…?"

"You're an inhabitant of two worlds now, Kane," Brigid explained, "just like me. Two different realities, the one you knew and the one that the Igigi see and hear and touch. They see it all so differently, they don't have our frames of reference. They are alien, Kane. This is what it is to be alien, truly alien."

"They overwhelmed those people," Kane reminded her, "overwhelmed the Incarnate. You're the next one, Baptiste. They're overwhelming you, and then they'll come for me."

"I know," she told him, smiling wistfully, "and it hurts and I know that I'm not strong enough to take them, but it's all so fascinating. I don't want to just go, to leave here."

"Which is probably the only thing keeping you alive," Kane told her. "You don't remember things the way other people do. Lakesh thinks, because of that, you must have a stronger image of self than just about anyone else on the planet."

"The looking-glass self," Brigid whispered, as Kane continued.

"I don't have your ability, Baptiste," Kane said. "I need you to remember who I am, or we'll both wither and die, in here, in this place."

"In this memory," Brigid said wistfully, the girlish smile playing across her lips as she stretched out on the grass.

"I'll need to know what this is," Kane told her, gesturing all around, "if I'm to destroy it."

Brigid sat up, outraged. "Kane, you can't!"

"It will kill you, and me, and everyone it touches, the whole of Cerberus, the whole world, before it's all played out," Kane said. "We have to stop it, and Lakesh thinks that we—you and I—are the key."

"How?" Brigid asked.

"Show me everything, Baptiste," Kane told her. "Show me what it all means, what this place really is."

Lifting herself from the grass, Brigid stood beside Kane, holding her thin, pale hand down to help him up.

Together, the two of them walked, arm-in-arm, across the verdant hills of memory.

INSIDE THE GAS-FILLED chamber, Lakesh watched the dark-skinned creature as its chest slowly rose and fell. "It makes sense now," he said, turning to DeFore in his blocky gas mask.

"What does?" she prompted.

"It was born in those caves—the man-made caves, the kiva—in Arizona," Lakesh said. "The quake freed it."

"How can you be so sure?" DeFore queried. "They're two disparate events, miles and miles apart."

"Because I dislike coincidence, Reba," Lakesh told her. "Coincidence is only when we fail to put all the pieces of the jigsaw together, when we don't realize that we left one piece inside the box."

"So, if this thing escaped from Arizona—from its prison there—then how did it end up in California?" Reba asked.

"It moves," Lakesh said simply. "It moves fast, often underground, draining victims of life, overpowering them and using them up like batteries."

"What makes you so certain?" DeFore asked.

"The kachina that Edwards brought back," Lakesh said, smiling beneath his mask. "This thing overwhelms personalities with its own, leaking personality into the minds of others until they are subsumed and killed. And what are the kachina but tiny representations of different personalities, different character traits? A leakage felt by the Pueblo people in their visions, their dreams, carved into form and substance."

"That is either utterly preposterous," DeFore said, "or a revelatory leap of logic."

"I just pray that Kane and Brigid have the ability to put the genie back in the bottle," Lakesh said ominously.

Chapter 18

They walked for a while, across grass-covered slopes, until they reached a smooth obsidian wall that glistened with reflected sunlight. The wall stretched across the landscape, seemingly as far as the eye could see. On closer inspection, Kane saw that it was covered in tiny characters, cuneiform lettering carved across the vast length of the ten-foot-high structure. Kane turned to Brigid and asked her what the wall was.

"This wall surrounds a special site," she explained. "A temple, I suppose."

"It reminds me of the high walls that surrounded Cobaltville," Kane said, feeling uneasy.

"The patterns repeat themselves, Kane," Brigid told him, the trace of a smile crossing her lips.

"Where are we anyway?" Kane asked. "Some memory?"

"This is prehistory," Brigid said. "Or, at least, this is how the Igigi remember prehistory, back when the Annunaki—their masters—first ruled the Earth. Their minds are in uni-thought here, recalling the old days."

"So this is, what," Kane asked, puzzled, "five, six thousand years ago?"

"Possibly more," Brigid proposed. "The records from this time are patchy, to say the least. That's the very reason that we've been unable to counter much of what the Annunaki have set in motion."

"But how can this exist," Kane wanted to know. "How can this…memory be so complete? So tangible?"

"It's a group memory, Kane," Brigid explained, "a unithought, and we have become a part of it. Soon we'll be absorbed into it, ourselves no more. So we may as well look around."

Brigid led the way along the smooth obsidian wall, running her hand along its surface as she walked. Kane followed, looking all around him, marveling at the completeness of the illusion. The sun was high in the sky, a shimmering white ball of flame, and the sky itself a clear blue, so clean, totally free of the pollutants that had ravaged the Earth. The air had a freshness that Kane could taste, could feel against his skin, and the colors of nature were vivid, all around him.

"In Sumerian belief, there were two layers of gods," Brigid told Kane as they walked across the meadow to the side of the wall. "The Annunaki were at the top, rulers of Heaven and Earth. But beneath them were the Igigi, 'those who watch and see,' lesser gods who ruled over the day-to-day affairs of man."

"Bureaucrats, you mean," Kane realized.

"Bureaucrats, slaves, is there a difference? They each do their masters' bidding, with little opportunity to share in the true reward," Brigid said. "The Igigi built this wall."

Kane admired the smooth surface of the wall, the intricate patterns carved into it.

"The Igigi were placed on Earth to construct things like this," Brigid continued, "monuments to their masters, so that Homo sapiens would know their place. But after a while the Igigi became bored with their tasks, building and farming, and so they ascended back to *Tiamat* and left humankind to continue at such backbreaking work."

Kane listened, and yet it was as though he knew all of this. It was inside him already, seeping into his pores from all around. The Igigi memories were washing over him like the tide, taking hold, filling and replacing him.

"The royal family treated the Igigi very poorly," Brigid continued. "They were never even given names, just Igigu singular and Igigi en masse."

"So, the Annunaki treat someone else badly," Kane growled. "My heart bleeds for them."

Brigid stopped, pointing to the far end of the vast wall. Kane stared and saw figures working there, carving at the wall. As they strolled closer, Kane saw that these were alien creatures, lizardlike in part, and yet strangely graceful, beautiful. They reminded him of the hybrids and of the Annunaki, the wonderful aspects of both with none of the things that repulsed him.

"Enlil killed them," Brigid explained. "Massacred all three hundred before the royal family left the planet to the mercies of his Great Flood. He killed his servants, his most loyal servants."

"Is that them?" Kane asked, pointing to the beautiful, graceful figures working at the wall.

Nodding, Brigid explained, "They're reliving the best moments of their lives."

"Servitude," Kane said with a harsh laugh, "on their knees for their masters."

"They love the Annunaki," Brigid told him, and there was no suggestion of judgment in her tone.

Something moved out of the corner of Kane's eye, and he turned to see what it was. There, shining in the sunlight, a metallic bronze aircraft zipped by overhead. It was a Manta, just like the ones he and Grant used, its surface covered in cuneiform characters. The slope-winged craft landed on the far side of the wall, and Kane took a few paces back to try to see what was over the high structure. He could see the summit of a step pyramid there, a flat surface with a little box structure of pillars and roof atop its apex, the whole thing carved from the same black lava as the wall. As he watched, a low sound cut through the air, an animal horn being blown like a trumpet. All of the Igigi working at the wall looked up as one, and then they got to their feet and rushed to the temple, like children being called home.

"Dinnertime?" Kane guessed.

"The Annunaki are here," Brigid said. "They love them, would do anything for them. We're in the days before the betrayal by their masters."

"But this is just a memory," Kane said, confused.

"This is a group memory," Brigid reminded him. "This is everything that they remember, replaying over and over until, once again, they're betrayed by the gods that they love."

Kane and Brigid Baptiste made their way through the open gateway in the long, obsidian wall, and walked to the high pyramid that towered before them. The Igigi bowed in the grass, their foreheads touching the ground, as three Annunaki came slowly down the steps of the temple. Kane watched the lizardlike aliens as they walked majestically down the steps, and instead of revulsion or anger, he felt what the Igigi felt. He felt love.

The three reptilian creatures moved with such effortless grace, their scales rippling in the air, shining as they captured and seemed to hold on to the rays of sunlight. They seemed so tall, oozing power and control and wonderment.

Kane recognized the lead member of the group as Enlil himself. His scaled, armorlike flesh was a molten gold, tinted with red as though washed in blood. His body was lean and muscular, and Kane found himself fascinated by the way the wonderful creature's muscles moved beneath his flesh. Deep in his face, Enlil's eyes stared out imperiously, surveying his lands without ever acknowledging the Igigi bowed before him, merely treating them as part of the landscape, like the trees and the rocks. His eyes gleamed like molten brass, bisected with two, black horizontal stripes, as he stared ahead of him.

Kane knew then, beyond any shadow of a doubt, that here was a god. A god who walked the Earth.

"In less than a thousand years," Baptiste said, her voice breaking in on Kane's thoughts, "he will kill all of them."

Watching the god Enlil then, as he listened to Brigid's ominous words, Kane couldn't help but feel that this was his right. Nothing that this beautiful, exceptional creature did could ever be wrong.

"Don't let the Igigi's thoughts get to you, Kane," Brigid whispered.

He shook his head, trying to snap out of it. "So beautiful. I never saw…" he began, and stopped himself. He turned then, looking at the familiar face of Brigid. "Baptiste, what's going on?"

"I absorbed as many of the memories as I could," she

told him. "I pieced it all together, but I don't think that I can fix it."

"Fix what?" Kane demanded.

"They had an escape plan," Brigid said. "Led by a little group of rebels, perhaps twenty of them who knew of Enlil's scheme. They were nameless, Kane, valueless things in the eyes of their masters. What would the Annunaki care if they ran away?"

"The Annunaki can be very possessive," Kane reasoned.

"They stole technology from *Tiamat*," Brigid continued, "bootlegged it for their own ends."

"What technology?" Kane asked.

"The personality download system, the method of Annunaki rebirth."

"Shit," Kane muttered.

"IT WASN'T a prison," Lakesh told DeFore thoughtfully. "The amniotic fluid proves that."

Reba shook her head, the bulky gas mask swaying to and fro as she tried to shake the realization that had occurred to her at Lakesh's words. "A birthing chamber," she said finally. "Dear me, you think…this thing was born?"

"It's not fully formed," Lakesh said. "The way it breaks apart in sunlight, the chemical reaction that constantly burns the eyes—it's a temporary shell, nothing more."

"A damn powerful one, if Kane is to be believed," DeFore pointed out.

"A tank's a powerful vehicle but you don't want to use one on the school run," Lakesh reasoned.

"But you can't change bodies the way you can change automobiles," DeFore responded, after a few seconds.

Lakesh looked down at the black-hued monstrosity lying on the floor of the chamber. "Can't you?" he posed the question. "This is a whole different life-form. We don't know what it's capable of."

STANDING WITH THEIR backs close to the wall, Kane and Brigid watched as the radiant gods walked across the fields around the black pyramid, Enlil, his young bride-to-be, his brother, Enki.

"That download system is the very process that allowed Enlil and his family to be reborn," Kane said darkly. "Their personalities held in stasis, waiting to be placed in new bodies. We've spent years locked in an ever-expanding battle with the Annunaki in various stages of development."

"Exactly," Brigid agreed.

"And now you're telling me that the Igigi have done the same thing?" Kane growled. "That the three hundred so-called lesser gods are about to reemerge?"

"No, Kane," Brigid said softly. "They're already here."

Kane pulled Brigid to one side as Enlil and his entourage walked past them, but the Annunaki didn't seem to see them. "So where are they?" Kane whispered. "Are they the virus?"

"The Igigi uploaded their personalities—their souls—into the equipment that they cloned from *Tiamat*," Brigid told him, "hid it in the mountains of the place we call Arizona today. The personality file—the Shadow Box—was linked to Tuatha de Danaan technology. It was programmed to reawaken them into glorious new bodies once the Great Flood had passed, so that they could inherit an Earth washed clean of the blight of humankind."

"But?" Kane prompted.

"The technology must have failed," Brigid told him. "They stole the materials, made a copy under the noses of their masters—they must have misjudged something in their haste."

Kane surveyed the area around him, this glorious past created from the memories of the trapped Igigi. "Then this is all they have," he realized. "Memories."

"They've been trapped for thousands of years," Brigid said. "Trapped in a mass of corrupting files. They've lost their individual instincts, Kane, they've lost the very thing they strove to gain—uniqueness, individuality, *names*. Slivers of personality leaked out of the Shadow Box over the millennia, but there was no body to inhabit, and so they just died. The Tuatha de Danaan system never rebooted."

Kane shook his head. "How can you know all of this, Baptiste?"

"Listen to them," Brigid told him. "In here," she said, pointing to her left temple. "First the memories swarm, then they overwhelm. You just need to listen."

Kane closed his eyes, acknowledging the pressure inside his skull, that same old feeling of being underwater. And he felt something else, the floor beneath him, the box shape of the room around him. He opened his eyes and now he was crouched in the storage room that served as a cell, his fingers entwined in Brigid's, pressing both of their hands against the black carapace of the hulking creature that stirred restlessly in unconsciousness before him.

Kane looked around, saw the walls to the room, the thick, curling wisps of anaesthetic smoke. And he saw the two hairless apes standing over him. No, not apes—people. His friends. Lakesh and DeFore. They looked ugly to his eyes now, foul, alien things, their features all scrunched up in their faces, clearly different and yet too similar to define.

"Lakesh," Kane breathed, barely audible through the gas mask that obscured his features, "Reba."

Lakesh stepped closer, leaning down to better hear Kane, but keeping a cautious distance from the creature lying beside him. "What is it, Kane? What's happening?"

"They're in me now," Kane told him. "They're taking over."

"I need you and Brigid to be strong," Lakesh instructed. "You can reinforce each other if you try. Your bond will reinforce the other."

"It's like seeing another world," Kane said, his eyes widening.

Lakesh drew back as he saw Kane's eyes properly for the first time through the smoky gas. Where once they had been slate-gray-blue, now the ex-Mag's eyes were a pale crystal blue, the color of a baby's blanket.

"Hold on to yourself," Lakesh told him firmly. "Hold on to yourself, focus on your bond with Brigid."

"Baptiste?" Kane said with confusion. "She's just an ape, a jumped-up monkey-thing, like you, like Reba."

"No, Kane," Lakesh said. "No, she's not. She's a part of you and you a part of her. Remember that now. Remember that."

It was no good—Kane's eyes had already closed and he was drifting back into his own thoughts and the memory template of the Igigi.

"THE MONSTER is their vessel," Brigid was explaining to Kane as they strolled along a path by the crystal clear waters of the Euphrates River. "It holds them all inside."

"How?" Kane asked. "Why? And what happened to the pregnant woman, the farmers and the Incarnate guardsman out in the desert?"

"They were meant to be given their own bodies, three hundred of them, strong and new," Brigid said, "but this is all that was created. A glitch in the system, the Tuatha de Danaan read their personalities as one great, amorphous, schizophrenic mass. It created a body that could fulfill all of the requirements it was reading."

"Then they're trapped," Kane stated, "together in that Frankenstein's monster. They're no longer individuals."

"The individual personalities are trying to break loose," Brigid told him. "They latch on to anything they touch, leaping into that body."

"A mind virus," Kane muttered.

"A lesser god is still a god," Brigid stated. "We cannot contain them, our bodies are too weak, just pathetic shells for a weakling race of clever monkeys. They burn through us like flames through tissue."

Kane stopped walking, and he stood there, looking out across the clean waters of the ancient river, the birthplace of the Sumerian religion that man had built up around the original appearance of the Annunaki. It was all just a memory, a memory created by the many personality files of the Igigi. A memory of better days, before their massacre at the hands of the adored one, Enlil.

"It's not just our bodies that they burn through," Kane said. "It's our souls. That's why Lakesh sent me here with you. That's what he meant when he said to use our bond."

Brigid placed an arm around Kane's back, looking up at him. "How, Kane? How can we do this?"

"The *anam-chara* makes us eternal," Kane told her. "No matter how many of these things attack the core of our being, we can bolster the other's soul, regenerating throughout eternity, overwhelming them until they're all absorbed into us."

"But how can we kill them?" Brigid asked. "*Why* should we? They're so beautiful, so much better than us, and they only want to live."

Kane turned to her, his expression solemn. "They're in your head," he said, "making you see things their way."

"No, Kane," she said, a tear trickling down her cheek.

"I feel it, too," Kane admitted, pulling Brigid close to him as the river rushed by. "Part of me doesn't want to do this to them, either, Baptiste, but I know it's the part of me that's theirs now. And I need to get that back before they drown all of me, wash me away like the silt in this river."

Brigid stood in Kane's arms, shaking her head back and forth. "I won't," she said. "I can't do that to them."

"The technology failed, Baptiste—you said so yourself," Kane told her. "They're stuck inside that monster. Their true personalities are already lost. This is a mercy killing, that's all. That's all it is."

She looked up at him, her emerald eyes locking with his as a flock of birds flew over the mighty river, cawing to one another.

"We're the only ones who can do this," Kane told her quietly.

Holding his gaze, Brigid nodded slowly, the air of resignation to her movement.

INSIDE THE CHAMBER, the creature was stirring, its movements becoming more agitated as it struggled to wake up. Seeing this, Lakesh stepped toward the door, tapping his hand against the tiny window of reinforced glass.

Outside the room, the noise of Lakesh's tapping was too faint to be heard, but Domi saw her lover's hand rapping at the reinforced glass and she stepped closer, calling attention to it as she peered through the little window.

"What is it?" Grant asked, the Copperhead assault rifle in his hands as he tracked her movements.

"Lakesh needs us," she said, her voice muffled by the gas mask.

Domi stood on tiptoe to peer through the little pane of glass, and she saw Lakesh looking back at her, the rebreather covering the lower half of his face, tilting his head to look through the window.

"What?" she shouted before realizing that Lakesh couldn't hear her. She reached up, fingers working at the strap of the gas mask to remove it, but she saw Lakesh shake his head vigorously, wagging a warning finger at her through the glass pane.

Domi looked at him, watching as he mimed movements. Lakesh placed his hands together as though to pray, then he rested his head against them at an angle, eyes closed as though sleeping. Suddenly he was moving, eyes wide, awake again, and then he pointed to where the creature lay on the floor of the storeroom.

"Lakesh says it's waking up," Domi said, waving for Grant and Donald Bry to join her. "The monster's waking up."

As she watched, Lakesh created a tube from his bunched fist. Then, with his other hand, he indicated something spraying from the end of the tube.

Domi nodded her understanding. "He says to use more gas," she told Bry.

"I don't think we have that much more to pump in," Bry said thoughtfully. "We'd be hard-pressed to increase the feed any more than we have."

Domi looked at Lakesh through the glass, reaching her hand to touch it. "Find a way," she said. "Just find a way."

In silence, Bry nodded before heading for the stairwell to speak to the scientists and engineers who waited there, out of harm's way.

As the River Euphrates flowed by their feet, Kane and Brigid took one last look at the world that the Igigi had created from their grouped memories. "The Earth was beautiful then," Brigid said, marveling at the clear skies, the aromas of the flowers that grew along the riverbanks.

"It still is," Kane countered.

"But this," Brigid said, gesturing all around her, "it's like new, like something untouched."

Gently, Kane pulled her around until she was facing the towering step pyramid that nestled behind the high obsidian wall in the familiar pattern of oppressive Cobaltville, where the pair of them had been raised. "No, it's not," he told her. "It's already been spoiled."

Brigid closed her eyes, taking a long breath of the crisp air. "You're right," she said. "A memory is only a dream that we attach significance to. It's no more real than that."

When she opened her eyes once more, Kane was

standing before her, his face very close to hers. "Look at me, Baptiste," he said. "Look at me and tell me who I am."

"You're Kane," she said firmly. "Kane, my truest friend. Kane, son of Kane. Once you were a Magistrate in Cobaltville, a protector of the system until you learned that the system was corrupt. And despite your rough edges, despite your gruff exterior, I know you. I know that you believe in the inherent goodness of man. That's what you fight for, that's what you've always fought for, and that is what you will continue to fight for, in this life and the one that follows."

Kane nodded, feeling her words, her emotion, bolster his sense of self, feed his soul.

"Baptiste," he said, "Brigid Baptiste. Librarian, archivist, knowledge seeker. Bravest of the brave. Knowledge is your weapon, and you would stop at nothing to gain it. A more loyal companion I could never ask for, in this life or any other."

"Oh, Kane," Brigid breathed, her voice cracking with emotion. "I can feel it, deep inside. It's not them, it's you. They're departing, leaving me."

"I feel it, too," Kane told her, *anam-chara.*"

Around them, the world of the ancients was fading, becoming insubstantial, like a dying candle flame. In its place, misted with white smoke, the storage room began to re-form, its white walls and tiled floor coming back into focus as Kane and Brigid watched.

Kane could see his hand once more, encompassing Brigid's as they touched the hardened skin of the jet-black creature. Hand, creature, walls, floor. It was all coming back to him, normal once more, the knowledge so basic that it was hardwired in him as the most primal recall. The monster was shaking, but as Kane watched, the shaking became less and less until finally it stopped moving.

Kane looked up, examining the creature's pained, awful face. The last wisps of green smoke were floating from its eyes, no more being emitted.

"Did we kill it?" Kane asked aloud, and his voice came to his ears as though from miles away.

He turned then, as full awareness returned, and he saw Reba DeFore working a new IV line into Brigid's arm, frantically tapping for a vein.

Letting go of Brigid's hand, Kane stood, facing the beautiful woman lying on the gurney. "What happened?" he asked, his voice still coming to him as if down a tunnel, its usual resonance lost.

DeFore glanced at Kane for a moment before returning to her work. Her mouth moved, and Kane could make out the words with effort: "She's crashing."

For a moment, Kane couldn't understand. Crashing? What did she mean by crashing? Then understanding dawned, and in a second he had pushed the medic gently aside and taken Brigid in his arms, pulling her into a sitting position on the gurney.

"No, she's not," he said, his voice a bark through the filters of the gas mask.

Kane shook Brigid's limp body in his arms, shook her with increasing violence until her eyes opened. They were yellow, like a cat's, peering out at him like alien things in that beautiful porcelain face.

"Brigid Baptiste," he said. "Brigid Baptiste."

Brigid blinked, a long, slow movement of her eyelids,

long lashes closing like curtains over the windows to her soul. "Kane," she said, the single word muffled by the mask.

As she opened her eyes, Kane knew it would be all right. Her eyes were glistening emeralds once more, that wonderful, beautiful shade of green that was etched into his very being, the eyes that had watched over him, guarding his soul throughout eternity.

Chapter 19

Kane and Brigid had found a quiet corner of the canteen, and they sat together, eating pancakes and maple syrup and drinking strong cups of black coffee.

"I'm so hungry," Brigid admitted between mouthfuls. She was wearing a loosely fitted shirt, white and left unbuttoned, over a vest top and loose pants, and Kane was dressed similarly, in the nonconstricting gym clothes he had found in his wardrobe. Lakesh had suggested the pair of them take leave from duties until they felt fully recovered from their ordeal.

"Me, too," Kane said, gulping down the piping-hot coffee. "Whatever that thing did, it took a lot out of us."

"Gave us a lot, too," Brigid told him after a few seconds' thought. "Reminded us of what we are to each other. *Anam-chara.*"

Kane just nodded, pouring more coffee from the tall carafe he had brought from the service area of the canteen.

As they worked their way through more pancakes, Domi and Grant came through the canteen doors. Seeing them, Domi waved and rushed across the room to join them at their table. Grant followed a little more sedately, but he was clearly pleased to see his friends up and about.

"So?" Domi asked. "What happened? In the storeroom, I mean."

Kane waited for Grant to join them, carrying a cup of coffee for Domi and a little cup of steaming, watery liquid for himself.

Grant shrugged as Kane looked quizzically at the little, steaming cup in his hand. "Green tea," he said. "Something Shizuka got me into."

"Well," Domi said impatiently as she dropped into one of the molded seats at the plastic-covered table, holding the coffee cup closely in both hands. "What happened with the monster? Spill."

"Lakesh had this theory," Brigid said as she reached for more syrup for her pancakes, "that went all the way back to Decard's initial description of the people he had originally found. 'Mindless, soulless wretches,' he had called them."

"Emphasis on the 'soulless,'" Kane chipped in.

"Whatever this thing was, Lakesh figured it was feeding on the souls of its victims, using them up," Brigid explained. "So, he needed to find a soul that was somehow impenetrable to the attack. And that's where Kane and I came in."

"Plus," Kane said, "Baptiste was already infected by then anyway. So, it was pretty much a fait accompli that I was going to help."

Grant shook his head. "Well, that's a load of horse crap," he muttered, looking uncomfortably at the contents of his cup.

"The way that Lakesh explained it," Kane continued, "is that the Igigi souls were looking for escape. But when they met with two souls that couldn't be overwhelmed, they found themselves with nothing to take over and nowhere to turn back. They couldn't go back into the monster."

"But why you two?" Domi asked.

"The *anam-chara* bond," Brigid said. "Soul friends, eternally. We somehow complement each other, reinforcing the other's soul."

Grant snorted.

"Something wrong, partner?" Kane asked.

"I'm sticking with my previous statement on this," Grant said. "Horse crap."

Brigid looked at Kane, resting her hand on his forearm for just a second. "I think someone's jealous," she said, and they both laughed.

Grant sniffed at the green tea, then put the steaming cup down. "You two are going to be impossible about this, aren't you?" he said before pushing himself up from the table. "I think I need a proper mug of java."

As they watched him go, Domi pressed Brigid for more information. "So how did your *anam-chara* bond thing stop the attack?"

"Lakesh said it was like holding up two mirrors against each other and trapping the light between them," Brigid said.

"Only with souls," Kane added. "They can bounce between us, but they can never get free."

"So they're inside you?" Domi asked, clearly intrigued. "Can you feel them?"

"No," Kane said, and Brigid shook her head, as well.

"I don't even remember them," Brigid admitted. "All that knowledge, all those incredible things we saw, and they're all like a half-remembered dream. I can feel emotions, things calling to my heart, but I can't really recall them anymore."

"But *you* remember everything," Domi said, astonished. "It's your whole thing, Brigid."

Brigid closed her eyes, their emerald luster back in place after those hours where she had been possessed. "Sometimes it's better to forget," she concluded, and Kane nodded in silent agreement.

ROSALIA HAD WALKED across the California desert for most of the morning, creating distance from the smoldering ruins that had been Tom Carnack's base. Her limbs ached, and her stomach felt empty. She had gone too long without food, and spending the night on the cold, windswept desert floor had done nothing for her temperament.

As she made her way toward the little settlement where the monster had originally appeared, attacking Kane and Decard and the group of warriors in their ludicrous fairy-tale masks, she stopped, gazing at the churned-up sand where the monster had burrowed its tunnel. The tunnel had caved in on itself now, just a heap of sand to show where a hole had once been excavated.

The five-shack hamlet was empty, the buildings abandoned now that their owners were deceased. Two of the shacks had taken massive hits, and one was just a jumble of fire-damaged wood where a grenade had felled it since Rosalia had last been here. To one side of the little settlement, a tiny marker had been placed in the sand—a gravestone.

With her long, dark hair catching in the wind, Rosalia stepped into the shelter of one of the shacks and made her way into its main room. Swiftly, professionally, she opened the cupboards, looking for supplies, for something to eat. There were some strips of cured meat, and some vegetables that had been pickled in brine, and Rosalia took these to the little wooden table and sat there, eating them between swigs from the water in her hide flask.

As she sat quietly, gnawing at the cured meat, the beautiful dancing girl became aware of another presence, and she looked up to see a dog, some kind of mongrel that looked as if it had some coyote in it, looking up at her from the doorway, its ears back and its head tilted inquisitively. It had the palest eyes of any dog that Rosalia had ever seen.

"Here, boy," she said, holding her hand low to the floor, smiling with encouragement. She had seen the empty kennel outside, and she guessed that this hound belonged to the previous owner. It had probably been in hiding ever since the monster attacked and killed its master.

Warily at first, the pale-eyed dog sniffed Rosalia's hand. Then, it nuzzled at her, and Rosalia tore off a strip of the cured meat and held it out for the hound.

"Nice little dog," Rosalia said soothingly, watching as the mutt worked the hard meat strip around with its jaws, trying to bite into it, salivating in great gobs on the floor. "Nice little dog."

The dog looked back at her with those pale, intelligent eyes, and Rosalia wondered at what her new companion was thinking.

Stupid, ugly, furless ape-thing, the dog thought with the Igigi soul that had invaded and overwhelmed it. Soon, you and all your kind will make room for your new deities.

The Executioner
Don Pendleton's®
LOOSE CANNON

A man's quest for vengeance knows no limits....

A jungle ambush leaves several Indonesian security forces dead, setting off a political firestorm in the volatile region. When a disgraced former U.S. ambassador emerges as the mastermind behind the attack, Mack Bolan is called in to find him, before the country descends into civil war. It's not long before the Executioner realizes that the ambush was only the beginning of a deadly scheme....

Available June wherever books are sold.

GOLD EAGLE®

GEX367

TAKE 'EM FREE

2 action-packed novels plus a mystery bonus

NO RISK

NO OBLIGATION TO BUY

GEO

AleX Archer
SEEKER'S CURSE

In Nepal, many things are sacred. And worth killing for.

Enlisted by the Japan Buddhist Federation to catalog
a number of ancient shrines across Nepal, Annja
is their last hope to properly conserve these sites.
As vandalism and plundering
occur, police become
suspicious of Annja—but
she's more concerned with
the smugglers and guerrillas
trying to kill her. As she treks
high into the Himalayas to
protect a sacred statue, she's
told the place is cursed. But
Annja has no choice but to
face the demons....

Available July
wherever books are sold.

GOLD EAGLE®

GRA19